AN EYE FOR AN EYE

BLINDED IN THE PURSUIT OF REVENGE

Published by Brolga Publishing Pty Ltd
ABN 46 063 962 443
PO Box 12544
A'Beckett St
Melbourne, VIC, 8006
Australia

email: markzocchi@brolgapublishing.com.au

National Library of Australia
Cataloguing-in-Publication data
   author. Klepfisz, Arthur
   book title: An Eye for an Eye
   ISBN (paperback) 9781925367713
   Subjects: Revenge--Fiction
   Dewey Number: A823.4

Printed in Australia
Cover design by Alice Cannet
Typesetting by Elly Cridland

BE PUBLISHED

Publish through a successful publisher. National distribution, Macmillan & International distribution to the United Kingdom, North America. Sales Representation to South East Asia
Email: markzocchi@brolgapublishing.com.au

AN EYE FOR AN EYE

BLINDED IN THE PURSUIT OF REVENGE

Arthur Klepfisz

AN EYE FOR AN EYE

BLINDED IN THE PURSUIT OF SCIENCE

Arthur Klopbar

An Eye for an Eye presents a riveting story of a questionable death set in Melbourne in the 1970s. The characters in the story are alluring. They come from different cultural and social backgrounds. The story leaves one wondering how nature, nurture and relationships contribute to life's experiences. *An Eye for an Eye* is a very insightful book and a very good read.

- DR. MINA SHAFER, *Psychologist and published Author.*

Part thriller, part pulp fiction type novel - it's a page-turner. Human frailties, which are sometimes brutally, sometimes subtly experienced and exposed by the well-rounded characters, are described with gentle insight. Moral dilemmas, consequences of vindictive actions and the obsessive pursuit for revenge drive the story to a suspenseful resolution. It had me hooked from page 1.

- VICTOR MAJZNER, *Artist and Author.*

CHAPTER ONE

Tuesday, 8 January 1988
3.02 a.m.

'I could be screwing a dead mullet!'

The profanity polluted the air and drained away any remaining dignity in the room.

He rolled off the slight shadow, his right foot angrily shoving aside the girlish figure. No clothing masked her small, slender body and no emotion penetrated her doll-like features.

'If you want to stay in this country, you're going to have to do better than this. Otherwise you're out. Back into your leaking boat, eating noodles,' he snarled.

Still no response.

Brett knelt naked on the bed. He pushed up the girl's eyelids. Staring vacantly at him were non-comprehending almond eyes, no longer witness to her life's shame. He searched for the missing pulse in her neck.

'Fuck!

He was oblivious to the sadness and squalor of his surroundings. His concern was protecting himself and the sight of the young woman's body lying naked amongst the stained sheets did not arouse any other emotion. His mind raced, weighing up the options available to him, whilst the slivers of early morning light intruded through the tattered blinds, unable to purge the image contained in that room.

The light was cast mainly by the sentinel-like street poles surrounding the dingy boarding house, which doubled as a brothel and

1

was run by Brett's business partner, Vladimir. Outside, the darkness of the night was beginning to fade, whilst inside, it would never lift.

For a heavy, thickset man, Brett could move quickly. He felt he needed to, in his line of work. Detectives in the Victorian Homicide Squad didn't always get a second chance, dealing with the lowlife they encountered.

Brett Maloney was not one for introspection. He figured that he would leave that to the effeminate Chardonnay set, but he knew that he had a bit of a problem here. He'd left his signature in the dead girl. He guessed the media would highlight her youth, manipulating reader's emotions. As far as he was concerned, chinks always looked younger than they were.

He brushed aside any vestige of doubt, reassuring himself that he could not be held – lots of it – to make her come alive when they screwed, and had taken some himself, enjoying the high that it gave him. He'd promised her that she would get a fix of heroin if she pleased him.

It was only later that a vague memory elbowed its way into his thoughts. He reluctantly recalled her whispering some words as he entered her, but they were words he ignored, as he had no interest in what she was saying.

Now, the only faint recollection was her mentioning drugs, and he recalled her popping further pills of her own. At the time, her words were only a distraction which he ignored, allowing her voice to drift away. Belatedly, he now wondered if she was telling him about drugs she had already taken that day, but reassured himself that she had only herself to blame if that was the case.

He left her lying naked in the bed, believing that any attempt to hide the body would only heighten suspicion about the cause of death. This way, she would be found within hours at most, leaving open the possibility that she had suicided or accidentally overdosed on drugs she had taken herself.

Brett believed that the other girls working at the brothel would be too scared to give evidence of him having been there the night of Candy's death on the 8 January, 1988, and he knew his name was not listed in the brothel appointment book on that date, nor on any other date.

Brett's features were a caricature of a cop, highlighted by a beefy red face, and a bulbous nose with his upper lip covered by a traditional moustache. He hated being asked why so many cops had moustaches – but wondered the same thing himself.

He avoided mirrors, except when imposed by the necessity of shaving. His was a face that scared the shit out of people, he'd realised years ago, and it wasn't a face that even he particularly liked. However, he was stuck with it, much as a Bull Terrier is slave to its own features and personality. His consolation was that you can't fight genetics, absolving himself of any responsibility for the ravages that he'd inflicted on his own body. Deep down, he knew that the cigarettes, the alcohol, the lack of sleep and the screwing around had not helped the way he looked. What he refused to acknowledge however, was how much of the inner person his features reflected. He used to joke with his mates that he had a face only a mother could love. Not that his had.

4.30 a.m.

Approaching dawn, Brett slipped into bed, grateful for the stuporous form lying beside him.

His wife Jenny had probably loved him early on. She didn't know better at seventeen years of age. He was a twenty-five-year-old constable when they met. *They all love uniforms,* he had thought to himself. Their love, passion, or whatever it was that held them together in those early years, was long gone. What remained were the two children, Penny aged fifteen and Craig, nineteen. The children were witnesses to a marriage anaemic of love; any desire they might have had for marriage forming part of their own lives had surely been curbed.

Brett guessed Jenny had meant something to him early in their relationship, but doubted that he would have married her if she hadn't become pregnant. At that age you thought with your prick and not your head, he often told himself, as he gazed at her sagging breasts and the droplets of saliva dribbling out of the corner of her mouth whilst she lay on her back snoring.

He struggled to get to sleep, with the events of that night running through his mind, jostling for position. He got up several times to get a drink of water and checked the children, as if this would magically bring on sleep.

He regularly lamented to himself that the children were slipping away from him as he and they got older. In earlier days, whatever remnants of time that he had free, he largely devoted to both children. To be truthful, the time was not evenly divided as he spent far more of it with his son. It was mainly physical stuff, wrestling, footy and having a beer together, much to Jenny's disapproval. He had always found male companionship easier than relating to women. Now he shared nothing with either child and they both seemed to side with their mother. They hated cops and barely grunted a greeting whenever they crossed paths with him.

Strange how the kids liked him when they were young and grew to hate him as they got older, he reflected. He suspected they might be into drugs with their friends – probably marijuana. He attributed a lot of their surliness and poor school performance to smoking grass. Penny was repeating Year 9 and Craig lasted only eight months in his plumbing apprenticeship. According to Brett, Craig was a "bum", sponging off his parents and the government.

Brett continued to pace around the house wondering if – what the fuck was her name – had been found yet. He had never cared enough to ask her real name when she was alive, but had a vague memory that the Richmond brothel where she worked had given her the identity of Candy. If he wanted her, he would flick through the book lying on the front counter and point to her picture. None of the girls working there went by their birth names. She wasn't the only one he screwed there – but he had favoured sleeping with her lately, enjoying the rough sex and the dilating look of fear that transfigured her face when he arrived. *As wide-eyed as a chink can get,* he would chuckle to himself.

They didn't pay him much for being a cop, he felt. But if one added to that shitty wage the perks of the job such as free sex, protection money from brothel owners, and the take he got from turning a blind eye to illegal brothels and drugs – well, it made the job tolerable.

He had moved from the Victorian Vice Squad to the Homicide Squad three years ago, but maintained his contacts. There was also a small drug trade that he was building up. He even had what one would call a "silent partner" in Vladimir – very silent if the partner was ever stupid enough to talk, the thought bringing a smirk to his face. Vladimir was part owner of a number of brothels, including the Richmond one where Candy worked – or used to work. Fear and power were the tools of Brett's trade, feeling even better than sex, and he was confident that Vladimir wouldn't talk.

Before leaving the brothel, Brett had told Vladimir to clothe Candy's body with a nightie and after waiting a couple of hours to contact the ambulance and police, informing them that he had checked on Candy and found her unconscious in bed and couldn't feel a pulse. There would be no record to show that Brett had been with Candy that night, except what he had left in her body. As it was a licensed brothel, no further difficulties would arise by contacting the authorities.

Brett had arrived at a stage in his life where he prided himself on not giving a damn about anyone else. He'd chortle privately that he lived by the law of the jungle, where "kill or be killed" became his mantra. He was determined to survive in the world he occupied, whatever the cost. Winning without conflict had bypassed him entirely and he was reluctant to reveal to anyone that he cared for another human being. An exception was Jesse, who was the son of his younger sister Eileen.

Eileen had lived in London since 1968 where she worked as a housemaid in a large hotel. When she had been in London for 15 months, she met her partner, Phil, a builder's labourer, and they moved in together. He was a hard drinker and a habitual gambler, so their existence was precarious and the arrival of their son Jesse in mid-1972 was an unwelcome surprise.

Around Christmas 1976, while drunk, Phil was critically injured one night in a car accident. His death two weeks later did not touch Eileen deeply – in fact, she realised that it gave her the freedom she had yearned for but had lacked the courage to seek. She had stopped dreaming of a better life many years before; she had no friends and did not look for a new relationship, remaining in the same flat with her young son, playing Bingo once a week and watching TV on the other nights.

Jesse survived as best he could in this emotional vacuum, struggled at school and began to develop behavioural problems associated with intermittent episodes of rage. At first his anger was expressed verbally, but as he got older and his frustration increased, his anger grew increasingly physical in nature.

At age eleven he was placed in a Government-run home but appeared to deteriorate further in that environment. Eileen wrote to Brett out of desperation, as they had not communicated for quite some years. She asked for his assistance in having Jesse transferred to an appropriate institution in Australia, preferably Melbourne, in the hope he would receive better management there. Brett was as surprised as Eileen when he agreed to her request. As youngsters living at home, they had been friends, with Brett often shielding her from the household trauma, and some remnants of this bond had remained.

Brett didn't seek Jenny's permission nor did he discuss the issue with her in any depth, a passing comment as he sat with his beer watching TV was the first she learned about Jesse coming. From past experience she did not question Brett any further and left it to him to discuss it if and when he felt inclined. Brett knew however that supporting Jesse was something she would have agreed to if asked, as she was a kindly soul by nature and any sign of caring by Brett, even if directed to someone else, gave her faint hope that things could improve their marriage.

Jesse was already 13 when he arrived in Melbourne and entered a Government institution about a 30-minute drive from Brett's home. Brett organised to have him fully assessed by a specialist paediatric doctor who diagnosed Jesse as being intellectually impaired. The birth notes were retrieved from the London hospital and revealed a complicated birth where the umbilical cord had caught around his neck at birth. The Melbourne paediatrician wrote out a program for Jesse but was unable to predict if he would ever be capable of independent living.

Over the following years, Brett saw Jesse regularly and took him for outings each week; kicking a football in the park, buying an ice cream, and sometimes going to football matches to watch Essendon play. Brett also took Jesse home to mix with his own children, who enjoyed the outings as Jenny plied them with treats and they related to him as one of the family.

By the age of seventeen Jesse was living in a supervised group home and coping well with casual work as a builder's labourer. It appeared that he might continue to need some degree of support and supervision in the years to come. Brett continued to pay for most of the ongoing costs, and Jenny lived with the faint hope that this seed of caring might germinate and spread further into her own relationship with Brett.

CHAPTER TWO

Thursday, 27 June 1990
4.59 a.m.

On the other side of the Yarra River, in a Melbourne suburb described in journalistic terms as "the leafy suburb of Hawthorn", Dr Andrew Wright rolled over in bed, absorbing the warmth of his wife Karen. Andrew worked as a consultant psychiatrist in private practice, outwardly appeared to have a stable family life, and had nearly been monogamous in the past.

It is difficult to imagine how a river such as the Yarra, long described by locals in negative terms such as "floating upside down" could have become an indicator of social standing in the city of Melbourne.

As the tumultuous period of the 1970s receded, with Australian troops no longer engaged in an unwinnable war in Vietnam. Andrew's life had appeared to be going smoothly.

This period of time was said by some to be the worst post-war decade, and as the 1980s progressed, there was a glimmer of hope that world events were improving. In the lucky country, Australians revelled in the historic America's Cup win, but in the rest of the world, natural disasters such as hurricanes, earthquakes and floods vied for prominence with man-made disasters. Each time there was a glimmer of hope for peace as one war ended, another conflict arose. Like a brush fire, every time the world dared to hope that things were improving, events erupted to dash those hopes.

By November 1989 the Cold War had ended and the Berlin Wall

had been pulled down, whilst at the same time in Tiananmen Square thousands of protesting students had been killed in June 1989. For some, the 1988 downing of a Pan Am plane over Lockerbie Scotland, by terrorists, appeared to be a foreboder of things to come. The decade had begun with John Lennon being shot dead and his killer pleading insanity, in what many considered an insane world.

With a world refusing to be free of conflict and disaster, by 1990, some degree of chaos had also intruded into Andrew Wright's life, whilst Candy's death had created potential future problems for Brett Maloney. In the normal course of events, one would not have expected the paths of Brett and Andrew to have intersected. However, the factors which determine these outcomes, whether they be divine intervention, the position of the stars and planets or pure chance, could not guarantee that the lives of these two men wouldn't cross, and they had.

Andrew gently lay his hand on Karen's right buttock, and watched her full breasts rising and falling with her breathing. Gazing at her aroused him, but he was reluctant to wake her at 5 a.m. He had been waking up far too early in the last few weeks. They never made love in the morning, though he would have liked to. Lovemaking always occurred at night when they were both tired, and this didn't enhance the experience or his performance. He felt that women had it easier sexually, as their level of arousal was not on public display as it was with men. *Hard to avoid noticing a limp dick,* he thought.

His thoughts went back to the nightmare of the last few years and he chuckled as he retreated from this goulash of thoughts – love, sex and nightmares – a précis of his working life as a psychiatrist.

He had one hour to go before his usual get-up time, when he would dress, shave, grab something for breakfast and dash out of the house to do his hospital ward round, before going on to his rooms to see patients for the rest of the day.

In spite of the early hour, he decided there was no point lying awake in bed exposed to his maudlin thoughts. He'd go and have a coffee at the hospital before starting his round.

As he got ready he reflected, not for the first time, on the corrosive events that he and his family had experienced over the past two years. He, his wife Karen and their two children – Jed, age sixteen, and Bobby, age fourteen – had been through "the mill". *Where the hell,* he wondered, *had that saying come from?* It was one thing to say that pain could be a growth experience and part of life's rich fabric, and another to actually be in the middle of that experience yourself; rich fabric for the lawyers, maybe.

He hated clichés. Karen's older brother Ralph was a walking cliché – anything to clothe and mask his inner-self. Feelings and emotions were not to be shared or exposed as far as Ralph was concerned. Andrew was aware that his own thoughts and feelings had been indiscriminately tearing down fences, often piercing boundaries at unpredictable and inappropriate times, as they scattered in all directions.

There was probably only one cliché that appealed to Andrew. It was said to be an old Arabic saying: "You can piss on me but don't tell me it is raining." He considered it to be a good way of describing the bullshit that masqueraded as honesty in many people. Not only people, he reflected, but also organisations, such as the media and politicians. But then, one shouldn't stereotype he believed. God, he was wasting hours – no, days, or weeks even – of his life going through all this stuff. He knew he had to cut it loose as it was close to two months since the court case in late April 1990.

He reflected that if one of his patients had presented with these thoughts, he might have been inclined to suspect that they were suffering from some degree of psychiatric disturbance, with features of paranoia, in suspecting an orchestrated conspiracy against themselves. He hoped that he wouldn't judge his patients in this manner, as he worked on the principle that it was their reality and not for him to reject in any clinical way. Today, he allowed the thoughts to stay. He recalled that it was a day like this – but then it wasn't. No two days are ever the same.

Two years ago, on a Sunday in early 1988, he and Karen had been walking leisurely through the streets of Brunswick, reflecting on the tribal nature of suburban life. Occupying the sidewalks and cafes were members of the local tribe; distinguished by tattoos, piercings, scrappy torn jeans and hair gelled into gravity-defying shapes. He and Karen wryly reflected that in attempting to demonstrate their independence as individuals, these young people had in fact become homogeneous. This was their uniform. Andrew found himself staring at them, whilst they appeared oblivious of him. He wondered if they were merely tolerant of his differences or whether they were indifferent to his existence.

He noted how trendy this area of Brunswick had become, where in the past it had provided housing for manual workers. Small workers' cottages had been done up and the suburb had become so expensive that the same workers would have found it out of their financial reach if they were looking to purchase now. Some remnants of the past remained, and the occasional vagrant could be found sleeping rough on the street, wherever they found shelter, although from time to time, this was actively discouraged by the authorities.

Suddenly the shrill tone of Andrew's phone pierced his reverie and life was never the same. A nasal voice introduced itself as a male journalist from the Age newspaper, with the lofty appendage of investigative journalist. Without a pause for any social niceties, the voice challenged, rather than questioned – was Andrew aware that the family of a patient he had cared for, who died in hospital in 1977, eleven years before, were pressing the coroner to investigate her death and alleging Dr Wright had subjected their relative to deep sleep therapy.

As the smug voice rolled on, Andrew recalled a woman in her late sixties, who had been a psychiatric inpatient under his care. He remembered her being hospitalised with severe depression and in spite of having a family history of heart problems, she had stressed her body for many years with excessive food and alcohol. Andrew had been working as a consultant psychiatrist for over eleven years at that stage, having commenced private practice in 1966, and his thoughts revisited the scene of the patient dying suddenly from a cardiac arrest and failing to be resuscitated, in spite of frantic efforts by himself and several other doctors in the hospital. Her death had upset him greatly and he felt for her family, but the cardiac arrest had been so sudden that nothing could be done to save her.

He recalled supporting her family in their grieving and having some family members coming to him as patients in the years that followed. His relationship with the family continued to be good and it baffled him how the coroner would be investigating her death eleven years after it occurred, and why the patient's family were pushing for an inquest now. Having planted the seeds of anxiety, the journalist chose to say nothing further.

Andrew then found it difficult to explain to Karen what the call had been about, as he was struggling to make sense of it himself. The sunny day had now turned grey for him, as if all the oxygen had been sucked out, and he didn't feel inclined to continue their outing. He regretted buying his walkabout mobile phone the year before. It was relatively new technology, and it certainly made him more accessible should emergencies arise. It cost him a packet, over $4000, if his memory served him right, and it meant that not only could he be reached for urgent patient care, but it also allowed intrusion from people whose calls could have waited. However, he knew the journalist would have made contact one way or another.

As Karen and he walked rapidly to their car, they were shrouded in silence.

CHAPTER THREE

Brett's family had migrated from Ireland several years before he was born. He was the second of eight children, two girls and six boys. Unlike some large families, the siblings did not fend for each other, and each child struggled to survive as best they could. Brett's two sisters lived in England, and his five younger brothers lived in Australia, but as far as Brett was concerned, they could have lived on Mars. He had minimal contact with his family and both his parents had died in 1981, about five months apart. It didn't feel like a loss to Brett, as for him they had barely existed before then.

Brett's father had worked as a labourer in Australia and was an aggressive man, prone to excessive drinking. Most of the money he earned was lost at the local pub or with the illegal SP bookie down the road. Brett's mother had been a pretty girl in her youth with many friends, he'd been told, but life had sucked her dry, and like her children, she lived in fear of her husband's anger.

Brett was not overly concerned about the death of the prostitute as the investigation appeared to be petering out. However, he was prone to periodic black moods where he would sit alone at the kitchen table nursing his beer, immersed in troubled thoughts of the past. Jenny knew to avoid intruding at these times, as she feared his blistering rage.

Whilst misery loves company, his did not seek the company of other people. During these down times, Brett's thoughts would drift through a range of bitter moments in his life, of which there were many.

Recollections would surface of his alcoholic father beating the daylights out of their mother, and treating his children with the same brutality.

Brett recalled the time when he felt his own body had grown big enough to take his father on. He relived the vivid images and sounds of the day he heard muffled screams escaping from his parent's bedroom, and the whimpering that greeted him as he pushed open their bedroom door and then wished that he hadn't.

The light that he flicked on revealed the punching bag of misery that was his mother, her body deflated by her husband's blows.

'Get the fuck out of here, you little turd!'

Brett now had a man's body – a young man's body – though he still trembled as his anger fought to douse the flames of his fear. He moved forward as his father leapt out of bed dressed as the day he was born. Somehow a naked man looks more beatable and vulnerable.

They stood less than a metre apart, glaring at each other, one body giving in to the ravages of age, gravity and lifestyle. A junkyard of wasted souls and missed opportunities. Brett looked down and his right foot connected with his father's testicles, the way his father had taught him to drop kick a football. As the older man doubled over, Brett smashed his fist into the balding head. His mother stayed on after that, whilst his younger brothers were too young to break away.

That night, Brett slept under a bridge and ceased going to school. He did a range of labouring jobs over the following months and survived, but the emotional scars remained, covered with a veneer of aggression and at times his own brand of brutality. No one ever dared suggest to Brett that he resembled his father in any way. He never spoke to his father again.

Before the year was out, Brett came to share an apartment with another young labourer, who introduced him to Deborah and The Union. The Union was a sect led by Deborah Duval and was housed on a 10 acre wooded property in the outreaches of Warrandyte. Brett was ripe for the picking, lacking a family structure and immersed in self-doubts. Deborah's group became his family and he lived with them for a while and resumed his schooling, taught by a number of sect members. About two years later, Brett left The Union after commencing a cadetship with the Victorian Police Force. The schooling he received whilst living with Deborah's group, and the connections she provided within the Victorian Police Force, helped to ensure that his cadetship application was successful.

Brett took to the structure of the force as if it was the last missing piece of his life's jigsaw puzzle. He particularly enjoyed what he saw as the legitimisation of his urge to wield power and exert physical force.

Brett married Jenny when he was twenty-five. She came from a similar violent background, which left her damaged and needy, but not tarnished with the same anger that polluted Brett's life. She initially mistook his sexual demands for caring and they married soon after, when she became pregnant.

Brett did well in the Victorian Police Force, rising to the rank of detective sergeant in the vice squad and then homicide squad, at the relatively young age of thirty-two. He maintained contact with Deborah, and she had decided he was of more value to her outside the sect, as his position gave her a measure of protection. He chose to move to the homicide squad feeling he would be subjected to less scrutiny than in the vice squad.

For a long time Brett had puzzled over Deborah's past and his inability to decipher it. Then, several years ago he struck gold.

His name was Matt – a petty criminal who had been picked up for alleged armed theft. Brett had become involved with his case after the elderly man, who Matt had robbed at knifepoint, died from a severe heart attack during the robbery. The details poured out of Matt in response to Brett's interrogation, and he described his failed marriage to a sixteen-year-old girl. Matt dramatically drew a picture of life repeatedly letting him down – including his young wife deserting him after only two years of marriage. He explained with an air of disbelief that his ex-wife was now fabulously wealthy and ran a sect up in the hills.

Brett's interest was suddenly piqued and he learnt that Deborah had reinvented herself, where in spite of her limited schooling she had become a Guru to hundreds of people, many of them with tertiary education. Brett's features revealed nothing of the excitement that now tingled his body, but he filed the information away for future use. He well knew that the dirt of the past can become the poison of the present.

Matt described Deborah as a 'pretty young thing' that he and others thought was somewhat empty headed, referring to her as 'Nancy', which was her birth name. Her intelligence did not show up in her academic results, as she had little interest in school or the subjects they taught there. Her parents were not troubled by her lack of achievement at school, as they had not performed there either. They saw no reason why she would need an education when it had been denied to them.

Likewise, her teachers were not troubled by her lack of performance, as they themselves felt trapped in careers and school that had not fulfilled their aspirations. They believed that even her looks would not elevate her above the stagnation of emptiness and poverty that surrounded her.

Brett gained the impression that her parents envisioned her being crushed by the weight of a lack of education. Her mother became embittered by recurring betrayals and her father succumbed to being pickled in his alcohol as a way of numbing the bitterness surrounding his upset of the hand that life had dealt him in being railed constantly about being a labourer in all kinds of weather for very little pay and having to follow the idiotic orders of people he didn't respect. Her mother wore her body down further, working as a cleaner in other people's homes.

Deborah, or "Nancy" back then, learnt to refine her anger to the point where it was silent, because to acknowledge such things made them appear real. She quarantined herself from her family's failures, as if they were infectious viruses that could be passed onto her. She was an only child, as her parents felt further children would be a drain on them.

She could see her parents withering under the pressure of existence, where nothing in life tempted them any longer. She had no memory of them having been any different, but people who knew them, said they had been alive and vital in their youth. Nothing drives some people more than the vision of what failure can bring.

She chose to leave Northcote HSC midway through Form 4, eager to enter what she called the real world, and commenced her life from then on. Prior to that time, to those who prided themselves on their ability to pick losers, she appeared to be one. Her parents never got to know their daughter Nancy had reinvented herself and disowned her past as soon after both her parents died from medical causes.

Deborah worked in a variety of short term unskilled jobs that she considered trivial, until two years later she began working with a group running yoga classes. Within a year of starting she went on to develop her own small but increasingly popular yoga school, and this opened the door to having contact with people possessing positions of power.

To those who came to know her, it was never clear when she made the decision to head a sect, and possibly she herself could not have pinpointed the time in her life when such a momentous determination developed. Most likely it was a seamless transition generated by her desire to escape her parents' fate, where she realised that like chess, at the end of the game, the queen and the pawn go back into the same box, but whilst the game was on, she was determined to win.

On Deborah's 10-acre property, there were scattered huts and a larger house where she and her partner Bill stayed. Over 35 young children lived on the property and were clothed in exactly the same manner, all with their hair dyed blonde. A number of the adults in the sect were responsible for supervising and educating the children, as they did not attend outside schools. These supervisors were mainly women and meted out punishments in a strict manner, at times bordering on cruel. Any sign of rebellion by the children would be suppressed by the use of solitary isolation and canings.

Deborah also possessed a store of illicit drugs obtained from medical and paramedical contacts, and she allowed these to be used at times to sedate the children, as a means of controlling them. The drugs used ranged from tranquilisers and antidepressants to LSD.

The goal of the children's schooling was that one day they would become nurses, social workers, teachers and the like. These were all occupations that could be used to assist Deborah in building up and protecting her group and her control over them.

The children were all given her surname of Duval. Brett learned that some of the children had been taken from young unmarried mothers, where social workers connected to The Union had convinced the distressed mothers to give the babies up for adoption. Other children were progeny of the adults who belonged to the sect and lived on the property. The remainder of the children originated from a breeding program instituted by Deborah, where she dictated which man would sleep with which woman on any particular night. These children also took on her surname and were dressed identically with the others.

Brett wondered if Deborah really thought she was developing a master race or whether she just viewed them as a bunch of screwed up kids that she could control, as she did the adults.

Immersed in his alcohol and maudlin thoughts, Brett recalled the conversation when Deborah had rung him the day before.

Wednesday, 20 January 1988
6.30 p.m.

Brett sat himself at the counter of the DT's pub with two of his workmates. DT's was a pub he often frequented, a satisfactory waterhole and hiding place that he chose in preference to rushing home.

He nursed his beer, though the urge was to drink something more numbing but for the fact he had to drive home later. Though he had his workmates alongside, he might as well have been on his own, as the fog of his black mood began to engulf him.

He was no stranger to these moods and this night the alcohol and black mood blurred the world around him. Not by choice, the piercing sound of his phone dragged him back.

Deborah's angry voice penetrated the fog, engulfing Brett.

'I've had it with those media rags reporting a bunch of lies from the termites who've deserted. They're out to destroy me and The Union. I've heard that many of those deserters have been seeing that quack psychiatrist Dr Wright and complained about The Union, and he's promised them to try and get the authorities involved.'

Brett remained silent, stunned by the angry outburst. *What the fuck can I do about it, Deborah?* he silently queried, as his mind translated her words into a demand.

As if reading his thoughts Deborah reminded him that in the same manner she had pumped air into his career, she could also readily deflate it. Her message was clear to Brett that he either assisted her with this problem "or else". He knew the "or else" was not an idle threat.

'I want you to drive up to see me no later than 8.30 p.m. tonight so we can discuss the best way of dealing with this problem.'

Brett again heard this as an order, rather than a request.

He went through the motions of letting Jenny know that a major case was taking him out of town and he wouldn't be sleeping at home that night. When his call went through to message, allowing him to leave a scripted response without questions being raised, he felt a sense of relief. Not that he would have felt any pressure to answer truthfully, and having left the message, neither he nor Jenny would broach the matter again.

Brett's career had stalled in its original upward path as initially he had moved up the ranks, scoring significant convictions of drug peddlers, petty criminals and a rapist/murderer who ran a prostitution racket, even if it involved using unorthodox measures at times. If it came down to their word against his, then he knew he was safe, but he was tiring of the hassles of dealing with the Police Ethical Department.

Recently a young hoon had laid complaints against Brett, alleging he had "belted him up". It wasn't Brett's job to catch idiots like this but he was driving home at the time, saw the hoon doing skids down a North Melbourne street, and decided he'd bring him in. The case was due to go to court, where he knew some smart-arse lawyer would attempt to give him a hard time. He knew how to handle himself in the witness box and believed he would get out of it, *but who needed that shit?* He thought to himself.

About a year and a half ago, he was put in charge of a task force whose main aim was to investigate The Union sect and the allegations of abuse voiced by a number of ex-members. Naturally he had undermined the investigation at every turn, but it had now come to a point where he needed to produce a scalp or his superiors at Police Headquarters would start asking questions. There had already been some grumbles that he'd been able to deflect, about the lack of progress.

So far he had never found a right time to tell Deborah about the prostitute who had died, and he wasn't sure there would ever be a right time.

8.15 p.m.

Brett drove slowly up the long winding driveway of Deborah's commune. He felt more comfortable calling it that, rather than that stupid, pretentious name of the "Union". It was a large property, set up high, so one could see the lights of Melbourne shining bright in the distance like jewels above the city sewers.

Brett didn't want his own kids ending up like this, like him, hating the world around them. He knew that he could probably stop work even now, as he had saved and invested carefully. The perks in his job had enabled him to accumulate a considerable sum of money.

No more than he deserved for dealing with the scum that were part of his work, he felt. He couldn't be too obvious with the way he spent his money, couldn't splash it around, or questions would be asked. It would be stupid to buy expensive cars or houses, but he could still enjoy life's pleasures without drawing attention to himself. Shopkeepers, pub owners, fast food outlets, and prostitutes – they all felt the need to give him gifts. No way would he end up like his father – as broke as a compound fracture.

Deborah's white colonial style house stood at the end of a winding path, set in 10 acres of wooded land. Poplar trees elegantly lined the route leading to the house, whilst the other sect members lived in scattered huts at least 100 yards away or more. The children's dormitory was placed amongst the huts.

Brett's visits to Deborah were not on a regular basis, but averaged about once a month, and were always associated with a mixture of excitement and apprehension. Much as prey is mesmerised by a cobra about to strike, so Brett felt inextricably entangled in an erotic mesh that drew him to Deborah.

As he climbed out from his parked car, he became aware of a tall bearded man approaching him. Brett felt an instant dislike building up, as the needles of the unfamiliar man's hostility pierced the air around him. The man's features appeared disconnected to each other, with teeth jostling for space and a furrowed, overpopulated forehead.

He had narrow, slit like eyes and his nose suggested pugilistic involvement in the past. The man's body was enveloped by a cloak of aggression and brute strength. Brett knew he could handle himself in a fight, but he didn't particularly want to take on King Kong, as he had instantly named him.

'Wadya doin' here?' he demanded of Brett. 'Can't you read the sign? No Trespassing.'

During the asphyxiating silence, Brett weighed up his options and then explained in a controlled and outwardly calm manner, that he was Deborah's guest.

Without a reply, the man backed away as seamlessly as Deborah materialised behind him. Not for the first time, Brett marvelled at Deborah's appearance, as the saturnine darkness enveloped her. She was totally different to the type of woman he was usually attracted to, nor was she the type that he would have expected to be interested in him. He knew that their convergent needs drew them together, spiced with a sense of threat, feeling stronger than sex but incorporating it at the same time.

He had read that intense negative feelings such as fear could stimulate sexual arousal, and he was aware of being pulled to Deborah like the powerful force of magnets drawn to each other. It continued to puzzle him, as he was used to being the one in control.

Although not usually given to speculation about such matters, Brett had no doubt at all that Deborah did not leave her looks to the vagaries of ageing, but regularly used the skills of a plastic surgeon. *It was money well spent,* he thought, as she was certainly a woman that turned heads, with people who passed her twisting to get a second look.

However, he knew there was something else about her, another dimension altogether, that endowed her with the power to lead and control others – including himself. But he found that he was unable to put that extra dimension into words. Like a chameleon, she seemed able to change her external appearance, as the outside environment altered, and as her followers in The Union grew and revamped, so did she. When Brett threatened people, it felt obvious to him and them; but with Deborah, there was a smouldering sense of danger that he could sense but had difficulty putting it into words.

As Deborah approached him Brett noticed that her dog – he couldn't remember the name of the mongrel – stood in the shadows nearby, guarding his owner. Its parentage was unknown, at least to him, though it looked to Brett as if a bull terrier had played some part. It was the ugliest dog he had ever laid eyes on, a dog that not even a bitch would love. Its body was misshapen and it had a skin condition causing part of its body and most of its chunky face to be red and inflamed. It was a thrusting ball of snarls, and the very opposite of the dog he would have expected Deborah to have, given her obsession with disguising her past and presenting perfection to the outside world.

Deborah moved slowly away from the car park, along a path, and Brett knew he was expected to follow in her wake. He anticipated where she was heading, as it was Friday, and he was aware that every Friday night at 9 p.m., The Union members congregated in the church-like hall on the property.

When he entered, he found the congregation were already seated, shrouded by the semi-darkness of the hall, with not a sound to be heard.

Brett walked to the back pew whilst Deborah glided towards the front, where a bluish light shone on the throne-like chair that she sat on. In the glow of that light, Brett could see that Deborah was now enveloped in a long, dark blue robe. Her assistant, a pale woman of almost transparent appearance, joined her and stood alongside, clothed in a similar coloured robe. The shining light created an aura around them, and scattered candles cast an eerie, flickering illumination around the perimeter of the room.

The smell of incense hovered in the hall as Deborah rose from her chair and the congregation pushed their benches back and knelt, crossing themselves in the unique manner that she had decreed.

With his past involvement in the sect, Brett choreographed his own movements to keep in time with the congregation. The congregants knelt for five minutes, making the sign of the cross in reverse and in silent prayer, before resuming their seats. No one made eye contact with any other, and each person appeared immersed in their own world, as if hypnotised.

Deborah still had not uttered a word and to Brett, it felt as if the heavy silence pressed the congregants to their seats. Brett himself felt weighed down by the atmosphere in the room.

The service lasted close to 45 minutes, mainly made up of meditation, until at the end, Deborah and the congregants knelt and chanted together the mantra of The Union.

> *"To thy Last Supper*
> *Shall we be allowed to stay*
> *We have not given thee a kiss of Judas*
> *Nor betrayed any secrets to thine enemies*
> *We shall outlive them and topple them*
> *So the lesson shall be learnt."*

For all his doubts, in the subdued light and surrounded by the smell of incense, Brett always found himself suspending disbelief and drawn into the ceremony, leaving him uneasy as he left the hall at the end.

After the congregation filed out, Brett followed Deborah to her house, which appeared empty apart from the two of them. He knew that she had a partner, Bill, but he was never visible at times like this. For the first time since Brett's arrival Deborah's languid voice addressed him as she passed over the glass of red wine that she had just poured. Her statement that she was giving him wine to drink required no response from Brett, nor had she felt the need to ask him if he wanted to drink.

They sipped their wine in silence, not looking directly at each other, and Brett found it hard not to be mesmerised by the leaping flames from the log fire close by. Having drunk half her wine, Deborah got up and in silence walked to her bedroom. Brett knew without asking that she expected him to join her.

He felt like a bystander viewing the unfolding events, and marvelled how different this was to any other interaction he had had with a woman or even with a man. At all times Deborah led and Brett followed – as if he were partnering her on a dance floor. She was the queen bee of their relationship. Brett was never sure what she got out of having sex with him, not that he really cared, but he was curious. Did she get any physical pleasure or was it merely another way of controlling him? Come to think of it, what did he get from it?

She dictated their sex as she did every other part of their interactions. From the time his naked body met hers, the precarious journey began. He felt excitement akin to the shiver and feelings he experienced with any extreme activity where danger lurked—such as sky diving, which he'd done several times, or dealing with a criminal who could be armed. He equated it with the coupling of some spiders or praying mantises, where the male would be consumed at the end.

He knew his mates at work would have been amazed to learn of the things that he read and knew, and they certainly would have found it difficult to believe that he could have a relationship like this.

As Deborah mounted him, she placed a pre-prepared ice block between her lips, and then let it slide into her mouth. Her tongue skated around its cold, smooth surface as her buttocks moved rhythmically above and around Brett. In the past, Brett had felt spooked by this ritual, but was now more at ease with it and aroused by her body. He knew that the ice block would contain a slip of paper with the typed name of a perceived enemy. He gave them the name of 'misfortune cookies'.

He climaxed as he heard her reciting her mantra:

"To Dr Andrew Wright
I bequeath this curse
May he forever return to dust and earth."

As bizarre as it all sounded, Brett knew that her capacity for malice and revenge outweighed even his own.

As Deborah rolled onto her side, she deposited the ice block into a glass beside the bed. Brett was unsure whether she had also climaxed, but what she couldn't control was the response of her body, the moisture and skin changes revealing to him that she had been sexually aroused. He waited for her to break the silence.

'Go to sleep, Brett. I'll wake you in about an hour and we'll talk then.'

CHAPTER FOUR

Thursday, 22 August 1986
1.25 p.m.

In theory, Andrew's appointment book allowed for him to take a lunchbreak of half an hour, but theory can evaporate in the face of reality. Frequently his break for lunch was gobbled up by going over time with some appointments or using the break to return phone calls that he felt shouldn't wait.

He had personally drawn up his own timetable and he wryly noted that there were occasions where an outside observer would have expected him to be in charge of his scheduling. However, to Andrew, it often felt as if the timetable controlled him, and for a long time it remained unaltered in spite of feeling that it wasn't working out.

Today he decided to take charge and managed to secure his lunchbreak by taking himself down the street to buy his lunch, choosing some sandwiches together with a coffee. On most days he had brought the traditional paper bag lunch to work, and when possible, ate it at his desk as he wrote notes and made phone calls. He now realised that the only way he could secure a break during the day was to leave the building. He chuckled to himself how something that was bleeding obvious had felt like a revelation.

As he left the building and closed the door behind him, he became aware of a prickly discomfort, as if he was a truant wagging school, and realised guilt was at play, and uncertain why.

Just before he left his medical rooms, Andrew asked his secretary Rosemary whether he could get her anything down the street and told her he'd be back in time for the next patient. Rosemary had been with him for close to ten years now, and he felt she was a wonderful secretary, admired by both his patients and himself.

Years back, a work colleague had told him that the criteria for picking a perfect secretary was to find a middle-aged woman, possibly in her mid-forties, someone who had never married and wasn't in any current relationship – a "spinster". God, Andrew hated that term – single men didn't have a label put on them.

'You need to find a single woman who is generally unhappy in her personal life and would be married to the job,' came the unsolicited advice from his colleague. At the time Andrew thought these comments were cynical and in poor taste, and he continued to feel that. Yet Rosemary in fact did fulfil those criteria, and Andrew reflected on how unfair life could be, as Rosemary showed so much warmth in her dealings with the patients, and yet, away from work, this warmth dissipated in the barren waste that was her personal life.

1.41 p.m.

Andrew seated himself at the back of the local coffee shop where he was able to observe the other people and not be disturbed. He had always enjoyed watching people and their interactions. The waitress brought the sandwich and blueberry muffin that he had ordered, as well as a strong coffee. He thanked her politely before opening a copy of the Sun Herald that he had picked up from the counter. It was not a paper he rated highly and felt it was a rag, but ease won out over content, as he found the page size a lot more comfortable to read.

Not like some of the other daily papers where turning a page might cost you a coffee, accidentally knocked over, or impair the vision of the person sitting next to you.

On page 4 of the paper, he noted an article by Penelope Dee, who was distinguished by the title of "Investigative Journalist". This label provoked a knee-jerk cynicism in Andrew as he had the impression that a lot of contemporary journalists cannibalised material from other outlets, often rehashing it and then presenting it as the fruit of their own labour. He reflected to himself how journalism was no longer seen as a noble profession by many in the community.

Personally, he conceded that there were a number of admirable journalists still around, but like many, he had the tendency to lump them all together and to judge journalism by the lowest common denominator.

What commanded his attention now was Dee's article describing how many young females, often university students, worked as strippers or prostitutes to raise the money required to pay for their keep and ongoing education. The article alleged that in some brothels up to 50 per cent of the prostitutes working there were students.

Andrew could accept the premise that some female students did use prostitution as a source of income, but he strongly doubted the high percentages given. *And at what price?* he wondered.

It worried him about the possible long-term harm to these young women, risking the distortion of how they viewed men and even how they viewed themselves. The strength of his opposition to such practice was unclear to him, as the article presented many of these young women making a free choice, yet it left him feeling uneasy. He had often reflected on the complex force that sex could be. It could form part of a loving relationship, or it could be used for control. It might be a way of obtaining reassurance about one's self-worth, or used manipulatively to climb the promotion ladder at work. It could be used as a means of escaping poverty, or to feed a drug addiction. In fact, the range of outfits that it could be cloaked in resembled a Dulux colour chart of reasons and emotions.

Given all the above scenarios, Andrew couldn't help wondering whether one should really be judgemental about the use of sex in prostitution compared to all the other ways that sex was used. Still, none of this took away the discomfort he experienced about the idea of university students using sex as a means of paying for their studies, given that most were not escaping poverty nor caught up in drug addiction or sex slavery.

He noted with a sardonic smile that medicine was often shifting from full time employment to sessional work, something that the so-called "oldest profession" had been doing for a long time.

He glanced at his watch and was startled by the time, realising he had better rush back as his next patient was due at 2 p.m. and there were only two minutes to go. Once again he had been kidnapped by his meandering thoughts. He phoned his secretary to warn her he would be at least five minutes late, and asked her to let his next patient know.

Not for the first time, he reflected about the difference between his practice and that of some of his colleagues in other specialties, where multiple bookings for the same time were not unusual. This certainly maximised the time efficiency for the specialist without any apparent concern that patients might have to wait one to two hours to be seen. By contrast, some of his patients would complain if he was over five minutes late. He could understand how patients objected to having to wait one or two hours, as they felt it showed a lack of respect towards them.

2.16 p.m.

As Andrew sat listening to his first patient after lunch, a Mr R, he found himself struggling to maintain concentration, as a wave of drowsiness started to envelop him.

The strange part and one that he didn't fully understand was that there were three other patients in his practice who appeared to have the same effect on him. He would struggle to listen carefully to what they were saying, a feeling he owed that to all his patients. Lately he had given a lot of thought to possible reasons for this, and excluded the possibility of it being caused by a lack of sleep the night before or a heavy meal or other factors along those lines. If it wasn't a factor within himself, he wondered, then what was causing this effect?

It troubled him that he had to struggle to listen carefully to what these patients were saying. It wasn't that these few patients spoke in monotones or that he found their histories boring, so why was there this impenetrable screen forming, creating a barrier between the patient and himself. He had begun to suspect these patients were coasting, and comfortable in not working on their problems. He heard them comfortably describing the same problems each session, appearing untroubled by their lack of progress. Rather, they appeared to be comfortably slipping into a groove where they recited the same problems in the same manner each session, without any sign of being troubled by their lack of progress. There was undoubtedly a level of frustration that he experienced, and probably, like those patients, he was becoming detached from their real issues. He knew that if he was going to be of benefit to them in therapy, he would need to start sharing his observations about their lack of progress, and their inclination to see themselves as victims, whilst they appeared to be only paying lip service to working on personal change.

Andrew was aware that it was easy as a therapist to be seduced into keeping a patient comfortable and winning their approval by just coasting along, but he also knew that the sessions would become meaningless if he was to do that. On the other hand, confronting the patient could result in them terminating therapy and obviously one couldn't treat a patient who did not attend.

Still, this wasn't a valid reason for avoiding facing issues with the patient. He was determined to start confronting Mr R in a manner that hopefully would not drive him away, but would make the sessions more meaningful for him.

Mr R suffered from a moderately severe obsessive-compulsive condition with associated depression and anxiety, but he did not have the emotional fragility of say, a young schizophrenic patient, where confrontation would be inappropriate.

Mr R's life and emotions were severely shackled by his psychiatric condition, where he could not cope with the intensity of his emotions or the uncertainty of what each new day might bring. He had developed a rigid and restrictive set of rituals to create the illusion that everything in his life was predictable.

Andrew realised that his thoughts were drifting and that he had stopped listening to his patient. It was close to the end of the session, but he had come to a decision that from the next session onwards, he would commence sharing his thoughts with Mr R, including describing how the sessions made Andrew himself feel, thus providing a mirror where Mr R could commence looking at himself, to facilitate seeing the real person underneath all the restrictive defences he had built up.

4.06p.m.

By the time he reached the last appointment of the day, Andrew had to admit to himself that he was looking forward to finishing work and going home. His last patient, Samantha, was a 41-year-old woman with a Rubenesque build, who tended to be clinging in therapy, and had been attending for close to 12 weeks now.

As Andrew gently guided her to the door at the end of the session, his hand on her left shoulder, she turned towards him, addressing him by his first name and asked if she could have more frequent sessions. She explained that she felt she would make more rapid progress that way. Hesitantly he clarified that it wasn't necessary and wouldn't speed up her progress, but he knew that the query would arise again.

6.08 p.m.

Andrew nervously fiddled with the car radio, trying to distract himself from the flood of the many emotions and thoughts enveloping him, and he felt as if there was a weight on his chest causing his breathing to be shallow and rapid.

Just before entering his driveway at home, he stopped his car and heard himself phoning and talking to Samantha, as if a stranger to his own thoughts. He was aware of an awkward, detached voice telling her that he had thought about it some more and decided they could give weekly sessions a try.

Prior to then, Samantha had been attending therapy every three to four weeks, so Andrew reassured her that he would avoid her being out of pocket by continuing to bulk bill the sessions.

Each progressive step Samantha took towards intimacy met no resistance, so she continued. Two months after her weekly sessions began in August 1986, they commenced having sex in a motel room that he rented not far from her home.

By now Andrew was experiencing a kaleidoscope of feelings and found himself immersed in lies that brought him no peace. He had difficulty looking Karen in the eye, and the blue ink shadow of guilt slowly enveloped his life from 1986– a year he would never forget.

He became increasingly anxious about being trapped in what felt like a sexual spider web, where he began to fear that the moment he attempted to stop the relationship with Samantha would be the very moment she would retaliate, reporting him to the Victorian Medical Board. Not that he wanted to leave the relationship, as he clung to her throaty laughter, to the scent and feel of her fulsome body. He allowed her to continue calling him Andrew and whilst he referred to her as Mrs Richards, he thought of her as Samantha. In their intimate moments, he did not call her by any name. He didn't usually address patients by their first name and didn't encourage them to call him Andrew, but a few, like Samantha, chose to do so.

He had always strongly believed that it was important to maintain a doctor – patient relationship, where his own personal life and needs would not intrude on the therapy, nor would there be inappropriate intimacy. *At least that's the theory,* he said to himself with heavy irony.

After several months of therapy and sex, unsurprisingly, Samantha continued to be a needy soul, prone to recurrent bouts of depression and occasional suicidal thoughts. Her childhood appeared to have been a normal one until her father died from a massive heart attack when she was eight years of age. Her mother then struggled to cope with four young children, aged from fourteen years down to the youngest, aged three. There followed a procession of men intruding, as her mother attempted to replace her husband with an urgency akin to a woman dying of thirst. Unfortunately the men she chose were totally different to her late husband, and had no interest in supporting a young family.

Samantha married when she became pregnant at the age of nineteen and escaped the family home, but found no solace in her new home either. Her husband was four years older than her, worked as a bricklayer and outside of work his only interests were the local pub and the local football team. They separated soon after their daughter was born, following three years of a loveless marriage.

Samantha and her daughter lived on their own at first, but in time, like her mother she began inviting a regular stream of men into her life. They accepted her invitation, took what they wanted and left.

Six months after the affair began, Andrew found himself becoming increasingly concerned about ending the relationship with Samantha and encouraged her to form a relationship with another man that she had recently met, in the hope that this would offer Andrew the escape route that he so desperately sought now. Privately, he wondered why he wanted to end the affair, and the best explanation he could arrive at, was that with diminishing excitement he had started to look at the destruction he was causing to his marriage and to the ethics and morals that had guided his life in the past.

For twelve months, his manipulation (for he could not call it 'therapy') failed to achieve what he so desperately craved by then. Then when he had stopped hoping, Samantha stunned him with the news that she had met a widower with two young children, who appeared to genuinely care about her. She rang Andrew, and told him that she wanted to terminate therapy as she was not prepared to risk damaging her new relationship. She no longer needed Andrew's therapy nor his sex.

Having penetrated that moral barrier once, Andrew struggled to avoid doing it yet again – and it was a struggle at times. He determined that if a difficult transference developed in treating a female patient, where either he or they developed a strong attraction to the other, he would refer them on to another psychiatrist. He was aware that in psychiatric practice, there was only he and the patient in the room and no nurse to chaperone the situation. Whilst errors tend to occur in the company of other errors, he knew that this was not the type of company he could afford again, as he would risk losing his family, his profession and his self-worth.

Andrew now felt a foreigner in his own moral landscape, struggling to make himself understand what had occurred and why. Karen and his friends noted that he appeared distracted and at times daydreaming. He came very close to confessing to Karen, but avoided giving in to that urge, knowing it would be disastrous to do so.

He had believed for a long time that to confess all was self-serving and the wrong approach. He had seen it happen in many of his patients, where in the guise of an open relationship they confessed wrongdoings, dropping the grenade in the lap of their partner. For a short while it seemed to ease their own guilt, but at the expense of burdening their partner and destroying the relationship.

Andrew had felt for some time, probably since late 1986, that things had cooled in the way Karen related to him. Silently he queried whether Karen could have possibly suspected he had been having an affair, and he continued to live with a lie that brought no peace. He knew he had to sort it out himself, possibly with professional help, rather than dumping the problem onto Karen.

During his medical training he came to understand that the basic goal in medicine was to cause no harm, and then to try and help the patient. He struggled to understand why he had failed to adhere to these guidelines when treating Samantha. Certainly he had recently lost both parents, and struggled to grieve over the loss of his father, a man who had only been a shadow in his life. He was wary of possibly using this as an excuse for behavior that only he could be responsible for. Andrew had been fascinated about the concepts of good and evil for many years, pondering the question of whether people were intrinsically good or intrinsically bad. If they were good, was it the fear of punishment that made them act so? He had come to believe that anyone was capable of doing bad things if their controls were loosened and depending on the circumstances around them. He knew about the mob effect where large numbers of people could be dragged into an environment where they carried out acts of evil, often feeling safe to do so under the umbrella of anonymity that a mob generated. He believed that there was a ripple effect, where having done one bad thing it would be easier to do more of the same.

Apart from his own behaviour, he thought back to his family's experience during the Holocaust where seemingly educated and cultured people could become sadists and murderers. He reflected on how the victims of these atrocities could also be part of a ripple effect, where the damage the victims suffered could cause further damage to the generations that followed because of how they related to each other.

Hannah Arendt's concept of the banality of evil was something he totally agreed with, and recalled how during the Holocaust the people who murdered their victims could have been a former friend, or a teacher whose class the victim attended or even a doctor who used to treat them. People who once had been close to their victim now became their brutal executioners.

Andrew wondered how his own behaviour in having sex with a patient fitted into these concepts. Had his resolve been weakened by events in his life or was he totally to blame? What did it say about him as a person? He worried that he was becoming too preoccupied with these thoughts and whilst they addressed important issues, he feared that he could be buried in an avalanche of emotion. Once the thoughts squatted in his mind, it was difficult to evict them. They were issues he would eventually need to confront, but he increasingly believed that involving a therapist would be a safer approach. The idea of a psychiatrist needing to see another psychiatrist did not sit comfortably with him, but he acknowledged it was necessary. He knew that the saying "physician heal thyself" didn't mean going it alone but rather, admitting to himself that he required outside assistance.

He had never felt so alone before.

CHAPTER FIVE

Wednesday, 20 January 1988
11.56 p.m.

'Get up.'

The command from Deborah met no resistance, and Brett was immediately alert. He checked his watch and guessed that the extra few hours sleep he'd been allowed were more to do with Deborah needing the time rather than any concern about his tiredness.

He knew that whenever Deborah invited him up to her compound, it was never just for a social outing. There was always some underlying issue that she wanted to speak to him about, and on this occasion he suspected that it had to do with psychiatrist Dr Wright and her concern that he might be involved in trying to expose her group.

Through his work with the Victorian Police Task Force, Brett had heard rumours that a number of aggrieved ex-sect members were attending Dr Wright, and it was therefore not a surprise to recently hear from Deborah that she was becoming increasingly troubled by this. She had become more and more concerned about the volume of ex-sect members airing their grievances about The Union to Dr Wright.

Brett had initially drawn her attention to this, but it was highlighted as a concern for Deborah when a sect member Beverley went to see her dermatologist, Dr Lee, who did sessional work in the same building as Dr Andrew Wright. The patients of Dr Lee and Dr Wright shared the same waiting room. Deborah described how Beverley had recently reported back to her the details of a coincidence that occurred when she attended her dermatologist.

While waiting for her appointment, Beverley had noticed an ex-Union member, Tracy, sitting at the other end of the waiting room. (Deborah tended not to believe in coincidences and felt many events were predestined rather than occurring by chance.) Beverley told her excitedly that on the spur of the moment she decided to go and sit next to Tracy. There were no other patients in the waiting room at the time, so Beverley chatted, asking Tracy how things were going in her life. Beverley recalled that Tracy and her partner broke away from The Union 10 months earlier, and after the brief startled silence that followed Beverley's greeting, Tracy began responding cautiously to Beverley's chatter. As she started describing the recent breakup of her relationship after leaving The Union, Tracy's eyes filled with tears and her controlled answers lost out to the rage inside, leaving her inconsolable even with Beverley's arm around her.

Beverley reported to Deborah the bitter allegations that Tracy had made about the role of The Union in destroying her relationship with her partner. In a rage undiluted by her tears, Tracy expressed the wish that Deborah would be punished for the havoc and damage she had inflicted on other people's lives. With a humourless laugh, Beverley told Deborah that for the first time in her life she gave silent thanks that her dermatologist was running late, as it gave her the freedom to listen to more of Tracy's story. She described to Deborah that it was like the waters of a dam escaping the walls that had held them back, so that the torrent of Tracy's words and emotions spilt out unfiltered.

Over the next 15 minutes, Tracy's pressured voice described how she and a few other former sect members had poured out their stories to Dr Wright, describing their hurt and complaints about The Union. Fighting to regain control, in a whisper that was more like a hiss, Tracy told Beverley how Dr Wright reassured her that he understood and shared the concerns of people damaged by The Union. He promised that he would try and speak to the appropriate authorities about the issues the ex- sect members had related.

After Beverley said that, Tracy suddenly clammed up, probably realising she may have said too much. Minutes later, as if orchestrated, Beverley's doctor called her in for her consultation.

After Beverley told Deborah about the chance encounter with Tracy and what was said, Deborah organised some of her members to monitor the building where Dr Wright worked, recording which ex-Union members were entering. She also arranged to have the rooms of Dr Wright broken into and was able to obtain a list of his current and recent patients, revealing the names of nine former sect members.

On the drive to Deborah's compound, Brett had decided that he wouldn't mention the death of the prostitute. He wasn't sure that he would ever discuss this with her, for even though she adopted a priest like a role in her group, where members opened up to her, she was not inclined to dispense forgiveness following their confessions. What he or The Union could do about Dr Wright wasn't clear to him at this stage.

Brett was fully alert after Deborah's voice jarred him awake, so he dressed quickly and joined her in the kitchen, where she had already prepared a coffee for them both. The hot liquid warmed him and he inhaled the aroma of the coffee beans, whilst her mongrel dog jumped up and licked the back of his hand, though Brett was on guard, knowing the mutt could readily switch from lick to snarl.

Deborah looked at Brett in silence, before asking directly what he thought should be done about Wright and his threat of interfering with her group. She said that she was now very aware that more and more ex-Union members were attending Wright and voicing their bitter complaints about her group to him. She revealed that about a month ago she had arranged for one of her current female members to be referred to Dr Wright as a patient, pretending to be unwell and posing as an ex-sect member, so she could gauge what Wright knew and how negative his attitude had become towards the group.

That visit demonstrated to her that Wright had become increasingly furious about The Union activities and had a strong desire to expose and close them down. Her stooge confirmed that the situation was as bad as she had feared.

Haltingly, Brett attempted to reassure Deborah that he was working on the issue, but her dismissive questioning pinned him down and he had to acknowledge that he really had no clear plan that would guarantee success in stopping Wright.

A task force headed by Brett had been set up close to one and a half years previously, with the primary purpose of exposing The Union activities and their alleged criminal behaviour. The Victorian Police Force had for a number of years put aside complaints and rumours relating to the Union, but eventually felt that they needed to investigate possible criminality associated with the group.

Brett had successfully undermined the investigation without detection, but needed a scalp to divert attention from the task force's apparent lack of success. Brett was also concerned that if the doctor managed to bring an increasingly hostile focus on the Union, then there was a danger that he, Brett, would be caught up in it. In addition, there was also the associated risk that if Wright involved higher authorities, then it would be a lot harder trying to stall their probing.

Slowly and deliberately, Deborah filled Brett in on a scheme she had devised and already set in motion, before telling Brett about it, though this action didn't surprise him as he had never seen her as a team player. He had to acknowledge that the scheme was brilliant.

Through her contacts, Deborah had learnt that there was a vacant position for a night-time cleaner/security person at the coroner's court. She directed Peter Robinson, a 38-year-old follower of hers, to apply for the position, which he succeeded in obtaining. The brief she gave him was to be on the lookout for any information that could be used against Dr Wright. As Robinson worked as a night-time cleaner, he was often on his own in the building and was able to snoop around the various offices, and hopefully access files and data at times, as the security was porous. Deborah was optimistic that something useful would be unearthed eventually that would destroy Wright's credibility.

Brett had hoped to stay with Deborah until at least the next morning, but she abruptly terminated their meeting, saying something unexpected had sprung up, and he needed to leave. He had not made it clear to Jenny when he would be returning home, and these days she didn't expect to receive that kind of information. There were times he might walk out the front door at home, calling back over his shoulder to no one in particular, that he was visiting a friend. Jenny would hear this and choose to say nothing, as it had become a ritual where the terms "friend" or "work" could represent going to a brothel or the local pub or whatever, in the language they now used.

For Brett, these pronouncements in a Catholic sense were akin to a confession and absolved him of guilt, if any existed. At times he wondered why he bothered, as he no longer cared and Jenny no longer believed him, nor took note of what he was saying. Her life had been set in concrete. He decided not to go straight home.

He pondered if it would bother him to have Jenny screwing another guy. *Probably not,* he thought, as their relationship had become meaningless. But the ego thing – wondering if the other guy had satisfied her – that would get to him. What if she got to love the other guy? He doubted that there was another guy. So what if she didn't love the other guy but liked his sex?

Sex and feelings had long ago divorced each other in his life. Brett drank from sex like he drank from beer. You bought it, you downed it, and you threw away the empties. But he knew that he wouldn't tolerate anyone taking something that belonged to him, whether he wanted it himself or not.

It troubled him that he couldn't get it up at will these days. The Viagra helped, but he felt it shouldn't be like this, and he believed his manhood was leaking away. It took more to arouse him now and he was aware that inflicting pain on a woman and seeing the fear in her dilated pupils – that turned him on. Trouble was, he was piss scared that his body was failing him and that people were no longer frightened of his authority. The thoughts sat on him like a brooding bird which one day might fly off altogether, leaving him an empty shell.

1.50 a.m.

Brett pulled up outside the Cherry Ripe, one of his favourite clubs. It was situated in King Street in the central business district, where investors had commenced converting warehouses into clubs and bars offering adult entertainment. Some of the clubs in this area stuck to the letter of the Law, such as Goldsmith's nightclub, The Underground, but the Cherry Ripe was at the sleazier end of the spectrum. It was located in the same street as The Underground, and only about 80 yards away from it, but the two clubs had little in common. The Cherry Ripe was a watering hole open well into the morning hours, with scantily clad waitresses who were rumoured to perform other duties as well, while The Underground was not even rumoured to be of any ill-repute.

As Brett walked in, he took note of who dropped their gaze and who edged away. Steve the barman knew him and gave him free drinks, but you wouldn't call him a friend, *He didn't have any real friends,* Brett's thoughts muttered to him. He nursed his beer at the counter and watched a repeat of a boxing match on the TV behind the bar. He felt the match was staged and that he could have taken on either of the boxers involved and laid them out without difficulty.

His grandmother used to say that misery needs company. *Rubbish,* he thought. *Company would just make you even more miserable –* maybe that's what they're trying to say. Sometimes he chatted to Steve or whichever barman was on, but tonight he couldn't be stuffed doing it. Steve was good that way. He didn't speak to you unless you spoke to him first.

There were few people in the club at this hour and only one scrawny, scantily clad waitress. Brett looked across at the wreck drinking at the other end of the bar, whose face looked familiar. He vaguely recalled a list of petty crimes and drunkenness. The derelict was dressed in rags and had probably slept under a bridge though Brett imagined the bum was not as old as he looked.

The man sidled over towards him and was obviously pickled,

and Brett knew if he let the fool talk, then it would be a temporary diversion from his own maudlin thoughts. The world wouldn't miss this wreck, but he wasn't going to be the guy that took him out.

By now the alcohol had weighed his own thoughts further down. He decided to buy the guy a few beers and what happened after that was no longer his responsibility.

The remnants of a man had layers of face folded over each other and giving in to gravity. His ugly mug was just asking for a fist to come smashing into it, but Brett decided it wouldn't be his. He had often reflected that it was fortunate people couldn't be charged for their thoughts; otherwise we'd all be in the clink. The stench from the swill of beer, sweat, vomit and cigarette fumes insulted Brett's nostrils. He felt really pissed off. Just one guy looking the wrong way at him and he'd let him have it. If it didn't happen here or in the street later, then it would happen at home. He felt tempted to go for a screw in the brothel and get it out of his system, but in one of his better decisions he convinced himself to go home, remembering he had an early morning shift the next day. One more beer and he would bomb out the moment he hit the sack.

Thursday, 21 January 1988
8.30 a.m.

Having cut short her meeting with Brett, sending him home during the early hours of the morning, Deborah was able to get a few hours of light sleep. She carefully concealed the circles under her eyes and painted on her dark red lipstick.

This morning she was to meet with Peter Owen, the owner of a well-known private gallery, which he founded in the mid 1970s after retiring from business. Telling Brett to leave early, without any explanation, had freed up time for an earlier arrival at Peter's gallery and allowing her more time to meet with its owner. However, she knew she could have arranged this meeting on another day, remembering how it had thrown Brett off balance when she told him he would have to leave and a puzzled, hesitant veil had spread over his features as he had done what was asked of him.

Exercising control over Brett and creating uncertainty was the stock of her trade. She had surmised that with people like Brett, it was safer to have them feeling unsure of themselves-to be reacting rather than initiating. It was a skill honed over many years. These days, she ensured she stayed in control, believing this reduced the risk of someone catching her unawares and hurting her.

9.57 a.m.

Deborah entered the Owen Gallery and seated herself to one side and towards the back, a strategic position where she could observe and not be particularly noticeable. This wish for anonymity seemed at odds with her presentation. Even in her early sixties, one could hardly fail to notice her. The high cheekbones and bright blue eyes, in a face framed by auburn hair, and a taut, slender figure that belied her age, made heads turn as she entered the room. She was comfortable with letting them look, feeling that at the end of the day they would know little more.

Peter Owen was a wealthy benefactor of the Union, having lived in the commune when younger, and then deciding to leave and make his mark in the world when he was in his mid-twenties. Deborah had been comfortable with his decision at the time, as she needed people of influence on the outside as well as the more pliable followers on the inside.

Peter was now married for the second time. After twenty-five years of marriage and two children, he had felt the need for change and new challenges in his life. He had achieved his financial goals as a land developer and investor, and as his marriage punctured and started to feel flat, he sought an injection of excitement. He lived alone for a year until in his late fifties he married a woman half his age. Their initial contact was made through an online agency with the not too subtle title of *sweetdaddy.com*, where attractive young women could make contact with very wealthy, older men.

Lilli, a young Chinese woman who was living in Hong Kong and had recently graduated from the University there, majoring in politics and economics, responded to Peter's advertisement and was happily chosen. She ran Peter's gallery proficiently, having entered into the marriage in the same manner, meeting both their needs. She had not been briefed about Peter's past connection with Deborah, but seemed wary of her, sensing that Peter's friendship with Deborah was something that she needed to keep an eye on.

Today she and Deborah had nodded their heads in greeting without the wish to chat further.

The gallery space had been filled with temporary seating for an art lecture, which was a monthly fixture at the Owen gallery. Deborah had come partly out of interest, but primarily to enlist Peter's financial help. The Union depended on benefactors for sustenance, as the group did not generate any significant income of its own.

Rather like a religious order, Deborah chuckled to herself, *but we are more creative in our bookkeeping.*

At the conclusion of the lecture, Deborah intended to follow Peter into his study for a brief meeting without Lilli, which she and Peter had prearranged. They could have met privately in a coffee lounge or wherever, but she enjoyed the thought of taunting Lilli, as well as publically promoting her image as a person of culture and learning.

Like herself, Peter was a physically striking man, over 6'1" in height, and with a physique that had once been athletic, but now was witness to the excesses of his life. Peter still had the same face but it had now doubled in size, and his girth had followed a similar path. It was many years since Deborah had slept with Peter, but the mutual attraction remained, and neither had ruled out the possibility of sex in the future. However, it was less complicated putting that aside for the moment and letting the desire bubble on.

Sex was always on tap for Deborah, beginning with her live-in partner, Bill, and a range of other men she might choose to sleep with. She continued to enjoy sex with Bill, with little else in their relationship and Bill accepted whatever crumbs were thrown to him. *His role in The Union was that of a maintenance/handyman-handy indeed,* she thought wryly to herself.

Deborah enjoyed watching the theatre acted out by the devotees of these art lectures. They appeared to use language of their own, and sincerity wasn't a word included in that language. As they chatted with each other, she could see people's eyes roving the room, looking to see who else might be present that they would prefer talking to.

The lecture for this day was on contemporary art and she heard a lot of words being uttered and observed people around her sagely nodding their heads in agreement. At the same time Deborah struggled to make any sense out of what had been said. *Could I really be the only one struggling to understand?* but she doubted that she was. She thought the whole scene was a jigsaw approach to culture, where one had to go through the whole maze of lectures and learning, trying to put it together and still exit unable to find the meaning that one had been seeking.

There seemed to be no limits as to what constituted Art, and she wondered that if anything could be called Art, then what criteria could the critics apply in assessing it.

Whilst considering herself an atheist of art, she still knew that with correct advice such as Peter was able to give her, it could be a lucrative area of investment. She believed that a squiggle on paper could be of value if one knew who had drawn it. A squiggle drawn by Picasso could be worth a small fortune, whilst the same squiggle drawn by someone totally unknown would be viewed as worthless and the object of scorn. Notwithstanding her sceptical approach, she realised that this was one area where it was worthwhile playing the game by other people's rules. If anyone knew the value of words and acting out a role, then Deborah certainly did. She was looking for value not sincerity, and knew that Peter was of a like mind.

As she looked at some of the art hanging in Peter's gallery, she was unable to detect any skill being required to produce it. Peter told her it was an example of the Sandcastle phenomenon. She was not prepared to admit that she didn't know what he was referring to, but he burst out laughing, confessing that he also couldn't see any intrinsic worth in that particular oil painting.

He said that so-called experts had told him that it was a significant piece of work, and that it was the underlying concept that made it important. When he heard that, it brought to mind a time years back when he was on holidays with his eight-year-old nephew, Billy, who had entered a sandcastle competition. As the judges approached to assess Billy's effort, the castle suddenly collapsed, leaving a pile of sand and no time to rebuild it. On the spur of the moment he had suggested to Billy that they call it 'I Never Promised You a Rose Garden'. Laughingly he said that he could hear the judges discussing whether it was likely that Billy had thought of this title himself or whether an adult connected with Billy had come up with the idea.

Still chortling, Peter said that the judges ended up awarding first prize to his nephew, and since then whenever Peter found himself confronted by art that appeared to consist of a pile of something without any differentiating features, he would refer to it as a 'Sandcastle phenomenon'. He explained that he only dealt with this type of art because art experts would extol its virtues and he sensed that he could make money out of it.

CHAPTER SIX

Before they married, Andrew had very little contact with Karen's family – not that it troubled him, as he barely noticed its absence. Only later did he become gradually aware that Karen preferred it that way, and the more he came to know her family the more apparent it became.

Not long after they married, Karen gradually began to describe the environment she had grown up in. She told him how her father, Tony Duncan, ran a small law practice in the downmarket, outer suburb of Broadmeadows, where many of his clients were hard working migrants who valued his assistance and demonstrated their appreciation with gifts of home grown vegetables, lemons and olives.

He enjoyed the feeling of helping people unable to help themselves, but Karen became increasingly aware that constantly niggling away at her father was his failure to achieve a lifelong dream of going to the Bar and building a practice as a high-flying barrister. She came to believe that what troubled him most was the knowledge that he had never found the courage to test himself, and try out for that goal. He had always come up with reasons for deferring his attempt, but when honest with himself, he couldn't avoid facing the harsh reality that underlying those reasons was his fear of failure. He came to believe that his marriage and family life had failed and fought against the feeling of career failure as well.

Of his four children, he regarded Karen, his youngest, as the one most likely capable of realising the ambitions that he had originally had for himself; some people are crushed by adversity, while others grow vigorously, as if making humus of the crumbling decay around them. Karen felt she had always flourished in defiance of her environment and knew her father dreamt that one day she would join his legal practice, make something of herself and give meaning to his own life efforts. She told Andrew that at first she felt weighed down by her father's expectations of her. She knew, for he had repeatedly told her, that he foresaw her being the shining light of the family, rising above her sibs.

At first she dreaded letting him down, feeling failure was not an option open to her. In time, she was able to redefine what success and failure meant to her personally. She recalled how at school she was mocked and called "goody two shoes" by the other children who were irritated by how excessively virtuous she appeared to be. Only in adult years did she come to understand that their reactions arose from a belief that she saw herself being better than them. She felt that the do-gooder description was partly out of envy, but not totally unwarranted, as she herself had probably believed back then that if one was very good, rewards would automatically follow – a variation of the Cinderella story.

She came to appreciate the inherent dangers of this philosophy, and how it could be turned inside out—namely, if something bad happened to a person, that it must have been because they had been bad in some way. She despised this approach of blaming the victim for whatever catastrophe befell them—whether a woman being raped had brought it on herself or Holocaust victims contributed to the disasters that they suffered.

As she matured, Karen became aware that she valued being good as the moral thing to do, rather than seeking a reward for it. She felt one had a choice of being good or bad and she had chosen to be good. Somewhat rigidly, she did not allow for shades of grey in between.

Karen described to Andrew how initially Tony searched for explanations of why his life had been derailed and not progressed in the manner he had hoped for. He would joke that it must have been an aberrant gene on his wife's side of the family casting a spell over his life, and it annoyed his wife and others who sensed that contained in the joke was a grain of belief.

Tony refused to ever consider that he might have contributed to his own failure, for that was how he perceived his achievements in life. He certainly attributed some blame to his wife for the problems the children had over the years, as well as for his own lack of work success. The fact that his wife, Violet, had been adopted made it impossible to test his theory about her introducing aberrant genes into the family, unless they commenced with her.

Andrew learnt that Tony's parents had migrated from Georgia, a Caucasian province of the Russian Empire since 1801, enjoying only four years of complete autonomy after the Russian Revolution in 1917, before it was occupied in 1921 and absorbed into the Soviet Union. Tony's parents struggled to extract a living from the small parcel of land they farmed and escaped in the early 1920s, migrating to Australia, hoping to rise above the dull, excruciating battle that had been their existence in the past, but leaving the remainder of their family behind.

In Australia they had two children – a daughter, and after a five year interval, Tony. He was essentially an only child as his sister died from congenital heart problems before he was born. His parents adapted their name to their new home, hoping in time to merge with the local community and altered their name from Dumbadze to Duncan. Tony was eternally grateful for this adjustment as he imagined what the other schoolkids would have done with the original name – starting with labelling him "Dumbo" and who knew what else. His parents told him that in Georgia he would have been Tamar Dumbadze, but they realised that Tony Duncan was a more sensible title for this new environment.

Andrew learnt how Tony's parents encouraged him to study, wanting him to enter the professions and enjoy a life different to their own life, which although financially more rewarding than their farming in Georgia, demanded they perform long hours of factory work. They were proud that he won a place at university where he studied towards a law degree. In the days before Commonwealth Scholarships, almost all students had to pay full fees for tuition; Tony knew that his parents could not afford to pay for his education and throughout the four years of his course he worked as a part-time labourer for builders and brickies.

After graduating, he gained professional experience in a number of city and suburban legal practices before purchasing a rundown practice in Broadmeadows, an area on the verge of rapid growth that he hoped would generate a steady flow of conveyance work, to underpin his earnings. The firm carried the solidly Anglo-Celtic name of O'Hearn, Billings & Ramsay, and although none of the original partners was still associated with the office, Tony had kept the name because he felt it had a solid British sound to it, which bestowed an element of prestige on the firm.

Tony had acquired the practice for a token sum of money, purchasing what was euphemistically referred to as "goodwill". The modest practice kept Tony and his family in a comfortable, middle-class lifestyle in Camberwell, where the children attended nearby public primary and high schools.

By the time Karen had completed her six years in public primary school, Tony had identified her as his hope for the future and enrolled her in the highly thought of Methodist Ladies College in Hawthorn, for her secondary school years. That decision generated long-lasting tensions in the family, as none of Karen's three older siblings had been offered such an opportunity; thereafter they resented Karen for having opportunities denied to them, and felt some bitterness toward their father.

Karen described to Andrew in more recent times that she had remained fond of her father and responded positively to his belief in her. She performed well academically without achieving great heights and subsequently went to Melbourne University where she studied for a law degree. Again, she performed above the average but not at the top of her class, so leading law firms did not seek her out or try to entice her for her year of Articles.

Tony had been keen for her to join him in his practice, but she decided wisely that she should go to another office for at least one year and it surprised Tony that she was prepared to act against his wishes, but he suppressed his irritation, knowing there was little he could do to persuade her.

Karen did not have unrealistic expectations of her year of Articles but nevertheless found that she hated the work she was called on to do, as it was mainly hackwork of filing and communicating messages, with minimal tuition offered to her. Initially, she found herself working 65 to 70 hours a week with little prospect of promotion in the foreseeable future, and resented making what she saw as indecent amounts of money for the senior partners of the city law firm employing her.

After three years of experience, Karen felt ready to join her father in his law practice in Broadmeadows, where he was a sole practitioner employing two part-time secretaries and one paralegal. Karen described how she commenced work in her father's law firm in early 1970.

On her second day, having been given her own key, she arrived early before the others and examined the office closely without her father present. The practice was housed on the first floor, with three rooms above a busy coffee shop in the main shopping strip. The second floor, above the Law office, housed many tenants over the years, but for the past twelve months had been occupied by an import–export business, though no one seemed to know just what they were importing or exporting. As she mounted the stairs, Karen gazed sadly at the mild decay and disorganisation of the space that represented her father's Law offices. A musty smell pervaded the stairway and wafted through the nearby rooms, where the windows were stained with bird droppings. The windowsills were caked with dust and rain spots, initially drawing attention away from the flaking paintwork on the ceilings and walls. With some mounting concern, she wondered if her father was gradually decaying like the building around him. She decided to arrange for the windows to be cleaned as soon as possible, and started preparing a mental checklist of things to be done. To this list she added magazines for the waiting room, as none of the tattered magazines there was less than two years old.

She wondered how her father could generate enthusiasm for his work in these surroundings and then asked herself why her father had tolerated these surroundings for so long. She chose not to ask him the very same question, knowing the pain it was likely to cause him.

When Tony commenced practice in Broadmeadows he needed only three rooms – an office for himself, a small conference room and a waiting area for his clients. Later, a space for the secretary had been partitioned off from his room and Karen's new office was carved from the waiting area. Apart from her father and herself, the practice had two part time secretaries and a paralegal, the latter doing a lot of her work from home. If the paralegal came in to work in the office, she was placed in the conference room. The contrast staggered Karen, as she felt Tony was always neat and tidy at home and meticulous about his appearance and surroundings.

Karen had arrived at 8.30 a.m., expecting to be joined by her father and then his secretary close to 9.30 a.m. when the office opened for business.

Before her father arrived, Karen had looked around his office. It was a small room which looked out onto a dingy alleyway. There was little furniture, not that there would have been room for more. He had a small, insignificant desk with two paper filing trays on it. There were no decorations or flowers and she noted the absence of family photographs of his wife and children. His degrees hung on the wall behind his chair and were mounted behind glass which appeared dirty and discoloured, and the printed paper of the degree certificates was markedly yellow. She supposed it was due to ageing, but could not recall ever seeing other people's degrees turning yellow like this as her own degree was now hanging on the wall also, its freshness in stark contrast to that of her father's. The only other item in the room was a small wall clock, which was surprisingly functional in spite of the glass covering it being cracked. It was strategically placed so her father could see it from where he sat, as the fee structure was time based.

She wondered how people in Broadmeadows could afford legal fees, but decided it depended on how desperate they felt. A lot of her father's legal work involved conveyance, wills and minor criminal charges heard in the local magistrate's court. Her father had done well in his legal studies, but this had not translated into the markedly successful career that he always felt he deserved.

In recent times his income had been eroded as cheaper methods of conveyance became available to clients. Karen felt that respect for lawyers was diminishing, which probably troubled her father, and she believed that the media was a significant contributor to this state of affairs.

Karen confided to Andrew how she wondered whether she really knew her father, as this decay scene was so different to his neat image at home, not that he spent a lot of time at home these days. She pondered where he went when he wasn't at work or home, but he appeared to have his own life outside of the family. She was uncertain when she first noticed this, but had only met one of his friends, assuming there were more than one.

Nick had gone through Law school with Tony, completed the course, and after a few years dropped out of Law, now running a successful business importing children's toys. He had been born into an establishment family and to Karen he appeared to be a dull but sunny person, even when intoxicated, which she had observed on one occasion when he came for dinner to her family home about a year prior. She'd noticed that her father generally didn't bring friends home.

Karen was puzzled why her father had allowed her to see the state of his office environment, as he had always been a proud man. She wondered if he had stopped caring, and possibly was numbed by seeing it daily, to the point where it ceased to exist for him.

Knowing that it would be a difficult task persuading her father to make major improvements to the office, she began with a complete review of the regular office cleaning and maintenance and only gradually rearranged the decor. She was pleased to see the immediate improvement in her father's attitude and she felt confident that as long as she remained active in the practice, it would not sink further and might even grow.

Though fond of her father, Karen described that she was occasionally troubled by his behaviour. Soon after commencing work in her father's Law firm, she noted on occasion one of the paralegals, Jodie, relating to Tony in a flirtatious manner.

Jodie was a buxom young woman of 30, who had divorced her husband two years ago and did not have any children. The clothing she wore to work appeared skimpy to Karen, and she was puzzled that her father allowed it. Jodie often wore a skirt well above the knees, and a tight, cut away blouse which left little to the imagination when she bent over Tony's desk to deposit paperwork. She was about 5'2" in height and wore stiletto heels, and as she tottered on these, her movements were accentuated by a prominent wiggle of her ample bottom.

Karen felt ill at ease with her father's reaction, as Tony appeared pleased to see Jodie in spite of what Karen considered to be the vulgarity of her presentation. Karen sensed her parent's marriage was a loveless one, but to see her father acting like a gauche schoolboy, who blushed whenever Jodie familiarly placed her multi-ringed hand on his shoulder, with her ample bosom not far from his face, distressed Karen.

She didn't believe her father was having an affair with Jodie, but it would not have surprised her to learn that he was having sex with someone other than his wife. She would not allow herself to ever condone such behaviour, but was aware that if she was honest with herself, she could understand how his barren marriage could lead him to stray. However, she strongly believed that the proper thing to do would be to leave a marriage before starting another relationship.

Karen had been in her father's practice for almost eighteen months when she represented a young man charged with assault. It was a serious matter, heard in the local magistrates' court; the offender was only twenty-three and had knocked another man unconscious in a local pub. Dr Andrew Wright testified for the defendant who had been his patient for a number of years.

When the court adjourned for lunch, Karen and Andrew Wright went together to the nearby Manny's Wine Bar for a quick meal and a chat. When they entered, there were no members of staff to be seen, but they could hear the noise of clattering plates in an area beyond a pair of swinging doors through which a gaunt young man soon emerged. He had a shaven head with two rings in each ear, and Karen wondered why so many waiters looked like this young guy nowadays – as she confided to Andrew, she had always associated food with plumpness.

With neither greeting nor eye contact, the waiter recited a litany of specials for the day before thrusting two menus in their general direction. Karen smiled when Andrew quoted a Marx Brothers' one-liner: 'If they're so special, why weren't they printed on the menu?' – a comment the waiter ignored. They both ordered spaghetti marinara and a cappuccino, explaining to the nearly mute waiter their need to be out of there in 30 minutes. The waiter disappeared wordlessly and they were pleasantly surprised to have the food arrive promptly. As a bonus, the meal was tasty and they finished it within the half-hour; they each paid their share and Andrew left what Karen considered an excessive tip. When Karen commented, he agreed with her that too often people lacked the courage to tip according to the quality of the service. In fact, he remarked, it was really self-imposed blackmail along the lines of. 'If I pay you all this money, then maybe you'll agree to do your job and make my outing pleasant.'

She wondered if he was trying to impress her.

Karen was attracted to this young psychiatrist who so readily displayed warmth and humour towards her. She and her girlfriends had often discussed what they were looking for in a man and she still wasn't sure, but knew that humour was an important part of the total picture, and this man had an open face which featured laughter lines. She also felt that Andrew seemed interested in her as a person even though they had only just met. In addition, he appeared highly competent in his work, as far as she could tell.

He was no hunk, she thought, but then reminded herself that she wasn't looking for one. Rather, he had pleasant features and though showing early loss of hair, he was not attempting to disguise it with the barcode look of brushing the existing hair over the bald areas.

During their short lunch, Karen had relaxed to the point where she confided that she was basically shy and had joined Toastmasters and consulted a psychologist for a few sessions, to learn how to be more assertive. With an embarrassed laugh, she told Andrew that the psychologist had asked her what animal she felt symbolised her personality and without further thought she had promptly replied, 'A hedgehog … because they are a vulnerable, shy animal with prickles on the outside.' When she turned the question to Andrew, he deflected the query, saying they needed to return to court; but as they strolled back, Karen was delighted to hear him reopening the discussion.

'A squirrel,' he said, with a slight change of shade in his cheeks. To her quizzical look, he explained that he saw himself as someone who made quick decisions, sometimes impulsive, and he believed he appeared non-threatening and could be playful, but added that he probably was more a mix of two animals – a squirrel and an owl, the latter appearing thoughtful and self-contained. Almost as an afterthought, he reflected to Karen that the two animals were widely disparate and their characteristics contradicted each other.

'So, what would you call such an animal and what would it look like?' Karen giggled with a deadpan face, Andrew answered her question. 'A Squowl, that's what you'd call it. There aren't many around these days, but they're a foot high, with bushy tails and big, round luminous yellow eyes. They're mute and have four legs, two big and two little. Can't say I've seen one as yet – they are very rare.'

The day ended with Karen's client being cleared of the assault charge due to the evidence presented by Dr Wright describing the taunting and provocation his patient had endured before the attack. The court referred him to the care of his psychiatrist, with the magistrate's advice that he avoid going to pubs in the future.

Karen knew that she would like to see more of this young psychiatrist, but wasn't sure how to go about it. She had friends who were seeking the perfect man to marry, which she felt could only be a fruitless exercise; she didn't believe there was only one partner for each person, but rather there were probably many potentially suitable partners, provided each of them brought goodwill and a willingness to compromise into the partnership, and she felt Andrew was definitely suitable. She quickly converted this thought into a fervent hope that he would prove suitable.

As they left the court, she quietly asked Andrew if she could see him again. His mind raced as he answered, 'Yes', not yet able to fully interpret the rush of emotions and thoughts that invaded his body.

Walking back towards her office, Karen noticed a svelte young woman on the far side of the busy street, her arms flung around the neck of her beau. The woman perched on her toes as if in some personal and intimate ballet, her body straining upwards and her blonde shoulder length hair caressing her lover's face. Karen smiled, hoping that it proved to be a mirror image of the happiness that would follow in her own life.

Just ten months later she and Andrew were married – Karen believed that she had found a lifelong partner. She continued working with her father until Jed was born in 1973. At the time, she felt no regrets at all about stopping work, as motherhood was time-consuming and fulfilling; the regrets came later when the boys began to separate from their mother, as part of becoming more independent, and she had the time to reflect on her life, and wondered if she should have continued with her career.

Every fortnight, Karen, Andrew and their children would set off to visit Karen's parents. Over the years it had become far more an obligation than a pleasure, so they had discussed the possibility of winding back the visits, to say, once a month, but they got no further than discussing the possibility.

Andrew enjoyed talking to Karen's father Tony. He was a warm man who enjoyed laughter. In stark contrast, Karen's mother, Violet, appeared to regard laughter as undignified and only suitable for the lower classes. She was inextricably trapped in the straightjacket of how she perceived her social standing – a prisoner with no wish to escape. Andrew felt her name Violet was incongruous, as she appeared to him to be completely and wilfully colourless. Tony and Violet had probably never been compatible and Tony maintained a totally separate life, socialising with his own circle of friends leaving Violet to pursue her own lack of interests.

Karen herself confided in Andrew that Violet seemed to live life by the sayings of a desk calendar, and added that Violet's most original thoughts were the ones she had read the day before, when turning to the date on her calendar; Karen then felt uncomfortable at how harsh this sounded. Over the years, Andrew had been able to silently observe Violet and had noted that Violet was not only prone to clichés but had used them to underpin her rules for life, even when it was clear that she didn't fully understand the sayings.

She certainly showed little or no interest in other people's thoughts or feelings – the moment another speaker drew breath to continue their story, Violet would jump in and kidnap the proceedings for herself. Whatever issue the other person was discussing, Violet would trump it and bring the discussion back to her own account, where she would describe the most boring and trivial incidents in minute detail, squeezing every last millilitre of air from her lungs until her voice died and she was forced to draw another breath. Andrew raised his eyes and gave silent praise to the God he didn't believe in that Karen was more like her father.

Karen was the youngest of Tony and Violet's four children; her two brothers and one sister all seemed so different to her in both nature and appearance that she had long wondered if they really had the same parents. Even after so many years, she had to admit that she still harboured some lingering doubts.

Karen's eldest brother Ralph was six years older than her and had worked as a postman, but was now retired on medical grounds.

He suffered from a severe obsessive-compulsive disorder, which presented in his work as a difficulty in letting go of the mail when trying to deliver it to the various households. He was too ashamed to discuss it with Karen, but his wife Connie had confided that by the end of Ralph's working life his postal round was taking three hours longer than the required time, because he would insert a letter into the letterbox and feeling unable to let go of it, he would withdraw the letter and then repeat the process over and over again. This made his round painfully slow and distressed him greatly.

CHAPTER SEVEN

Friday, 6 February 1987

Brett had little to do with his family since fleeing from home when he was sixteen years of age. He had no wish to maintain contact with the three younger brothers living in Australia, and his attitude ensured that they had no desire to see him. There was the occasional day where circumstances forced family contact onto him, and today was such a day.

His brother Roger had rung at a time when Brett was unlikely to be home, and had spoken to Jenny. She was surprised by his call as they rarely had contact with him, but was pleased to hear his voice. The call was a sliver of time, with no explanation about why he rang, but quietly, almost in a whisper, he asked Jenny to let Brett know that he had rung and needed to meet with him urgently, face to face.

Jenny knew Roger to be a tortured soul who was plagued by anxiety and periods of black depression, with his existence dominated by obsessive-compulsive rituals, tying his emotions and time in knots that he could not break free of. He had been diagnosed as suffering from agoraphobia, which made him a prisoner in his own home and the most menial task, such as shopping for a loaf of bread, could drown him in a lather of sweat. Jenny had heard that Roger used to be anxious as a child, but now as an adult was crippled by it.

In spite of all his problems and the infrequent contact, Jenny liked Roger and felt he was a gentler person than Brett. Later that evening Jenny apprehensively passed the message on to Brett who greeted it with silence, and then surprised her by asking if she would come with him to visit Roger. Like a sparrow hungrily devouring crumbs thrown in its direction, she eagerly said yes, hoping that Brett had not detected her excitement.

They had left almost immediately without bothering to call Roger, as Brett knew it was a certainty that he would be home. They drove in silence in Brett's battered Holden — he'd long said there was no way he'd buy one of those Nip cars. Without expecting success, Jenny attempted several times to start a conversation, until the heavy silence crushed further attempts.

Jenny had not seen Roger for over a year now, and was not aware that Brett hadn't either. She recalled how Roger had once worked as a bricklayer until he was superannuated out on medical grounds over twelve years ago. She knew that he lived alone on an invalid pension, enduring a very basic existence. As far as she was aware, he had never had any meaningful physical relationship with another human being, and his sexual needs were met either by prostitutes (which he could rarely afford), or more often by masturbation, whilst watching a pornographic movie at home.

She was puzzled, unable to imagine what urgent issue Roger needed to speak about, and was intrigued by the possibility that Brett might know, as he had responded immediately. Jenny was aware that Roger had only one person whom he could call a friend, and that was Tim, who also existed on an invalid pension.

She had met Tim several times in Roger's company and noted that he appeared to be functioning a lot better than Roger. Being emotionally the stronger of the two, Tim was the one who visited and would come to Roger's house regularly. He had a history of serious drug abuse problems, which appeared to be less of an issue for him now. In some ways, his illness had probably contributed to this improvement by reducing his income and his ability to socialise, and thus reducing his drug abuse. His relative withdrawal from daily life had diminished the pressure that he attempted to control in the past with drugs.

Jenny recalled that Tim had a troubled background with his father belatedly leaving Tim's mother, Maureen, about four years before he died, making her a divorcee and his second wife of one year, a widow.

Two years after the separation, Maureen remarried and moved to a farm in Gippsland where she appeared settled and happy for the first time in many years. Tim visited her regularly, relishing the shift from petrol fumes and pollution odours, to the smell of horse manure and yeast. He had no regular job at the time, before going on to an invalid pension, but he was able to extract a meagre living by trading … everything was negotiable. She'd learned his whole family traded one way or another. His mother had traded her independence for the illusion of security, only to have it battered into her, how poor a trade she had made in her first marriage. His older sister had traded intimacy for the lure of affection, thus short changing herself.

The drive from Brett and Jenny's home in Mitcham to Roger's small flat in Preston, took about 30 minutes. Jenny recalled how over the years Roger would ring her during the day, thus avoiding having to speak to Brett, expecting him to be at work.

For both she and Roger, it was a human voice that soothed their isolation as it penetrated the vacuum enveloping them both. From the conversations that she and Roger had, Jenny knew that there were times when Roger was troubled by thoughts of ending his life. The fact that he didn't act on these impulses, she attributed to his religious background as a practising Catholic. Suicidal thoughts made Roger feel fearful, but also laden with guilt about having such thoughts, which were not condoned by the Church. Often he was racked with guilt about his sexual activities and suicidal thoughts.

Though he no longer had the confessional to help him deal with these urges, she realised that he could never be totally free of the shackles of his early religious upbringing. He attended a psychiatrist on a somewhat irregular basis, and even though he was only billed for the rebate amount, he felt he was getting very little benefit from the visits.

Jenny had often pondered that she and Roger had things in common, and whilst she was nowhere near as desperate as he was, she believed they both shared the emptiness of isolation. Roger's small flat had become his prison, which did not require guards, as he was trapped and weighed down by loneliness and isolation, which were his constant companions. On the occasions he forced himself to walk to the shops with downcast eyes, he later paid the price for the sweat of his labour. He made himself do these walks in the hope it would build up his confidence, but his fragile building blocks invariably collapsed.

Roger had confided to Jenny that the sounds coming from his TV were the only indicator of life going on around him. He elaborated to her that he felt more alive when he masturbated, and she wished that he didn't have to share some of these graphic descriptions.

She tried to block out the images that arose from him telling her how he looked at pictures of women being used and abused, and how it engrossed him for hours of nearly every day. She didn't have the heart to tell him to cease talking about it to her, and in the absence of her resistance, his words poured out as if in a confessional. She couldn't help wondering if telling her also aroused him. Mistaking her silence for a continued interest, Roger described graphically how he would watch pornographic videos of naked women and listen to their screams of pain as they were being whipped and humiliated.

Jenny didn't judge him for it, reflecting that he lived in a vacuum where he had no life experiences to draw on, and hence no opportunity or clear image of what an appropriate and healthy relationship with a woman should be like. Roger also told her how occasionally he saw articles in newspapers that mentioned his brother Brett, and he described the surge of anger that they kindled in him. He related to her how years back he had attempted to reach out to Brett in the vain hope that some sense of family might generate support, but it only brought silence as the line was cut dead.

Jenny continued to puzzle over Brett agreeing to go and speak to Roger, and if he had been willing to confide, he might have confessed that he also was uncertain about exactly why he was going.

He would have failed to mention the possibility of one factor having to do with the knowledge that Roger used prostitutes at times, and whilst it was very unlikely, the thought niggled at Brett that Roger might have heard something about the death of the prostitute. He didn't think Roger had been able to afford prostitutes in recent times, but one never knew.

As they pulled up at Roger's house, Jenny gazed sadly at the mass of overgrown vegetation and the chipped paintwork on the building facade. She felt that it mirrored the deterioration of the person living inside.

'Stay in the car until I check,' Brett barked at her.

Jenny puzzled what he meant by "check" as she watched Brett pound on the door after trying the bell, which appeared to be broken. For a while there was no response, and she felt anxious as to what that might mean. Finally Roger appeared at the door and from a distance she thought that if anything, he looked calmer than usual.

Brett went inside and the door closed behind him.

It troubled Jenny that Brett, having asked her to come with him, had now left her sitting outside in the car. It made no sense to her.

About ten minutes later, Brett appeared, his face devoid of any warmth as he strode to the car, ordering her to come inside.

It hadn't taken him long to reassure himself that Roger's request of speaking to him, had nothing to do with the death of the prostitute. As Jenny entered the house, she noted the drawn blinds and sensed the heavy musty smell hanging in the air. She sat on a couch that turned out to have broken springs, and through the open kitchen door, she saw a large pile of unwashed plates. Brett remained standing as if he had no intention of staying for more than a few minutes, and neither Jenny nor Roger attempted to try and get him to sit down, having decided independently that there was little point in doing so.

Jenny found herself wondering yet again whether Brett really cared about any other human being, as there were no signs suggesting he cared for her or Roger.

'So, what's so urgent?' Brett barked at Roger.

At first Jenny apprehensively prayed that Roger could come up with something dramatically urgent, otherwise Brett would skin him alive – verbally at least. She shackled her mind and tongue from speaking out about the obvious – that in the ten minutes Brett had spent alone in the house with Roger, he surely could have clarified the answer to that question.

'You want to know what this is all about, do you?' Roger said quietly, with a subtle smirk shaping his lips, as he got up to stand facing Brett. He was 3 inches shorter than Brett and devoid of the muscles that Brett flaunted. What had been muscle in the past, now hung suspended He appeared not to have shaven for several days, and his clothes were ragged and perfused with the smell of sweat.

Jenny was not repulsed, but rather, experienced a deep sense of sadness, mourning the loss of both Roger's life and her own.

After what felt like an interminable silence, Roger looked up at Brett and held his gaze, announcing in a detached manner that he had recently been diagnosed with a severe form of leukaemia and required a bone marrow transplant.

He could have been talking about someone else, so removed did he appear to be from the story he was relating. He told them that so far the doctors had not been able to identify a suitable donor that was compatible with his body, and they had suggested to him that a family member might have bone marrow that could be used if they were willing to donate it. Roger then added that from memory, he thought that he and Brett were compatible and had the same blood grouping, leaving the last words hanging in the air as the trace of a smile played around his lips, Jenny noted.

She had continued sitting, somewhat physically removed from the drama that was unfolding in front of her. Having announced that Brett might have be a suitable bone marrow match, Roger said nothing further, avoiding coming straight out and asking whether Brett would agree to be assessed as a potential donor. That query was left hanging unsaid and followed them home.

Neither he nor they had raised the possibility that the donor issue might be considered in the near future.

In the silence on the way home, Jenny told herself that she would ask Brett, but not just yet – certainly not just yet. As they drove, the issue enveloped them inside the car, louder than any conversation, had Brett been willing to speak. Arriving home, as they walked through the front door, Jenny no longer needed to ask Brett as he dealt with her unspoken query in a dismissive surgical manner.

'No way am I going to have that test,' he snapped, exiting the house he had just entered, and slamming the door behind him. In the same way, he effectively closed the door to any possibility of being a donor for his brother in the future.

Jenny heard the screeching tyres as Brett drove off, leaving her reflecting that Brett was not only a man's man, but a bastard's bastard. She immediately got on the phone and rang Roger, who gave a bitter laugh and said he would have been amazed if the answer had been anything else. Haltingly, she expressed her regrets and Roger explained that Tim had pushed him to contact Brett, though Roger believed even then that it would turn out to be pointless. There was nothing more to be said and they left it at that.

Jenny took herself to the lounge room and poured a much larger whiskey than she would normally consider. She downed it soon after and felt the alcohol insulting her stomach, just as Brett's words had insulted her feelings. She turned on the TV for company, not caring what the show would be, as she struggled to fight off the feeling of panic that was building up within her.

As the whiskey dulled some of the blinding white light of her panic, Jenny found her black thoughts beginning to creep in again. Once more she revisited the barren waste that had been her parent's marriage and the emotional quagmire it created for her growing up.

Her father had been an abusive alcoholic, both to his wife and children, and her mother had become a non-entity as far back as Jenny could recall. She imagined or at least hoped that there had been more to her mother early on, but life appeared to have squeezed it all out, leaving only the empty shell. Both parents had now died, but she had already grieved years ago for the loss of the parenting she had wished for and never had.

Jenny was the youngest of six children, having three brothers and two sisters. Two of her brothers were violent criminals, currently serving time, whilst the remaining brother died from a drug overdose about six years ago. One of her sisters married an Indian student and moved to live in the family compound in India. Jenny believed this was due to her belief that any alternative had to be better than what she had grown up in. The other sister appeared to have survived the family upbringing in some miraculous fashion, and now lived with her two children and plumber husband in Brisbane, wanting nothing to do with Jenny or the rest of her family, as if family contact could contaminate her life.

By now, Jenny had given up hope of hiding the wreckage of her own marriage from her children. She knew that they were witness to how unhappy she was, and they appeared to be distancing themselves from both parents. She saw her family as a graveyard of wasted souls.

It hadn't always been that way, and she recalled herself being a bubbly, fun loving adolescent girl in spite of the family turmoil around her. She revisited memories of a teacher at school asking her what she wanted to be when she grew up, and the teacher shaking her head when Jenny replied, "happy".

Years later she came across the story of the Beatle, John Lennon, who had given much the same answer to his own teacher who then chastised him for not understanding the assignment. As Lennon's mother had always taught him during his childhood years that happiness was the key to life, Lennon informed the teacher that it wasn't him not understanding the assignment, but rather it was the teacher not understanding life. Jenny wished that she had the gumption to answer her teacher in the same manner, and wondered what the outcome of Lennon's exchange had been. It obviously didn't harm him, but then he had a mother standing in his corner.

Jenny recalled how difficult it had been as life became more complex the older she got. There had been no one to explain to her about her cycles, about dating, about not getting pregnant. Craving affection and closeness, she gradually became disillusioned with her adolescent flings with boys – boys who groped and pressed for more, with no interest in her as a person. Eventually and inevitably she fell pregnant and not yet sixteen. It was all her fault she was told by family and outsiders – she was acting cheap. She recalled the illegal abortionist they took her to, with more groping and lack of respect, her legs strapped to rudimentary wooden poles, lying on someone's kitchen table. She developed a mild infection, which later settled, and then had to endure the whispers of "slut" as she walked by. Her goal in life of happiness was receding, as her confusion and helplessness became more pronounced. Not long after, she again fell pregnant and married Brett. Onlookers to Jenny's poor marriage, wondered why she stayed on. The same query troubled her own mind, at least early on. However, as life depleted her energy reserves, she gave up wondering.

Jenny had several acquaintances, but only two women she could call friends. One was Goldie, an elderly Jewish lady in her mid-seventies who had survived the Holocaust of World War II, emerging from that nightmare totally alone, having lost her entire family. She was born in Frankfurt, Germany, the youngest of three girls and aged in her late twenties when war broke out. Her parents were both lawyers and felt very much a part of German society, but as the flames of the Holocaust took hold, they were brutally reminded that this was not how non-Jewish Germans viewed them.

At that stage of her life, Goldie was working in a three woman general practice, but as the Nazis took hold, her partners asked her to leave. They explained to her that their medical practice would collapse if she stayed on and that there was also a real threat that they would be punished. Her closest friend, who she had gone to school with, took her in and hid her until it became too dangerous. She then arranged for Goldie to live in a nearby monastery and pretend to be studying to be a nun. She was not betrayed by the decent women there, but after the war she searched without success for signs that her family were still alive. Eventually, to her horror, she discovered that her family had all perished in a concentration camp and from then Goldie had no wish to stay in her hometown as it no longer was *her* hometown, she felt. In fact, she no longer wished to remain in Germany and moved to England. She decided that she did not have the will to study medicine again, which would have been required if she was to practice in another country. She commenced nursing training and after graduating as a nurse, she did mainly private work tending to people in their homes. At that stage she had admitted she felt she was surviving rather than living.

Later she moved to Australia, leaving Europe behind forever. She travelled a little around the country to see where she wanted to live and ultimately chose Melbourne. In time, she met Herbert, another Holocaust survivor, who was about the same age as herself, but the union proved disastrous. When they married, she barely knew him and he seemed to fill a gap in her life, but she gradually realised he was highly suspicious and at times physically violent towards her.

Initially she attempted to make allowances for his behaviour, attributing it to damage caused by his wartime experiences. She also started hearing rumours in the local Jewish community that he had been a Kapo, assisting the Nazis in running a concentration camp.

Jenny knew that some of the Kapos were protective of the people in the camp, but feared for their own safety. They were meant to carry out the orders of the SS running the camps and supervised the other prisoners. Some of them were quite brutal, but they all knew that if they were judged not to be doing their work properly, they would be demoted back to being ordinary prisoners in the camp. If this occurred, then they risked being set upon by the other prisoners and possibly killed. Goldie did not know whether Herbert in fact had been a Kapo or not, and never had the courage to ask him. If he had been a Kapo, she was certain he would not admit it to her.

Thus the Jewish community shunned both of them, which left Goldie even more isolated than before, and trapped with a man she had grown to hate.

She believed it was fortunate that they had no children. Initially she had difficulty in conceiving and later stopped trying when it became evident that her husband didn't want children, nor did she want him to be the father to her children by then. So when Herbert died from a massive heart attack, there was really no one to grieve for him.

Jenny's other friend was Margaret, who had trained as a nun in Ireland, and left her calling when she became increasingly disillusioned by the behaviour of some of the local priests. She came to believe that several of them had molested some of the young people living in the orphanage where she regularly assisted. She then moved to Melbourne, Australia, where a somewhat distant cousin lived and hoped to start a new life there. She no longer practiced religion in a formal sense, but maintained the religious ideals she had developed in her earlier years.

She was about fifteen years younger than Goldie, and worked part-time in a supermarket. Both friends had been scarred in various ways by life, but were still capable of supporting each other. Jenny remembered that she had met the two women whilst assisting in a soup kitchen for the local disadvantaged. She chuckled to herself that it sounded like the beginning of a joke: Have you heard the story of the nun, the Jew, and the cop's wife? But it was no joke.

Whilst Goldie and Margaret were older than Jenny, she felt both of them were warm people who appeared caring and supportive in spite of all the pain they had experienced in their own lives – or maybe because of it. From time to time, they asked Jenny why she had stayed in such a bad marriage, and she had the feeling they had already answered the question themselves.

To begin with, she and they knew that Jenny lacked the resources to be financially independent, and at first they encouraged her to look for work. However, Brett immediately put a stop to it and angrily told her he wanted her at home – *for what,* she wondered. He did not explain why, nor did she have the courage to ask.

Both of the women, especially Goldie, knew there were probably multiple factors creating obstacles to Jenny leaving. *What if Brett came looking for her and became violent?* As a cop, he had extensive contacts and could readily find her, they believed. Also, from what

Jenny told them, she had never been in a good relationship nor witnessed her parents in one, and this left her doubting that a good relationship was possible for her. They could understand how Jenny might fear being on her own or forming another relationship which would be equally bad or possibly worse than the one she was in. It was apparent to them that Jenny's self-esteem was far too brittle to see herself as having something to offer in a new relationship.

Jenny spoke to her two friends on the phone most days of the week and met with them at least once a week, outside of home, as Brett had told her he didn't want them visiting. The three women shared a lot of personal experiences and feelings, and their interactions provided mutual support.

Occasionally Jenny had a phone call from Jesse, but he tended not to visit these days. In fact it was close to nine months since he had come to the house. When she thought about it, she had never seen him happy, and from what she had learnt about the earlier years of his life, it was possible that true happiness was an emotion he had never learnt to clearly measure. She wondered if for him happiness equated to the absence of pain rather than real joy. The years of growing up at home were experiences that damaged him from the brief facts she had gleaned. When Brett agreed Jesse could come to Melbourne, she believed Jesse and she both carried the hope that it could start to turn his life around in a positive fashion. In fact, Jenny dared hope that the small flicker of caring it revealed in Brett might herald the potential of it developing into a flame of kindness that all the family could benefit from.

Certainly Brett paid to help Jesse stay in a sheltered environment and would bring him home to mix with his own children, at which time Jenny would shower all the youngsters with treats. She had hints that Jesse liked her and knew she cared about him, but over half a year ago he lost a labouring job that he had for reasons that were never made clear to her, and soon after Brett divulged that he had introduced Jesse to The Union and this was where Jesse now lived and worked. She sensed that Brett was somehow connected with the sect and she wondered whether Jesse living there took away any need for Brett to be financially or emotionally responsible for Jesse.

The brief calls she occasionally had from Jesse revealed little information about how he felt or what if any work he did, but there seemed to be a harsher edge to his makeup that she sensed. If she had been asked whether she approved Jesse joining The Union she would have been strongly against it, but she knew her opinions counted for nought with Brett. She sensed that Jesse disapproved about the way she was treated by Brett, but feared him too much to say anything.

CHAPTER EIGHT

Wednesday, 3 February 1988
5.59 p.m.

Brett felt as if he was treading water, hating the uncertainty of what was to follow in executing Deborah's plan. Could it succeed?
He found himself drinking more than usual, and was aware that he had become increasingly irritable both at work and at home.

Walking out of the office, he decided to take himself straight to his favourite watering spot, the DT's in Richmond. Whilst this was the usual after-work routine for Brett and his mates, lately it had become an escape through the haze of his excessive drinking.

7.50 p.m.

Brett sat slouched at the bar. The only drinking partner still remaining was Luke O'Conner, another member of the Victorian Homicide Squad.

Brett was finding it difficult to avoid thinking that it was close to two weeks since his meeting with Deborah, and still no sign of any development in their plan for Dr Wright. He wryly corrected himself that in fact it was not their plan, but Deborah's plan. He was puzzled as to why it was troubling him so much. He knew Deborah would contact him as soon as something significant developed, but no one had given him a timetable as to when this would be. He hated being a passive player in anyone else's plan. He also sensed that in spite of this he strangely missed being around Deborah. Like a moth drawn to a flame, he felt deprived of the rush of adrenaline that he experienced when he was around her. He struggled to understand his reaction, believing that it wasn't just the sex, though that was certainly part of it, but there was also an element of danger that spiced their interactions, and unbelievably it felt as if he might be missing the sense of being controlled by Deborah. There was no point making contact with her, as she had made it clear that when anything significant developed, she would let him know.

He found himself unable to make any sense out of this morass of feelings and thoughts. Suddenly Luke's voice made itself heard.

'Which planet are you on mate? You haven't heard a word I've said for the last five minutes.'

Brett closed the trapdoor to his mind, gave his body a shake as a dog might do, and forced a grin. Leaning against the bar, he picked up his beer and cocked his head still grinning at Luke.

'You've got to hear this, Luke. It's better than a screw,' Brett smirked. 'You know I was in court today …' He paused. What he couldn't tell Luke was that Deborah had asked him to check out how a case was proceeding against one of her followers from The Union, a woman who allegedly received illegal social security benefits.

'… I told a friend I'd check how the case against her partner was going,' he lied. 'The prick allegedly stole thousands from social security. Well, his case didn't come up and that left me with some time on my hands, so I decided to sit and listen to a case that happened to be running. Better than TV it was. I recorded what went on and I'll play it for you now. If you can guess what it's all really about, then I'll shout you four.'

Luke's eyebrows lifted. 'Big deal, "Mr Generosity". You don't pay for the beer anyhow. You got permission to record in court, did you?'

Brett smirked again. 'Would you believe that I accidentally triggered that recorder – didn't know it was on.'

'I'm letting that go through to the keeper, mate!' Luke exclaimed.

Brett glanced around the room. 'I'll get Fred to let us use the backroom,' he whispered. He signalled to the barman who knew the score and brought the key over before being asked.

The room was small and stuffy, clouded with the smoke remains of others who had sought privacy. Brett began to describe how he ended up spending many hours in the county court, where a woman was facing charges of theft. She was a follower of Deborah, but it appeared to Brett that the police were not aware of that.

'It was no minor theft, mate,' he informed Luke.

'This woman had defrauded the State of over $30,000 by claiming disability payments that she apparently wasn't entitled to. But it wasn't the alleged crime that made it so interesting.'

'Yeah, so what did? Who was hearing the case?' Luke asked doubtfully.

'Justice John Cowdrey,' Brett replied. 'The sneaky bird's name is Mrs Phillips. This tape recording is of her in the witness box with the prosecution barrister Peter Egan going at her hammer and tongs. Wait 'til you hear this, Luke.'

'So, Mrs Phillips ...'

'That's Egan's voice,' Brett interjected.

'You do acknowledge not always being faithful in your marriage? Please enlighten the court further. You were married close to sixteen years – how many extramarital affairs did you have in that time? Please speak up so his Honour can hear you.'

'One – only one,' Mrs Phillips replied faintly.

'She sounds meek,' interrupted Brett, 'but you could see the anger flashing out of her eyes directed at Egan.'

Luke looked somewhat disinterested.

'Okay Luke,' Brett said as he stopped the tape. 'I guess you're wondering why the hell the bitch is being quizzed about her extramarital affairs. Well, her defence lawyer Ron Bentley decided to use as a defence the fact that she had a rotten marriage, which made her chronically depressed. Egan decided to try and discredit her as a witness by showing her to be unfaithful in the marriage, as if lying in the marriage could mean that she might lie in court. Pretty hopelessly long bow to draw, if you ask me. Wait, I'll just wind it back a little,' Brett said in a puffed up voice before resuming the tape.

Luke leaned in a little closer as Brett wound back the tape to replay the legal questioning.

'You do acknowledge not always being faithful in your marriage, don't you, Mrs Phillips? Please enlighten the court further. You were married close to sixteen years – how many extramarital affairs did you have in that time? Please speak up so his Honour can hear you.'

'One – only one. I'm not what you're trying to paint me as. This was someone I cared about deeply.'

'Cared about deeply, Mrs Phillips? Deeper than you cared for your husband?'

'By that stage of our marriage, yes.'

'And what exactly was that stage, Mrs Phillips?' Egan intoned, highlighting the "Mrs" before he mentioned her name.

'It began as a friendship …' Brett remembered that her eyes were downcast at this point and in a soft voice she continued. 'It was in early July 1967.'

'Well, Mrs Phillips, it's now February 1988 and you married in January 1960. So you're telling us that you had this affair for close to twenty-one years, starting seven years into your marriage? Tell me if my maths is correct Mrs Phillips … it appears to me that you loved another man longer than you loved your husband, but chose to live a lie with your husband. Is that so, Mrs Phillips?' Egan boomed.

'No!'

'No? Well, Mrs Phillips, tell me where my maths falls down. I have to remind you Mrs Phillips that you are here on oath. Should I repeat the question?'

Brett intruded with a look of orgasmic delight on his face. "this was the really good part!'

'It wasn't another man … it was a woman,' Mrs Phillips blurted.

'The silence was deafening in that court, I can tell you,' Brett smirked.

'Well, Mrs Phillips, you do surprise me,' Egan drawled, 'and I imagine your husband was surprised as well.'

'We can do without that piece of wit,' Justice Cowdrey snapped.

'She looked like a bloody beetroot and so did the judge,' Brett chuckled. He had stopped the tape again and painted the picture for Luke. 'So, Egan approached the witness box and stood right alongside the witness. He was so close to her she could probably smell the garlic from his lunch – you know his nickname is "garlic lips". He was so flamin' close to the witness that she could probably also see the black hairs in his nostrils!' Brett mused before turning the tape back on again.

'Mrs Phillips, where exactly did you meet this … woman?'

'He was speaking into her ear at this stage,' Brett interrupted, stopping the tape again, as he explained to Luke. 'Then Mrs Phillips turned to the judge and asked, "Do I have to answer that question, Your Honour? I don't want to identify her."'

'Jesus,' Luke muttered.

Brett took over from the tape and continued to explain the spicy courtroom scenario. 'Then the judge says, "Yes, you do have to answer that question and take care not to identify her." So Phillips stares at Egan and says – real defiant like – "She's a psychologist and was my therapist at one time."' Brett put the tape back on again.

'I went to her because of how unhappy I was with my marriage. Our relationship only began about one year after I stopped therapy.'

'Most convenient, Mrs Phillips,' Egan intoned, as he preened himself. 'The court respects the right of your lover to remain anonymous. So, without wishing to identify her, I shall ask you some questions regarding your relationship with this woman. Now, how old would you say she is, Mrs Phillips?' Egan asked smugly.

'I wouldn't say,' Phillips snapped. 'She's one year older than me. She's fifty-one.'

'He didn't ease up,' Brett volunteered. 'Am I correct in assuming your relationship was more than platonic … sexual, you might say?'

'Yes!'

'Where did these acts occur, Mrs Phillips? Her house or yours? When your husband was at work?'

Brett stopped the tape again and said with a snicker, 'At first I couldn't make head or tail as to why Crowley would allow this line of questioning to go on, but then the penny dropped and I knew!'

'Knew what?' Luke slurped over his beer.

'Just wait ...' Brett cautioned him, as he turned the tape back on.

'Neither house,' Phillips said. 'We met in neutral places. We might go for a drive, or have lunch or go to a movie. I knew she had two children and she knew I had three, but nothing more than that was discussed. We never talked about what jobs our husbands did or where the children went to school. We kept our family lives totally separate.'

'Very honourable,' Egan drawled. ' I assume she already knew the details from when she was your therapist. However, Mrs Phillips, when it was sexual,..... where exactly did the acts occur?'

'I said it was at neutral places. Sometimes we'd check into a motel. We decided it would be betraying our families to meet at either home.'

Brett interrupted describing how he saw the judge's head suddenly jerk and his face redden.

'And you wouldn't want to betray your family, would you, Mrs Phillips?'

'Would you believe that it was Judge Cowdrey who said that?' Brett gloated, as he resumed the tape.

'You don't need to answer that. It speaks for itself,' Cowdrey boomed.

'I could see her barrister's eyes gleam,' said Brett, as he continued his commentary. 'I bet he could see the grounds for appeal handed to him on a platter.'

'So you never went to her house or she to yours?' said the saccharine voice of Egan. 'Is that correct, Mrs Phillips?'

'I picked her up just once from her home in Brighton – God, I didn't want to say that! You flustered me! Can't this be kept out of the record?'

'Go on, Mrs Phillips ...' Egan encouraged.

'I just rang the doorbell and she came out and we drove to lunch. She'd been in a small car accident and her car was being repaired.'

Brett stopped the tape again and lifting his beer, said to Luke, 'Have you guessed what was happening yet, you idiot? No? Okay, let's finish the story. So Judge Cowdrey asks Phillips which month of the year it was, and the barristers looked at each other in amazement, but I knew by then what it was all about,' Brett chuckled.

With one eyebrow raised, Luke took another generous slurp of his beer.

'Still don't know what happened, you dill? I'll put you out of your misery,' teased Brett. 'This woman had been screwing the judge's missus! I met the judge's wife a couple of times at functions, and I knew where she lived and I also had heard she'd been in a car accident. Put all that together with what happened in court and even Blind Freddie could come up with the answer!' Brett's smirk had taken residence in his features. 'So Cowdrey then asks Egan if he has any further questions – which he did. I bet Egan knew by then and was sinking the boot in. It was bloody great!' He turned the tape on again.

'Did you ever discuss or complain about your respective spouses with your lover?' Egan politely asked.

Brett interrupted the recording. 'Egan really enjoyed that question and so did I.'

'No … apart from knowing we were both unhappy in our marriages, we never talked about our husbands or children,' the tired voice of Mrs Phillips explained.

'Excuse me, Your Honour, I missed what you said,' Egan asked in his most deferential voice.

'I said, let's recess for the day,' Judge Cowdrey growled. 'We'll resume at 10.30 a.m. tomorrow.'

The tape had come to a halt and Brett explained that the judge's wife worked under her maiden name, but it was possible Mrs Phillips suspected a connection with the presiding judge and that would have made her even more anxious.

'You know what, Luke,' Brett exulted, 'I only meant to stay for 10 minutes or so in court, but I couldn't drag myself away. Haven't had this much fun for years! You see those prickish judges looking down their noses at us lesser beings day in and day out, so it felt good seeing him squirm,' Brett said bitterly. 'Most judges have a weak point if you can find it, and it can be used as a bargaining point some time down the track. It makes them weaker and could be our insurance later on if we run into problems'.

Finishing their drinks, Luke and Brett parted ways. Though drinking buddies, Luke felt there was little about Brett that he liked. They rarely socialised outside of the pub, as Luke was a family man and pitied Jenny who he had met several times and liked.

CHAPTER NINE

The call finally came from Deborah.

Jenny had already gone to bed, whilst Brett was watching TV, slouching on the couch with a stubby in his hand. He knew that he was uptight and hated his body showing signs of that – the knot in his stomach, the tightness in his throat, even his bloody hands shaking a bit; why the hell was it getting to him, he questioned. The answer was already known to him – he was not in control – not in control of his body and not in control of the situation and plan that was about to unfold.

Getting straight to the point, Deborah crisply reminded Brett, as if he needed reminding, how she had planted one of her followers as the night-time cleaner in the coroner's court, which he was well aware of. *God,* he wondered, *was there anywhere she didn't have connections?* It had taken over three weeks, but she had struck gold, Deborah informed him. The cleaner worked alone at night and as he was the only one in the building during those hours, it allowed him the time and opportunity to access various drawers and filing cabinets containing files relating to the working of the court. Security in the record keeping section was somewhat lax and he was able to perform his scrutiny undetected. Some of the filing cabinets had been left closed, but unlocked, and others he was able to open with keys he found in a desk drawer. Eventually he came across a file of a female patient who had died in a private psychiatric hospital in

1978 whilst under the care of Dr Andrew Wright.

Brett could hear the smile in Deborah's voice as she described that the death certificate stated the patient had died from natural causes connected to her heart problems, which were further exacerbated by excessive use of tablets and alcohol.

Deborah said she had no doubt, and Brett agreed, that they could organise publicity to stir up concern and anxiety in this woman's family, and the community at large. They were both experienced in manipulating the media to spread rumours and half-truths. They had done this in the past in other circumstances with considerable success.

Brett was aware that he had nothing personal against the doctor, but he agreed with Deborah that a scalp was required, otherwise it might end up being his own scalp and that of Deborah. It wasn't that he felt sorry for Wright. Brett didn't believe in God, but paradoxically believed in hell. He believed that the righteous pricks who followed the rules and looked down on him should have to live in hell before they died, to make up for missing out on it after death.

"They believe in equality, so let them experience it", was his mantra. Brett had to hand it to Deborah. *She certainly knew how to get what she wanted and had the balls to do it,* he reflected. He often thought about Deborah and how she related to him, especially the dominant role that she adopted with him, and in fact, with everyone. He was used to dealing with submissive women, but there was no submission in this one, he knew, and yet, strangely, it seemed to turn him on.

She must have been a raving beauty in her youth, he pondered to himself, but it was more than just her looks that that excited him. When they had sex, with her sitting astride him, which was the position she always dictated in their encounters, he'd noted that her eyes remained open and her body appeared devoid of the groans and the usual sounds of lovemaking. However, he had searched for signs of arousal in her, and noted the goose bumps and flushing of her skin, bearing witness to her arousal, as did the moistness of her body.

It would have troubled him to believe that he had not been able to arouse her. *You can control most things, but not what your body says,* he often told himself. He would have loved to tie her up and have her bound to the bed, but knew he'd have to save that for the brothel women.

Deborah arranged, or rather, told Brett, to meet with her after work the following day, so they could fine tune how they would go about putting her plan into action. He knew that question marks were never part of her vocabulary. It had always been understood that when she said something, it was in fact an order to be carried out, and it continued to amaze him how readily he accepted that.

Brett slept in the spare room of his home that night, the phone conversation with Deboarh still playing in his head.

Sunday, 14 February 1988
6 a.m.

The alarm pierced Brett's ears, waking him from a deep sleep. He dressed and left the house half an hour later, intending to pick up breakfast in a cafe near work. Jenny and the children were still asleep when he left the house, the only communication being a short terse note, which he left on the kitchen table, stating that he had been called away for a case. He knew they wouldn't believe it, but it had become a ritual now, using a language of their own.

Brett went through the motions at work that day, and as soon as possible checked out to drive to his meeting with Deborah. He no longer had the knot in his stomach, nor the tremor in his hands, and in fact felt calmer than he had been for many days.

4.58 p.m.

As he entered the property and drove towards Deborah's house, he saw people walking around, but on this occasion no one questioned his right to be there. The late afternoon sun was shining and the vegetation created a fragrance and sense of tranquillity, which Brett was oblivious to. Again he found Deborah alone and wondered where her partner disappeared to on these occasions.

He sat where she placed him, facing each other across a coffee table, holding a glass of red wine which she had poured. Without any further delay, Deborah began describing how she planned to set her most trusted troops loose on the family of the woman who had died. Her followers were not bound by ethical rules nor restricted by feelings of guilt. They were adroit at manipulating people, especially at times of crisis such as a loss, even if it had occurred many years previously.

Deborah knew well that needy people were vulnerable to being manipulated. She explained to Brett that psychiatry was poorly understood in the general community, so if words such as "deep sleep therapy" were inserted, then the media would take the bait and run with the sensational term, and like blood borne bacteria, infective doubts would start building up and spread through the community.

Deborah reiterated her rage about what she called the treacherous termites who were eroding her life's work, referring to past followers who had not only left her group, but soon after became whistle blowers. The tranquillity of her façade suddenly disappeared, as her voice quivered with rage, railing against the ex-followers of The Union. Riding the crest of righteousness, she told Brett that they couldn't allow things to continue the same way with these traitors – adding after a short pause "for both our sakes", her words striking Brett with the implied threat.

Deborah organised for four of her followers to make contact with the deceased patient's family, and indicated to Brett that she wanted him to start involving the media, where he had a number of trusted contacts. Deborah described that by building up a head of negative feelings in the community, at the same time as her people worked on the family of the deceased patient, it would eventually back the coroner into having no other choice than to hold a coronial inquest.

In addition to silencing Wright, Deborah said she hoped to also discredit psychiatry to some degree, viewing them as her natural enemies and competitors. She believed that if psychiatrists were busy defending their own flanks, then they were less likely to be probing into her affairs. After meeting for two hours, Brett got back into his car to drive to Melbourne, as Deborah had not extended any invitation for him to stay overnight.

Monday, 15 February 1988
1.05 p.m.

The day after Deborah and Brett met to discuss strategy, Brett contacted his favourite journalist from The Age - Robert Sykes was termed an investigative journalist and Brett felt only contempt for him, but sensed he'd be useful.

Sykes was in his mid-fifties and had narrow pinched features. If eyes are a mirror to the soul, then Sykes bloodshot, glazed eyes, revealed a life of deceit and failure – failure in his career, failure in his private life and most damning, a failure in his own eyes. He was of medium height with sloping shoulders and thinning hair, which he attempted to disguise with a barcode hairstyle. Brett viewed him as a miserable sod but useful, as Brett could write the column for him and have it featured under Sykes name. He knew no one in the journalistic profession respected Sykes, but he sold newspapers and people seem to lap up the sensational crap that he fed them.

Brett's other main journalistic contact was Robin Hilary, who also worked for The Age newspaper. Like Sykes, she was a journalist that he didn't really respect and come to think of it, there were not many people in any field that he respected. If he had to describe Robin, the words that came to mind were a "cheap tart".

She was a trollop and full of lust, he felt. She hankered for an exclusive, to see her name in print alongside a newspaper article, any article. It had become apparent to her that she had assets that weren't taught in journalistic studies, but could elicit information that male journos could only dream about. Her success was largely with men that she interviewed; whilst with women, she encountered suspicion and resentment. Her tight skirts and sweater emphasised the features that she wanted noted and loosened many a male tongue. On warmer days, they got to see some of what the sweaters hid so poorly. It was rumoured that she was not averse to sleeping with some of the men that she was interviewing, if the journalistic need arose.

It was to these two journalists that Brett leaked information about Andrew Wright's alleged mismanagement of the patient who died, and they did the rest. Robin and Sykes' lurid and exaggerated conjecture became the news of the day that the public ingested. The piles of dirt that Brett fed them through these two journalists, built up to become mountains of exaggeration, and over the following 12 months, succeeded in creating sufficient pressure of doubt in the family of the dead woman, and in the general community, to provoke them into demanding a coronial inquiry. Prior to then, this family had maintained a good relationship with Dr Wright, and had no doubts about his treatment.

As is the nature of mobs, other media outlets took up the cry and the concocted accusations eventually saturated suburban newspapers with the same sensational news items as contained in the major papers. They spoke about Dr Wright using a discredited form of therapy termed deep sleep therapy where the patient is put into a coma for days on end by injecting barbiturates.

As Deborah suspected, because of the lack of knowledge of psychiatry in the public domain, it is seen often as something mysterious and potentially dangerous. The fact that deep sleep therapy in the past had been used with some disastrous consequences for patients, causing death and injury, and that at times it was combined with electro-convulsive treatment (ECT) added to public fear. ECT itself had a touch of black magic about it in the public mind, especially after the movies of mental hospitals in past years. Deborah was well aware of these anxieties and effectively tapped into them.

The hounds were let loose!

CHAPTER TEN

Monday, 1 February 1988
7.15 a.m.

Andrew and his family were greeted with a daily barrage of media allegations and headlines. They started to dread picking up the daily paper in the morning, and reading headlines that made them want to hide.

COVER-UP OF DEEP SLEEP THERAPY

PSYCHIATRIST ALLEGED TO HAVE USED ILLEGAL THERAPY

ILLEGAL THERAPY SUSPECTED IN DEATH OF PATIENT IN PRIVATE HOSPITAL

There were many variations of these headlines, all competing with each other for eye-catching sensationalism. At this point, Andrew's name had not been mentioned, but he knew that if it got to the stage of a pending coronial inquest, any privacy would be stripped bare.

At the height of the media barrage, Andrew found himself struggling at work and at home. His ability to concentrate diminished, and he found himself absorbed with his internal life, making it difficult to relate to the world around him. He could not remember the last time he felt happy and relaxed and able to let go with unrestrained laughter, as there were too many intense emotions and thoughts disrupting the normal circuits of his mind. The past, the present and the future started to become a bit blurred.

He became bogged down with recurring thoughts about retiring and on occasions rationalised that it was time to move on and let some of the newly trained psychiatrists have a go.

Years back, he attended a lecture on professional life where the statement was made that professions progressed through funerals. At that time, he thought it was a rather glib catchphrase attempting to make the point that there was a need for the older generation to make place for those coming up through the ranks. It worried him back then and even now, the thought that all that experience can be killed too early, before it can be shared and imparted to younger graduates.

He realised that his present urge to retire was most probably a disguised attempt to escape from the overwhelming pressure. He was determined to cease work at a time of his choosing and no way would he allow those bastards to drive him out. These thoughts were often followed by a rapid audit of past years, reflecting on the damage that working over 70 hours a week had inflicted on his personal life.

There was no denying that the long hours of work had only left him with drips and drabs of time to devote to family and friends and any remaining personal interests. He feared that once work was removed, the residual vacuum of his life might struggle to sustain him. He puzzled why he had cast aside so many important areas of living and now queried whether it was really just simply a devotion to his work or could it be that work was the only thing he felt good at.

His thoughts drifted back to more than ten years ago when he found time for family and personal interests such as tennis, reading and writing. He recalled Karen laughing at the time as she told him writing would inhibit their sex life.

'How can I make love to you when it could be described in the book you write?'

In the same period of over ten years ago, he would lunch with friends and regularly attended a psychiatric study group on a fortnightly basis. Nearly all these activities had gradually slipped away without protest, leaving him a one-dimensional man, he felt.

He realised that he had studiously avoided thinking about these things until recently when they forced their way into his thoughts. Even with Karen, the passion had evaporated. He believed that he had never stopped loving her, but somehow the excitement was missing and he wondered what she was possibly getting out of their relationship. *Not much,* he told himself.

In sessions with Dr Engel, his therapist had touched on the possibility that it was Andrew's insecurity that created a craving for patients' gratitude, whereas with family and friends, any praise needed to emanate from himself. Over and over Andrew found himself accosted by these thoughts and feelings, often coming without invitation. They could arise when he was on his own with a drink in his hand or they could intrude when he was at work seeing a patient. Like Russian dolls, there were stories within stories.

Thursday, 12 May 1988
11.10 p.m.

Though he now frequently experienced an urge to hide away, Andrew pushed himself to continue going to the fortnightly evening study sessions, where he and other psychiatrists got together to discuss patient treatment, difficulties in therapy and the like. He had sat through this evenings study session interacting in a somewhat robotic fashion, he felt. The other psychiatrists avoided asking him questions about his current problems and he sensed a degree of discomfort in the way they superficially related to him.

Having said goodbye to his friend Peter, Andrew now sat in his own car outside Peter's house, where the meeting had occurred. He didn't feel it was safe to drive yet and he wasn't sure whether he should call a cab or not, but hoped to sober up. He wasn't certain he would be fit to drive soon, given how derelict his brain felt.

In the rear vision mirror, he could see the yellow haze of a nearby streetlight softening his features and masking his inner turmoil. He leant back with his head on the headrest, closed his eyes and with the assistance of the alcohol found himself once again reflecting on the past, his jumbled thoughts shooting in all directions without any apparent rhyme or reason.

Past relationships with girls, or was it women, came to mind. He thought it was strange how, even in their fifties and beyond, women referred to themselves as "girls", but men continued to be called "men". He often wondered what drove people the most – was it the sex drive or the fear of death? Andrew had read that we are born alone and must die alone. He tended to agree that one of the most frightening things about dying was the unknown and the isolation, .and not being in control. He softened these thoughts by recalling Woody Allen's crack that he was not afraid of death, he just didn't want to be there when it happened.

However, he believed the sex drive was a powerful force, even when the body had difficulty responding adequately to it in the latter years. He reflected that maybe the sexual urge got stronger with ageing in a desperate attempt to avoid the feeling of failure, even if performance headed in the other direction. He could think about sex easily and often did, but death – that was something where he, like many others, scrambled away in an attempt to avoid thinking about it.

Andrew smiled inwardly as he recalled his first love when he was seventeen years of age – or was it more a puppy love or infatuation? He was immediately drawn to her warm, firm body and gentle, radiant smile. Andrew had been introduced to Rachel, which now felt like an old form of love making. It didn't take them long to realise they had previously known each other at school. He recalled liking her years ago and again when he was seventeen. They came from very different directions where she was born in Melbourne and was the youngest of three children to a Jewish couple. Her parents were hard-working people who had a clothing store in Victoria Market. They lacked formal education, but provided a very loving family environment.

Rachel and Andrew went out for about ten months, once a week. They never consummated their friendship, but explored with pleasure the steps leading up to it. However, it felt as if their earlier knowledge of each other somehow created a barrier to becoming lovers. Rachel's total acceptance of Andrew was starting to make him feel anxious, so he broke things off.

Looking back, he knew he had acted badly, and now wondered what more he was possibly wanting from a relationship. He suspected that it had progressed too rapidly and he feared taking on the responsibility that came with her appearing so totally committed to their relationship. His bumbling rejection hurt her and in time she met someone "less complicated".

Andrew remembered taking a break from any further relationships, became absorbed in his studies and spent more time with his male friends, sharing their interest in football and poker.

About two years later, he was introduced to Philipa, who was studying Arts – Law at the University of Melbourne, whilst Andrew was completing his medical studies. She was non-Jewish and it irritated him that he had to hide their relationship from his father, who would have strongly objected to it on religious grounds. He wondered where this prejudice had come from, as his father obviously had not been born with it, so where was it learnt? Was it possibly a reaction to how other non-Jews had treated him and his family in the past? If so, he felt that his father was creating a stereotype and rejecting others the way he himself had been rejected in the past.

Andrew relished some of the sensual memories of Philipa, when his eyes would absorb the fullness of her body, watching her sit down and taking off her shoes without a word being said. He recalled how, with her eyes lowered, she would sink back into the sofa. She had confided to him that she felt naked as she sensed his eyes undressing her, but confessed she enjoyed the feeling.

They had been going out for two months before the evening when they first had sex, and later she had told him that she had predetermined nothing more than some innocent flirtation would occur in that outing. Andrew recalled sinking into the couch next to Philipa, realising that she seemed to be holding her breath. Still nothing had been said. He remembered laying his head on her shoulder, with his hair brushing her cheek, and inhaling the elusive fragrance of her skin. He enjoyed the memory of how passive and submissive she felt just then, and how he had hoped at the time that she wouldn't say anything to break the spell. He recalled feeling his body hardening and reacting as he watched the curve of her breasts rising and falling, and how some anxiety crept in – was he reading her correctly, did she want him to enter her, and was he up to the task? He remembered worrying that his hardness might go. It was easier for women, he reflected. He had reached out and stroked her hair and kissed her ear and the back of her neck, as his hand cupped her breast and gently rolled her nipple. In some ways the build up and anticipation had felt better than actually entering her, as it all happened too quickly then, given his excitement, but he still enjoyed their moist bodies clinging to each other afterwards.

Somehow the promise and excitement disappeared as rapidly as it had built up, and four months later they both realised they were getting bored with each other. There seemed to be too many differences in their past and their present and probably their future. The confusion about what to do with the relationship was settled for them when Philipa's parents went overseas for several years taking their children with them, as the father was being transferred to a higher position in a large engineering firm in Manchester, England.

At the time and since, Andrew pondered whether religion pushed people apart or brought them closer together. *Are you with us or with them?* More recently he had begun querying whether formal religion was very different to a sect like The Union.

He had come to the conclusion lately that, at its best, formal religion was probably different to a sect in a positive way, by showing tolerance, but if it lowered its standards, which seemed to occur too often, he felt, then it started wielding its power in a harmful fashion, controlling, exploiting, and setting people against each other.

When religion followed the dictum of treating others the way one wanted to be treated, then it appeared more noble. However, all extreme forms of religion worried Andrew, as they appeared rejecting of other people's beliefs.

Still with his eyes closed and reclining in the car, Andrew realised that his thoughts and emotions were racing everywhere and recalled sipping at least four glasses of red wine whilst at the study group meeting, provided he was counting accurately. Prior to then, he'd probably had two or three glasses of beer on his own after work, and knew that drinking was becoming a problem since the media onslaught began, and and his awareness that Karen and he were drifting away from each other.

He was amazed how his thoughts had commenced conducting a precis' of his life and beliefs in such a short period of time. He felt that he was still not sober enough to himself home and had better call a cab. He had sat in his car for close to an hour now, and hoped that Peter had not looked out the window and seen him still sitting there for so long after they parted. He reassured himself that Peter had probably gone straight to bed and was well and truly asleep by this stage, otherwise he would have come out to see if Andrew was okay.

Peter was of Italian background and a fairly uncomplicated person, Andrew felt. During the evening meeting, Peter managed to magically lighten the mood for Andrew by diluting a lot of the seriousness that might otherwise have weighed Andrew down. Peter had a wide grin as he related that whilst the Greeks invented love, the Italians had improved on it and introduced the concept of women. The whole group had packed up with laughter, including Andrew, who could not recall the last time he laughed so heartily. Andrew told himself that he needed to resume living a life outside of what was going on in his mind. Opening his eyes, Andrew sat up and rang for a cab to take him home. He wondered how Karen would react to the late hour and his drinking – or had she also stopped caring?

Monday, 12 September 1988
2.15 p.m.

It had been eight months since the news broke in the media. As Andrew sat in his office with a young patient, he struggled to maintain his focus and keep other thoughts and feelings at bay.

On the other side of his desk sat Romy, a troubled young woman of twenty-three, her features showing residual prettiness partially ravaged by years of porous boundaries separating the imaginary from the real.

She had been hospitalised in psychiatric hospitals on four occasions since the age of sixteen, the last admission with a drug related paranoid psychosis occurring close to five months ago. At that time she was psychotic and having delusional thoughts that her boyfriend Bini and his mates were trying to kill her. It occurred soon after her dog Petrie died from natural causes, but in her delusional state she believed Bini had poisoned him and was hoping to do the same to her. At the same time Romy was planning to revenge her dog's death by killing Bini with a sharp knife that she had armed herself with.

The daily diary that she kept, proved to be her salvation, as in it she had described her plans to do away with her boyfriend. Her mother, already concerned about her daughter's deteriorating mental health, took to reading her diary entries whenever possible, and on coming across this worrying material, rang their family doctor urgently. In hospital, Romy's condition gradually stabilised on medication, and living away from the drugs she had been abusing. Since discharge, she no longer took the marijuana and occasional LSD that Andrew believed had led to her previous psychotic episode. Whilst being off the drugs, she still lacked insight and was not totally convinced that the drugs were harmful for her.

'So what do you think, Dr Wright?' Romy asked, her question invading his reverie and bringing him back to the present. Andrew felt guilty, realising he had stopped listening and worried what words he may have missed coming from her. 'What do I think about what?' he asked, trying to cover up his absence.

'What do you think about me living away from home now, with my girlfriend?' Romy repeated without any apparent irritation.

Andrew realised that in fairness to his patients, he could not continue working in this manner. He made an immediate decision that he would resume sessions with Dr Engel and try to continue working and seeing patients. He had ceased going to Dr Engel about one month ago, feeling they had gone as far as they could in therapy. He suspected now that it was one more thing that he had run away from.

Andrew began winding up the session with Romy, as the time had almost expired, and suggested that Romy consider the idea of her parents seeing another therapist whilst he continued meeting with her. He knew that he had to present as a real person to Romy in the future, so that she was not confronted by the emptiness in his eyes on the occasions where his thoughts had drifted away. For someone like her, struggling to differentiate between the imaginary and real worlds, it was vital that the boundary between the two did not appear blurred in therapy.

After Romy left his consulting room, Andrew's phone buzzed and he picked up the receiver to hear his secretary, telling him the next patient had cancelled on short notice. Such cancellations had irritated him in the past, as it was often time wasted, being too late to offer the appointment to another patient. The people he treated did not often cancel, so it made him wonder if this occasion was related to the barrage of media accusations, which, though not naming him, still had the potential to create anxiety about any psychiatric treatment. In addition, some of the reports had mentioned that Fairside Hospital was where the death had occurred, and many of his patients knew that he used that particular hospital.

He consoled himself with the knowledge that very few patients had cancelled their appointments in the past, and the current figures were much the same. He felt touched by the trust his patients were showing in him, in spite of the negative and at times lurid media reports. A few patients had left messages for him to call them, and he used the spare time from the cancellation to do this. The queries were mainly to do with medication, which he answered, but one of the patients, Sylvia, brought up some of the articles she had seen in the newspapers that had reference to Fairside. He listened to her soft, pressured voice as she asked him whether any of the allegations about a psychiatrist there using a discredited form of therapy were accurate. As the name of the patient had been mentioned in one media outlet during the previous week, Andrew acknowledged to Sylvia that it was indeed the hospital that he used and that the allegations were possibly aimed at him. He told her there was no validity to the claims, and without appearing to be defensive, he explained that deep sleep therapy was a treatment he had never used and felt it had no place in modern psychiatric care. He gently asked that Sylvia defer judgement until all the points were clarified in the future and was reassured by the warmth in her voice suggesting her continued trust in him.

He thought to himself how he wished his colleagues would demonstrate the same belief, as he sensed that following the publication of allegations in the media, many of his psychiatric peers appeared to have commenced backing away from him, as if fearful that his problems might contaminate their lives.

CHAPTER ELEVEN

Monday, 26 September 1988

Towards the end of September 1988, close to six months after the affair with Samantha was terminated by her, Andrew finally decided to seek help from a therapist. He had hoped to deal with the issue of the affair on his own, but had to finally acknowledge to himself that he was not coping well with his guilt and anxiety.

He referred himself to Dr Engel, a psychoanalyst whose work he had admired, but prematurely terminated with in the past. He saw Dr Engel on a weekly basis for two months, and they focused on his feelings of guilt over the affair with his patient, and his realisation that he had betrayed his medical oath of causing no harm to a patient, as well as his awareness of the damage he had inflicted on his marriage and the trust between Karen and himself.

Whilst the short-term therapy did not bring about any dramatic change, it did help to alleviate a lot of his anxiety by the very act of being able to confess what he had done. Confessing to Karen would have been selfish and damaging he felt. It might have made him feel calmer initially, but left Karen to struggle with the whole mess.

Andrew became increasingly aware that his thoughts and communication with his family was starting to have overtones of sounding like a psychiatrist, rather than the warm interactions he'd like to have with Karen and the boys. He was showing features of intellectualising and interpreting and somewhat detached from his feelings. Maybe he was scared that if he let go he could be flooded by his emotions.

Dr Engel was a secular Jew and a fully trained analyst who fled Austria during the Holocaust period of World War II. Thus his initial training was in Austria and he then undertook further training after fleeing to America. He lost his wife to leukaemia when their only child, a son, was ten years of age. He was solely responsible for the boy and they became very close. Thus, when his only son married and settled in Australia, it was almost a reflex decision to follow the young couple there.

Dr Engel was now a sprightly eighty-one-year-old and Andrew respected him as a wise and kind elderly man. The patients Dr Engel saw in analysis, usually attended him daily over a number of years. Andrew was grateful that Dr Engel had been prepared to stretch the rules for him by seeing him on a less frequent basis. Andrew smiled to himself whenever he recalled the story going around about Dr Kurt Engel's claim to fame being that he once stood at a urinal in Austria alongside Dr Freud. However, apart from this folklore, he knew that people in the profession respected Dr Engel for many more things.

Andrew looked forward to his weekly appointments with Dr Engel. At first their sessions focused on Andrew's guilt over the affair with his patient, as he realised that it was a betrayal of everything that he felt he stood for. He was aware that the variation of the Hippocratic Oath that he pledged allegiance to, emphasised the message that the medical practitioner cause no harm to the patient, and he felt he had betrayed this, just as he had betrayed the trust in his marriage.

As the sessions progressed, he spent increasing time dealing with his anxiety over the media allegations, but not yet knowing where it would lead, and what it might mean to him and his family. He was starting to build up increasing resentment towards the people that were generating these allegations and harming his family and himself, but remained puzzled as to what it was all about. He and his family were beginning to feel self-conscious and embarrassed, wondering whether friends and strangers believed the allegations contained in the articles. Would people trust and accept what they read and heard? He was starting to examine people's faces to gauge their reactions and discovered that Karen and the boys had similar responses, with the boys suffering taunts at school about their father being a murderer.

Initially Andrew felt that the sessions with Dr Engel were a bit like he imagined it would feel when going to a confessional, not that he had ever attended a confessional. What he knew about confessionals was based on reading and media articles as well as speaking to Catholic friends.

One session, as if reading Andrew's thoughts, Dr Engel looked at him with a kindly but penetrating gaze.

'So, given you're not Catholic. This is not a confessional and it doesn't absolve you if you happen to confess all,' explained Dr Engel. 'From these sessions, maybe, just maybe, you'll be able to stand back and look at yourself and your actions, as honestly as possible.' In addition to working on his feelings about his previous affair and his anxiety about the media publicity, Andrew hoped there would be side benefits from the therapy. He felt strongly that a therapist could help him improve his understanding of himself, which in turn had the potential of diminishing the risk of his own problems intruding into therapy with patients. He had to focus on their issues not his own.

Andrew didn't lie on a couch during the sessions, but was placed in a comfortable chair with Dr Engel sitting behind him. Andrew was aware that the purpose of this seating arrangement was to minimise Andrew's reactions to what he thought Dr Engel might be thinking or feeling. This in turn reduced the possibility that he would be inclined to modify his own responses so as to impress or please his treating psychiatrist, rather than expressing what he truly felt and thought

In the early sessions Andrew would squirm when Dr Engel sat behind him, saying nothing for what felt like an interminable silence. He was aware that it wasn't easy for a psychiatrist to be seeing another psychiatrist for therapy and he recalled one meaningful exchange he had with Dr Engel:

'So, Andrew, who benefits if you confess about your affair? Does it benefit you or your wife and children? Could it be that no one benefits and sadly, a lot of people might be damaged. Maybe, just maybe, you will have to work through the guilt yourself ... so, who gains from this?'

Andrew recalled how he sat quietly with furrowed brow and deepening grooves which strangely he had become aware of as he passed his hand up to his forehead to feel them.

Dr Engel continued 'Do you benefit? Possibly yes, as you dumped it all onto someone else and appeased your own guilt. Do your wife and children benefit? Could it be that no one benefits and it's just a self-serving exercise to make you feel better? Maybe you have to live with the guilt yourself and learn from it.'

Andrew continued to sit silently for a while and knew that the silence in the room would remain until he, Andrew, spoke. After a few minutes he found the silence asphyxiating.

'You know, I always believed that I never lied – not deliberately anyhow. Before this – this – affair ...' Andrew imagined that behind him, the doctor's lips had formed a faint smile. 'Dr Engel, the only lie that I can recall was something I would call a white lie,' he confessed. 'It occurred when I tried to protect someone else's feelings.'

'Tell me about that,' Dr Engel encouraged.

'Well, it was years back and my son was about, I guess, eight or nine years old. I'd decided to buy him a set of weights and I was somewhat concerned whether he might be too young to have weights and unsure whether the weights could cause him some physical damage, such as developing a hernia. So I asked the salesman about these concerns and it turned out he was also the owner of the business. He volunteered a flood of medical advice, which I knew to be, well, absolute rubbish, but I let him go on. Suddenly he asked me what I did for a living. I knew that if I told him I was a doctor, it would make him feel like a goose – so I told him a white lie to protect his feelings. "I'm a teacher," I said. Unfortunately, he was one of those individuals who couldn't leave well enough alone and he followed up each of my answers with a further question. "So where do you teach," he enquired. I told him I taught at Essendon High School, hoping he'd run out of steam for any further questions. That hope proved to be in vain. He asked me what I taught and for some inexplicable reason, I said History, Polish and Politics. I saw him staring at me at this point. "I didn't know they taught Polish at Essendon high school," he said, going on to explain that he actually worked as a live-in caretaker at the school. "Strange I haven't seen you before," he queried, sounding more like an accusation than a query. So I decided to cut my losses and said I needed to rush as I had another appointment coming up and could I please have the bill to pay. With another piercing glance at me, he went off and returned with the bill, which he handed over to me.While I was making out the cheque I tried to explain that I had only been at Essendon high school for a few months. He took my cheque, glanced at it, and said in staccato tones – "it says you're a doctor." "Yes," I explained, my voice now a few octaves higher than I would have chosen. "Yes, I've got a Ph.D. in languages." My voice trailed off as I grabbed the set of weights that I had purchased and held my son's hand, and rushed out of the shop. My son fortunately was too young to realise my embarrassment. So you see, Dr Engel, what began as a white lie with the noble motive of not embarrassing this guy, ended up with me sinking into a quagmire of lies.'

'So what did you learn from this experience?' Dr Engel asked after a moment's silence.

Andrew imagined that there was a smile playing on Dr Engel's face after having heard his story.

'What did I learn – I learnt that they don't teach Polish at Essendon high school and that I'm a poor liar. Maybe that's a good thing,' Andrew smiled.

'Andrew, would you believe that everyone lies throughout their lives, whether it be by distorting the truth of what they say or whether it be by selectively leaving out things. Sometimes the truth may be more harmful than the lie. We'll discuss this more in further sessions.'

Andrew felt that if nothing else, the pouring out of his thoughts and feelings in these sessions had to be a safety valve, as previously he had subjected Karen to a barrage of his thoughts. This was especially likely if he had been drinking, which he had to admit was happening more frequently than he felt comfortable about. The other evening Karen had been staggered by his onslaught of words and emotion, and gasped in disbelief over his monologue.

'What on earth triggered that,' she asked with a look of amazement on her face. Before he could respond, she did it for him. 'Must have been the curry we had.'

She tended to do that now, he felt. Couldn't cope with the intensity of his feelings and just wanted to go calmly ahead. He corrected himself, feeling that his assessment didn't seem fair It was more likely that examining his own thoughts so frequently often when he had alcohol in him made it difficult for Karen and others to relate to him. He wondered if the barriers meant to contain his thoughts and feelings were becoming porous, and like the boy who put his thumb in the dike, he was struggling to stem the flow.

He let the curry remark go, apparently unheeded, and seeing the worry etched into Karen's face, he forced himself to talk about day to day things such as the kids, friends, social outings that were coming up – anything to distance both of them from the torrent that was threatening to escape from within him. He knew that he wasn't easy to relate to at present, and hadn't been for a while, crumbling somewhat under the stress of the media barrage that was building up.

When friends were due to come over, Karen would make him promise that he wouldn't talk about politics, global warming, religion or any subject that might become heated. He regretted being flippant in response to her request with comments such as, "I'll brush up on garden fertilisers and talk about that". He knew that in the past he had always enjoyed playing the devil's advocate, but now with the stress he had become more abrasive. He was aware that whilst he might call it being a devil's advocate, others might refer to it as being a cynical provocateur.

In subsequent sessions with Dr Engel, they branched more and more into areas beyond the guilt over his affair with a patient, which was the initial reason for attending. Now, with the media build up, Andrew was particularly glad to be seeing Dr Engel, as there was no one else he could really freely discuss these issues with.

In the previous session there was an initial period of uncomfortable silence, which was broken only when Andrew started describing his anxiety about the possibility that the allegations could lead eventually to a coronial inquiry. He confessed that he was probably "a bit scared" and wondered if he should be taking some medication to settle himself down.

'So, you want to be a psychopath, do you?' Dr Engel queried.

'Of course I don't,' Andrew hotly denied.

'So, who do you think is free of anxiety and fear?' It was more a statement than a question and before Andrew could respond, Dr Engel went on to elaborate. 'People need responses like anxiety and fear to stressful events, otherwise there is really no motivation for wanting to change or adapt,' he explained. 'Psychopaths are devoid of fear and therefore lack the impetus to change some of their patterns of behaviour. Provided that whatever anxiety and fear you are experiencing is not overwhelming, then it's best not to medicate. If people didn't have anxiety or fear about the consequences of their actions, then heaven help us. What do you think you can do to help yourself deal with the coming stress?'

Thoughtfully, Andrew replied, 'You know, I've noticed that the more prepared I am, whether it be giving a lecture or going to court to give expert medical evidence, the better I feel. I need to remind myself that if I stick to the truth and the medical issues involved, then it should reduce my nervousness in court. I have to remind myself that I know more about medicine than the lawyer cross-examining me, and use this to prevent him from making me feel bamboozled.'

'I have read studies,' Dr Engel said, 'that they are experimenting on ways to eradicate fear from soldiers in the field. That might sound good, but the downside is that the soldiers may no longer take the necessary precautions to avoid being killed or injured. Fear can prevent us from doing crazy things. So, how do you feel about letting yourself experience some anxiety or fear, within reason, as it will act as an impetus for you to defend yourself adequately. Like I said, only if it becomes overwhelming would you consider treating the anxiety or fear with medication,' Dr Engel reiterated, in response to the quizzical look on Andrew's face.

'I believe you're right, I didn't at first but now I do,' Andrew responded. 'Like I said before, if I give evidence in court as an expert medical witness and I feel prepared about the topic, then I feel a lot less anxious. It's the unknown that has been getting to me. Like who is responsible, and why are they saturating the media with all these distortions and lies about myself? You know, it's not easy when you're fighting and not really sure who your opponents are,' Andrew said softly.

'I imagine your barrister can help clarify those issues if and when the court process starts,' Dr Engel encouraged.

Andrew had to agree, as this had been his fervent hope for over a year now. 'But I can't stop wishing that I knew more about why things were happening than I do at present, but that's not going to occur, is it?' he asked, not really expecting an answer. 'At least not till the evidence is brought out in court hopefully.'

'No, if it goes to court, hopefully your barrister will lead evidence that clarifies a lot of those queries,' said the kindly voice behind him.

'I'll never forgive those bastards for what they've put my family through. At school, in the shops, in the streets they've had to fear people's responses, wondering if they would be shunned or embarrassed in some way. Would friends believe what they read and heard in the media? I keep examining the faces of people to see their reactions towards me. You know, Dr Engel, the other night after a few drinks I sat wondering whether I was capable of killing those bastards who are putting my family through this. I don't believe in God so it isn't God that's stopping me from doing it,' Andrew said heatedly. 'So what would stop me?' Would it be my own sense of right or wrong or the fear of getting caught? I really don't know ...'

Dr Engel allowed Andrew to talk and follow his thoughts and

feelings spraying in all directions, and they came in an avalanche.

'I know that if someone threatened the life of one of my family, then I would defend them to the death. Sounds a bit dramatic, doesn't it, but I really think I could kill in those circumstances.' Andrew's face was flushed as he spoke. 'But, you know what, I guess the best revenge is to prove that they're lying, which is what I hope will happen in court one day.' Andrew mused, 'You know the saying, "kill one man and you're a murderer. Kill 1 million and you're a conqueror." Not sure what made me think of that as it doesn't really apply to me,'

Dr Engel broke the silence that followed by reminding Andrew that the therapeutic session was up. On the way home Andrew reviewed the question of whether the sessions with Dr Engel were of benefit or not. He came to the same conclusion that if nothing else, the pouring out of his thoughts and concerns with Dr Engel was a safety valve, as he continued to batter Karen with his flood of emotion.

CHAPTER TWELVE

Friday, 2 December 1988
8.53 a.m.

Karen entered the gym, as she had entered it for the past seven years, going regularly at 9 a.m. on Monday, Wednesday, Thursday and Friday. She liked the routine and predictability of going four times a week, and was sure that she felt better for it. For two of those four sessions each week, she had a personal trainer Elliott. Having the appointment with Elliott ensured that she went regardless of how she felt that morning. She could let herself down, but not someone else.

Today was one of her appointment days with Elliott. He was a 30-year-old married man and she found him to be knowledgeable and pleasant to be with. She could forgive him not remembering what they chatted about in a previous session. With everything that he heard, you couldn't expect him to remember it all. She wondered at times if possibly he had remembered having heard her story before and was just being polite, pretending to be amused by the same story that had amused him the previous week.

So, as they chatted for the one-hour of her session, the time passed easily. Elliott was a good listener and had a sense of humour and his responses most of the time indicated that he did think about what she was saying. Karen got herself a glass of water and as she headed for the treadmill to continue her exercise, she spied a friend Nerida doing weights at the other end of the room.

When the session finished, she joined Nerida and a few other friends in the routine they followed each Friday after completing gym. They would have a coffee at the nearby coffee lounge, chat for an hour or so, and then go for a dip at the public swimming pool, followed by a sauna. Sometimes other friends would join them, such as Prue, Veronica and Sam.

It was approaching midday as Karen leaned back in the sauna, giving in to the well-earned fatigue of her vigorous exercise. Three of the women had left, leaving her alone with Nerida in the sauna.

Karen's eyes were pried open as Nerida's words pierced her reverie.

'You know, Karen, they say it's a man's world and it probably is, but we women have the power of sex. I believe sex is the Achilles heel of men. Sex is something we women can trade and that gives us power.'

It was a statement, more than a question, so Karen didn't feel the need to comment. The issue appeared to come out of nowhere, but it caused Karen to suspect that Nerida knew about Andrew's indiscretion at work. "Indiscretion" – such a cute word to cover a multitude of sins, she reflected bitterly. When the media came out with the publicity about Andrew's pending inquest, she had feared that one of her friends would feel that it granted them permission to dredge up the material of rumours circulating about Andrew's affair, which they would innocently pass on to Karen. That's one more thing he's guilty of, would be their implied statement! She did not doubt his innocence where the death of his patient was concerned, but struggled to cope with the knowledge of his infidelity.

In fact, Andrew's betrayal had been imparted to her by a so-called "friend" approximately six months ago, and Karen carried the weight of that knowledge in silence, not really knowing what to do with the information. Now Nerida appeared to be dredging it up once again, as she pontificated about relationships between men and women. Karen's thoughts drifted off, wondering how many true friends she really had, that she could trust completely. Only two came to mind and even then she was not really certain. It wasn't long ago that she had believed she could trust Andrew completely, but not now. A heavy feeling, which she identified as sadness rather than anger, slowly permeated her being. She brought herself back and determined that she would play Nerida's game, but on her own terms. She was not going to give her the satisfaction of seeing how much upset she had caused.

The issue with Andrew she had put on hold, and was still unclear whether she should confront him with it or file it away for the time being. Whatever, it felt to her that something had been lost in the way she felt about Andrew, and she was not certain that it could ever be regained. She decided to test how open Nerida was prepared to be, and so she pointed out to her that sex could be a two edged sword. Whilst it could give women power over men, a man could emasculate or evaporate that power by moving on to the next sexual partner. Nerida remained silent and to Karen, she appeared uncomfortable. Karen went on to say that she had never personally used sex as a weapon of power in her relationship with Andrew. Nerida continued to remain silent.

It got Karen thinking once again how she had struggled about this issue in recent times, wondering if Andrew's affair was a reflection of her failure or his. Had the other woman exploited sex the way Nerida had described, going from being a dependent patient to a patient the doctor depended on? She leaned back on the hard bench and closed her eyes. The word emasculate that she had used seemed out of place, but she couldn't think of the female equivalent to describe robbing a woman of power. It was strange how some terms could only apply to men or women, she thought. Now, misogyny has been used to describe men's negative attitude towards women, but she had wondered, what on earth was the word used to describe a similar attitude of women towards men? If such a word didn't exist, did it imply that women never thought badly of men nor put them down? She knew that wasn't the case and had searched in various dictionaries, until she came up with the word "misandry". As far as she could gather, it was the term used to describe women who hated men. It irritated her that she had never heard of the word nor seen it written, and from questioning, none of her friends were familiar with it either She didn't see herself as a feminist, but for a long time it had annoyed her how there was bias built in to many words in the English language. For example, the term used to describe humanity was mankind. Likewise, the lack of balance demonstrated by people being familiar with the term misogyny and not knowing the term misandry, bothered her. It suddenly struck her that she didn't know the male equivalent of feminist—was there such a word? She didn't see herself as being pedantic or overly politically correct, but felt that bias in language could influence the attitudes of many people.

Suddenly she became aware that she had been silent for what felt like an inordinate amount of time. When she opened her eyes and glanced over to Nerida, she saw that Nerida was probably dozing and the silence would not have been an issue. In fact, she had probably only been quiet for a matter of minutes, though it felt a lot longer to her. She wondered where all this tangled spaghetti of thoughts was getting her, and decided – not far. However, she continued to ponder as to whether she had in fact used sex as a form of punishment towards Andrew – you behave badly and this is what you miss out on. She cast aside this possibility, feeling that it was difficult for her to be really intimate with someone that she didn't trust as much and who she felt had betrayed her.

She imagined their relationship would continue, but whether the damage could be repaired, remained to be seen, and whether any repair was possible without further discussion or any discussion, was something she had to work out as well. She chuckled to herself with a touch of black humour, thinking that if she was to publish all the thoughts that were racing around her mind, then it might produce a saucy novel that could be a best seller. She had read that the opposite of love is not hate but rather indifference. She knew that she didn't hate Andrew nor was she indifferent to him. Rather, it was a feeling of puzzlement and hurt, struggling with the question of whether he was still the man that she had once fallen in love with and married, years back. Was she living with a stranger in her midst?

CHAPTER THIRTEEN

Friday, 19 August 1989
7.30 a.m.

It began as a warm pleasant day, with the sun filtering through the trees as Andrew hopped on to the tram making his way to his consulting rooms. For the past three years he had found it easier to use public transport rather than the stress of searching for a parking spot, and had worked out that it was also less expensive, especially if one took into account the occasional parking fine that he incurred.

Generally he enjoyed the time he had to read and relax on the tram before commencing work, but constancy was no longer part of his life, and his emotions were becoming unpredictable with the media accusations that now greeted him on an almost daily basis. Some days he could put it to one side, though not for long, especially if he saw it getting to Karen and the boys. But today he was feeling buoyant, as the police had notified him officially yesterday that the coronial court hearing would occur, which in a sense, he already strongly suspected from the time he received the phone call in early 1988 from the Age journalist. Sure, the journalist had only indicated that the family of his patient were pushing for a coronial inquest, but as Andrew and his family were subjected to a barrage of media allegations over the weeks and months that followed, he became certain in his own mind that it would eventually end in the coroner being involved.

However, hearing it from the police somehow formalised the whole thing, and he learnt that the hearing was set for April 1990.

When it was first mentioned by the journalist, Andrew had felt shaken up and couldn't understand what was going on. Now, for the first time, he began to look forward to having an opportunity for the truth to come out, under the protection of a set of legal rules.

But what is the truth, he asked himself. He knew in theory everyone lied at some time in their life, whether consciously leaving things out or stating things that were deliberately false. Or people could lie accidentally, believing something to be the truth when in fact it was not an accurate representation of what had occurred. Thus, giving evidence under oath didn't prevent lies of some nature occurring during the court proceedings. However, he had the benefit of still possessing the patient file written at the time the events in question occurred in 1978. He knew that the court findings were never totally predictable, no matter how strong his evidence was, as Coronial hearings allowed hearsay and rumours to be presented under oath, provided the witness believed them to be true. It left him feeling anxious knowing that the process could leave some dirt tarnishing his reputation...

He was aware that the role of a Coronial enquiry was a fact finding mission to see what factors contributed to the death of the patient. Because one is not actually charged with anything, it is unusual for the Coroner to state a finding of innocence. If the wildest allegations are eventually shown to have no basis in truth, people following the case in the media may only remember the name of the doctor involved and the allegations made.

Doctors and lawyers familiar with the process made him aware how difficult it was to avoid a professional reputation being significantly damaged. However, he was buoyed by the knowledge that for the first time he could shed the role of being a passive dummy under attack, as if his hands were tied behind his back, and he looked forward to confronting his accusers and dealing with the lies and distortions that had bombarded his family and himself for the past two years. However, he couldn't help wondering if he could really return to a normal life again.

He wondered if his recent interest in constructing a family tree was his attempt to magically ensure that his family life could connect with the future and not perish with him. He was aware how introspective he had become during the past two years whilst powerless to fight his accusers. He often needed to remind himself that Karen and the boys were also receiving the body blows, though initially he felt it was his trauma alone, tending to make him blind to their pain.

Andrew shook himself out of his reverie and examined the other people in the tram that he was riding in. He enjoyed watching people and their interactions and fantasising what he could infer about them. He noticed that sitting almost opposite him in the tram were two ladies, probably in their sixties, who were quite animated and speaking with their hands, almost as much as with their tongues. He found himself eavesdropping with difficulty, as they were speaking in hushed tones, and he detected that they weren't speaking English, but probably were talking in Yiddish. He couldn't speak Yiddish himself, but he had heard the language often enough to be able to identify it.

His parents had spoken this mixture of German and Hebrew and he had a rudimentary understanding of the language himself. In the past it had been used mainly by Ashkenazi Jews, but these days it was the victim of assimilation and murder and far less Jews spoke it. He chuckled to himself as he recalled his parents using it instead of English, when they didn't want the children to know what they were talking about, like a secret code.

As far as Andrew could make out, these two women seemed to be talking about Jewish issues in the local community, but it was hard to be certain, as they were speaking very softly. It had troubled Andrew over the years that he had often noticed Jewish people, both friends and strangers, lowering their voices whenever they spoke about Jewish related issues in public. Like spies carrying out espionage they whispered, so that others did not realise they were Jewish. He doubted that it was shame that brought this on, but more likely it was a combination of fear and insecurity regarding how others might react towards them if they knew they were Jewish. He realised that on this occasion it could just be two women talking softly out of politeness, because it was in a public place. However, he felt his initial observation was accurate – that many Jewish people in Australia were masking their Jewish identities in various ways.

Andrew could understand that there was a real basis to this feeling of threat, as even he found himself whispering in the same manner at times, but he believed strongly that it should be resisted. Whenever he noticed himself starting to whisper for that reason, he forced himself to speak naturally, if force and naturally were not contradictory terms, he reflected. He could understand such a reaction amongst Holocaust survivors, where the scars of their past hell made them ultra cautious, but when he saw it happening with young people who hadn't been through those experiences, it saddened him why they felt the need to whisper. He acknowledged to himself that even in Australia there was an undercurrent of threat that a lot of Jewish people experienced. It had troubled him for a long time to see that Jewish functions and establishments had more security than most, but he knew that the need was there. He regretted that even in a democracy such as Australia, there was still a need for security measures if an individual or group were identified as being Jewish. It was painful to observe some Jewish people showing the twitchy vigilance of deer in the wilds.

Andrew himself had experienced situations where after a jolly superficial interaction with a stranger at a football match or in a shop, joking around with them, then finding that occasionally the warmth dissipated when the stranger learnt that he was Jewish It was something that he didn't dwell on and he realised that it was part of human nature to stereotype and have prejudice. However, even though he could understand it intellectually, it continued to trouble him that in spite of being the same person, the response towards him could alter for some people when they learnt that he was Jewish. It had occurred at school fairly frequently, at times he was aware of it during his medical course, and even occasionally noticed it with girls that he dated.

Andrew suddenly jumped up and pulled the bell cord, realising that the next stop was his. As he got off the tram, he reflected that at times recently it was like he was drowning in a flood of thoughts. God, he was taking his work with him wherever he went, like a tortoise carrying its shell; all these thoughts coming from observing two elderly ladies in a tram. The way his mind was at the moment, maybe he should write a book. He smiled at the two women as he headed towards the exit.

During the tram ride, thoughts about human behaviour and whether people were intrinsically good or bad had popped in to Andrew's mind. And as if it was a natural extension of his tram ride thoughts, his first patient for the day was Mr B, an Austrian tourist who had been a member of the German Hitler youth movement during the war years. He initially doubted taking this man on as a patient, fearing that the emotions he experienced about World War II would create an impenetrable barrier to therapy. He rapidly convinced himself that he could treat him professionally and found that treatment in fact progressed well, and he believed that he established a therapeutic rapport with the Austrian tourist.

9.16 a.m.

'So you're Jewish?' asked Mr B, only minutes into the session,

'Yes, I am.'

The answer seemed to hang in the air – and why shouldn't it, Andrew thought, given that his own reaction to treating this man was also delayed. It was as if they had exchanged their greeting cards and laid their credentials out for both of them to see, and could now put all that aside and focus on the medical problems. Andrew discovered that's Mr B had suffered the breakup of his marriage after many years, and was questioning what he had achieved in his life, now that he had passed the midpoint.

Here we sit, Andrew thought, *but how would it have been if it was in the early 1940s?* He pushed these thoughts away, acknowledging to himself that they weren't relevant to his therapeutic relationship with this man, and in fact would be destructive to it. The last thing he wanted was to exact revenge. At the conclusion of the session, Andrew found himself reflecting on how there was a fine line between caring and hating. He had often pontificated with friends how everyone is prejudiced and that it was part of the human condition. What counted, he felt, was what one did with the prejudice. It was only a couple months ago that he had attended a musical that he thought he was totally familiar with – South Pacific. For the first time the lyrics of one song registered with him. This was the song called 'You've got to be Carefully Taught'.

> *You've got to be taught.*
> *To hate and fear.*
> *You've got to be taught*
> *from year to year*
> *it's got to be drummed*
> *in your dear little ear*
> *you've got to be carefully taught.*
>
> *You've got to be taught to be afraid*
> *Of people whose eyes are oddly made*
> *and people whose skin is a different shade*
> *you've got to be carefully taught*
>
> *You've got to be taught before it's too late*
> *before you are six or seven or eight*
> *to hate all the people your relatives hate*
> *you've got to be carefully taught*

Andrew felt that these lyrics summed up the whole issue of prejudice. He was conscious that yet again he was finding a way to divert his thoughts from the pending court case, but starting to niggle away was the realisation that this might be an example where the defence of deflecting his thoughts and emotions could build up to a tsunami, and possibly become more damaging than the issue it was helping him escape. The buoyant feeling he had felt before didn't last as the pressure mounted and became more and more intense over the following days.

Monday, 19 March 1990

The date for the coronial inquiry having been set, Andrew found his name was now freely mentioned in the media, and he experienced waking daily to the sound of anxiety.

Each morning he or Karen would go to the letterbox to retrieve the daily paper, and almost each day their fears were realised. On the front page or close to it, headlines screamed the allegations that he had used an illegal form of treatment, leading to the death of his patient. Occasionally the accusations had attached a legal qualifier with the word 'alleged'. Sometimes there were general articles about deep sleep therapy and its dangers. Patients bought him clippings from suburban newspapers as well, and he was touched by their implied support and continued belief in him. Andrew was puzzled that he and the pending inquiry warranted such ongoing and extensive coverage.

Why was it happening, given that he had always enjoyed a good relationship with his patient's family, which continued after the patient's death, with family members turning to him for support. "Why", was the question he repeatedly asked himself, without being any the wiser. He was bewildered when Karen questioned if he had any enemies and said that it felt to her as if the media exposure was orchestrated.

Andrew needed to remind himself that Karen and the boys were also suffering, and that he was not the only victim in this nightmare. He noticed that his confidence was diminishing and that he had become somewhat self-conscious with people, at times tripping over his awkwardness.

As he looked at his face in the mirror each morning when he went to shave, his image felt unreal and cluttered with anxiety. He felt Karen appeared stressed too, and he regretted that rather than reaching out to each other, she had become withdrawn and cooler towards him. Occasionally she told him about friends making snide comments which to her suggested they believed Andrew was guilty of the allegations in the media. She told him that even harder to deal with were incidents where a group of friends might be talking and would fall silent as she approached.

The boys also appeared bewildered and hurt after reading the things alleged in the media about a father that they had always respected. Increasingly at school they were subjected to taunts about their father being a murderer. At this stage, not a day went by without the family being immersed in a fog of worry, and it was unusual for the air they breathed not to be polluted by anxiety.

Andrew felt himself unable to shield the family from the storm of accusations. He thought back to the tender moment years back, when Karen asked him to name the animal that most represented his personality, and he had created a fictitious animal which he named a "Squowl", a mix of a squirrel and an owl. Sadly, he reflected that if asked now, he would name an animal which was a mix of skunk and a feral cat, named a "Scat". He couldn't imagine anyone wanting to own or be around a Scat. He was not fond of the person he had become.

Not for the first time, he was amazed at the capacity of some people to be cruel, but was buoyed by the knowledge that his patients continued to believe in his innocence. As far as he could gauge, Karen and the boys also believed in his innocence after he had explained deep sleep therapy to them, describing it as a procedure without merit, but carrying considerable risks. He told them that he didn't believe it had ever been justified as a form of therapy, as it essentially put people into an induced coma and suppressed their breathing.

In contrast to the loyalty of patients and family, Andrew felt that colleagues, with the exception of his study group, were keeping their distance more and more, to avoid contamination from the allegations that were flying around, and being directed at Andrew.

Generally, he found himself withdrawing from people but kept on working with his patients, and the only outlet for contact with other people tended to be the fortnightly study group with his peers. A fair percentage of the group was made up of old friends, where one could be stupid around them and they would remain accepting of him. However, he didn't trust them completely to be non-judgemental. The study group had been going now for about two and a half years and up to 12 psychiatrists could attend on a good evening when everyone turned up. Most of those attending were about his own vintage, but several were considerably older and Andrew felt they brought experience and wisdom to the sessions.

The venue where they met was decided by rotating amongst the members' homes, and the person hosting the meeting would be in charge of the proceedings for that night. They had a rather loose arrangement as to what could be discussed at the meetings, so that it might range from difficulties one of them was experiencing with a patient they were treating, to discussions about recent medical journal articles, and could include discussion of specific psychiatric disorders and the recent advances made in treating them.

In the past, Andrew had enjoyed the meetings with the banter and camaraderie that existed in the group, even though he might have felt at times that he had not got very much out of that evening's discussion. There were a few in the group that Andrew didn't take to, but he enjoyed being around most of them sufficiently to not be troubled by those few.

Saturday 24, March 1990
9.45 a.m.

Andrew had taken himself for a walk down the street, going nowhere in particular but having the freedom to dwell on his own thoughts and feelings. Karen had gone out for a large part of the day with girlfriends, but he couldn't recall what they were doing. He reflected on the group meeting the night before, held at Peter Avery's substantial home, which he guessed many would label a mansion. It was set in extensive grounds in the establishment part of Hawthorn.

Andrew had long enjoyed Peter's company and their friendship went back many years, but on entering Peter's living room the evening before, he was aware of looks of disapproval greeting him, and felt hurt and confused by the response. He sensed that some of them were uncomfortable and guessed it probably had to do with the public allegations that the media was highlighting.

Friday, 23 March, 1990 was a date Andrew would recall in the future as a watershed moment in the way he tackled this nightmare, and when he decided to speak more openly about it on entering the room of his peer group meeting.

Andrew hadn't discussed the allegations about himself with anyone outside of his family at this point, and he didn't feel he was imagining the reaction in the room, as it seemed the most likely explanation as to why people would suddenly stop talking and look blankly towards him, but not saying anything. He knew at the time that he should broach the subject of what was being alleged and discuss it with them, but he didn't feel ready yet, and wondered if he ever would.

Soon after coming into the room, he found the relative quiet rippling through it to be more abrasive to him than any shouting could have been. He realised he had to curb the tendency to interpret people's silence in the most negative way. He decided that whilst he wasn't ready to open up and discuss the allegations against himself in the media, he would still share with the group some of the thoughts and feelings that he had been experiencing recently, as if in some magical way it would lead to a freedom to share what so far could not be spoken about. When there was a break in the conversation, he suddenly announced apropos of nothing, that recently he had begun thinking back to the earlier years of his working life.

'Those early days – it sounds like BC doesn't it?' he had said with a forced laugh. 'I was thinking, in those early days I used to see friends. Yeah, I had friends back then. Look, I know you guys are friends, but back then I also had friends unrelated to my work, some of them going back many years.' He took a swig of red wine, already his second glass that evening. 'You know, people lose interest in you if they feel it's all going in the one direction, them giving and you taking. Some friendships that go back many years still remain and it would only require a small flame to re-ignite them, but in our lives, most friendships are transient,' he had pronounced sadly. 'Yeah, you need to feed them, to nurture them, and a small flame can reignite them. It's not like flowers, you can't feed friendships shit.' Andrew heard himself lecturing to his colleagues rather than conversing – guaranteed to put barriers up. If the room had felt silent before, it was funereal now, Andrew had realised, even with the alcohol that he was imbibing.

The psychiatrists in the room let him go on, probably realising that for Andrew it was like lancing an abscess. He had continued rambling, telling them how he used to play squash and tennis, went to football games and had the occasional game of golf and how he spent time with his family.

'I do have one, you know,' he'd confided. The words were not slurred and they poured out unfiltered. 'I used to go and see the boys play sport. Karen and I went to concerts and operas. We'd go to plays and have dinner parties. It's a wonder I got any work done, so why has it all changed you ask – well, would you believe I don't know. But I've got some theories of course, like a good psychiatrist,' he had added bitterly. 'Could be my insecurity that caused it, a bit like kids who know they can feed their parents crap because the parents will still be there for them, so it's safe. But if they tried it on with friends outside of the family, then they would become former friends in the wink of an eye. So maybe with patients, to gain their loyalty I haven't said no, that way they'll like me and keep coming back. What I'm saying is that possibly it's easier saying no to the family than it is to patients, because the family won't give up on you in the same way.'

Still no one else in the room had said a word, as if mesmerised by what was pouring out of Andrew.

'You know, another theory is that there may also be an addictive element where you get a high seeing patients and having them like you and you need more and more to maintain that feeling. The other thing I have noticed, guys, is that when people ask you how you are, they're shocked if you tell them, assuming they're actually listening. You know what happened to me the other day,' he'd related to his captive audience, 'well, I met an acquaintance and she said, "How are you?" "I am terrible", I answered. "I've got these false allegations in the papers, I'm not sleeping, the whole family isn't sleeping, and I thought I'd throw in an extra to see if she was listening, and Karen has broken both her ankles." So my acquaintance says, "That's great. We have just bought this huge house and have started renovations and the stress is incredible." So there you have it guys, a package review of my life.' But he knew, that in the jumble of words and emotions, he had managed to start letting them know how bad things were for him and his family, and how alone he felt.

CHAPTER FOURTEEN

Friday, 30 March 1990
5.30 a.m.

Andrew awoke to the rumbling storm of anxiety, a pattern that was becoming much more frequent lately. It was still dark outside and no one else in the house had woken up as yet. It was a lot earlier than required for him to get to work at the correct time, which lately was 8 a.m. If he had patients in hospital, he usually saw them before going to his medical rooms and even then, getting up at 6:30 a.m. would be adequate. If he was running late, he could always have breakfast at a cafe close to work, or have it delivered to his rooms if he was very short of time.

Andrew realised that this early morning wakening might very well be symptomatic of a mild depression with associated anxiety. It felt strange applying psychiatric labels and diagnoses to himself. In recent times he had reflected with a touch of envy, that there were people, including friends, who appeared less aware of their surroundings and what was going on around them, and as a consequence seemed calmer than the majority of the population. Andrew noted how several of his friends appeared to calmly let the world go by.

He believed that it would surprise him if there wasn't a downside to being that way, as they did not always appear in tune with the world around them. He realised he was probably simplifying the situation, but on observation, these people didn't seem to be troubled by the complexities of daily life or burdened by introspection. They were not apparently weighed down by "what if" anxiety, and Andrew wryly reflected that he personally could not be accused of falling into such a group. It was a pattern that he had observed at one end of the spectrum in people born with Down syndrome who appeared happy and smiling and concerned only with basic needs, it would seem. At the other end of the spectrum were people with normal intelligence, yet oblivious to many events occurring around them and showing apparent peace of mind. Whilst Andrew had told close friends over the years that he preferred to deal with current issues that one could still influence, rather than working on past events or things that might happen in the future, he knew that in fact this was not how life functioned.

Actually, it was not how he himself worked when treating patients, as he was required to assist them in looking at past issues. The aim of therapy was to help the patient deal with past traumas that had been left to fester, whilst in other patients he might work to assist them in developing coping mechanisms for the future. However, Andrew knew that for himself and his family, it was the current conflict that had to be sorted out if they were to survive as a family unit. He realised also that in the not too distant future he would need to deal with issues beyond the current crisis. The phrase "physician heal thyself", was one he could no longer ignore, as he was becoming increasingly aware of many past traumas in his own life that he had just buried rather than dealing with them. All the recent stress had served to make him more aware of his own past issues, some dating back to childhood years.

As Andrew dressed for work, he gazed at his image in the bathroom mirror and it felt like he was looking at a stranger's face. It troubled him to witness what appeared to be the early ravages of ageing and the reminder that even though he had been attempting to build up his fitness level, he couldn't avoid noticing the slight paunch, and excessive weight, highlighting the continuing gap between desire and execution of this goal. He was troubled by the thought that the weight and paunch could be a down payment for problems to follow. He had come to terms with his early hair loss and didn't try to disguise it by the way he combed his remaining hair. He consoled himself by noting how many top sportsmen had billiard ball pates these days. There wasn't a lot he liked about himself at present. The hair loss had troubled him a lot more when he was younger, and in fact he had gone to a plastic surgeon, Dr Rigby, to get his advice about what could be done to halt his developing baldness.

The moment he entered the doctor's consulting room, he realised that the consultation would be of little value as he set eyes on Dr Rigby's shiny bald head. After Andrew described his concerns, Dr Rigby, a pleasant, energetic man of slight build, advised that the only option open to Andrew to save his remaining hair was castration. It was said seriously, but Andrew was certain the surgeon had said it in jest. Dr Rigby didn't charge a fee for the consultation nor would Andrew have expected him to.

Andrew found himself dwelling a lot on past memories lately, and though he believed his account of these memories was truthful, he also knew that time may well have chipped away to diminish the accuracy of what he recalled. It was not a lie nor was it the absolute truth, but it was the best that the years would allow him to do.

Still gazing at his image in the mirror, as if glued to it, he reassured himself that he also possessed a lot of positive qualities, though looks were not at the top of the list. He didn't believe that he was unattractive years back and probably even now, though it had become harder to convince himself of that in recent times. He believed that most people saw him as pleasant looking, and Karen had told him in the past that what appealed to her most, was his sense of humour and gentle manner.

Andrew himself had always considered that his most appealing features were probably internal, with a capacity for caring about people. He believed this was possibly related to what he knew about the traumas his parents and he had gone through during the war years and later, after arriving in Australia as refugees. He reflected that some people seemed to be built for their character, where observers might say they appeared warm hearted and had open honest faces. However, Andrew had never believed you could tell a person's character from their physical features. He had said to friends in the past that all one had to do was to observe how many pleasant good-looking crooks there were. He had often postulated that if one could tell a person's character by their appearance, then life would be a lot easier, as it would be possible to say, "I wouldn't buy a car from him. He looks like a crook" and "There is no way that man could be a murderer, when you look at him."

Andrew shook his head realising that allowing his thoughts to take over had robbed him of time, so that he was now verging on being late for work. Fortunately he didn't have any patients in hospital at the moment, so he could go directly to the medical rooms and arrive there just before 8 a.m. He quickly checked his diary and confirmed that after lunch he had an appointment with Dr Engel at 2 p.m.

Once again Andrew had stopped seeing Dr Engel, feeling at the time that he had probably gone as far as he could with the therapy. Now with a specific date having been set for the court hearing, and with the mounting media assaults, he realised that he had stopped prematurely and had better resume seeing Dr Engel. If he was honest with himself, he had to admit how much he was struggling in many areas of his life, at work, socially and at home, with anxiety and possibly early depression diminishing his concentration and energy levels and going hand in hand with increasing self-criticism. Today was now the third session since he had resumed therapy, and in the previous two sessions Dr Engel had encouraged him to speak about the traumas the extended family had all gone through.

Until recently, Andrew believed that he had come to terms with many of these memories and they no longer interfered with his daily functioning. However, a lot of pressure had occurred over a short period of time, apart from the recent hellish media allegations. He had lost both his parents since 1982, had the affair with Samantha and was struggling with the suspicion that Karen had somehow learnt about it. In addition, his two sons, Jed and Bobby had celebrated their Bar Mitzvahs in recent years, at a time when celebrating did not come readily. To Andrew, it felt as if his life had been compressed and was flashing before him, without time to feel part of it.

Andrew disposed the remainder of his coffee down the kitchen sink and let breakfast go,. hoping to possibly catch up with some food later on after he got to work.

7.15 a.m.

Andrew's fingers tapped gently on the steering wheel to the beat of the music from his car radio. He recalled how in the previous sessions with Dr Engel he described with difficulty what he knew about his family's experiences in war-torn Poland, and how his words came out in a fractured, hesitant way tripping over his own discomfort. Gradually, as he began recalling these events, he discovered that the flood of thoughts, memories and feelings started to become more accessible as if they had been waiting for an opening for many years. But there was a lot more to come, as he and Dr Engel had only touched the surface of these issues after two sessions.

Andrew checked his watch as he waited for the red light to change. He had an extra half an hour up his sleeve. Feeling caught up in the memories and emotions going through his mind, he decided to pull over in order to give himself some time to reflect.

Turning off the engine, his mind continued to replay the past two sessions with Dr Engel. He recalled describing to his therapist that, being so young at the time WWII hit his family and country protected him from some of the horrific memories of events that occurred then. However, over the years, as he acquired more details about what had happened to himself and his family, he began to fill in the gaps, and imagine the experiences that they must have gone through.

He was staggered by how much anger had bubbled up as he talked through his history with Dr Engel, and they had only just commenced. He was starting to realise that he had buried a lot of the bitterness and anger about the family experiences during the war, including the anger he felt about many of the perpetrators escaping punishment for the atrocities they had committed. He tried to get his parents to tell him more about the past, with only limited success, and came to realise that there are moments when the flames of evil create a light of such intensity that one has to do look away, sometimes forever.

His father, who had always been a shadow in his life, was unable to give him any history, and even his mother could only talk about the past for short periods and then hesitantly revisit those times later on. This was a pattern he respected and did not violate, and gradually he had joined the dots of her story together, but gaps remained at the time of her death. He was able to fill a lot of the gaps from records in Holocaust Museums in Australia and overseas, and from the history that his parent's close friends provided. As he learnt more and more, Andrew found that the protective barrier generated by being so young at the time of World War II was starting to be penetrated. He began to be troubled by images in his mind that arose from what he learnt had been done to other Holocaust victims. The emotions that he thought he had tamed were now escaping through the porous boundaries and insulting his conscious mind.

He told Dr Engel that probably the most horrific thought for him was the knowledge that if he himself had been killed for being Jewish, then his own children would not have existed, putting an end to the potential of future generations. If one multiplied this by the many millions that had been murdered, the experience became overwhelming to consider. Both his parents had lost many family members during the Holocaust and both of them had parents who had been shot dead in their own houses where they lived in Poland, in a small town close to Warsaw. In addition, his father had two brothers and a sister taken to Auschwitz where they were killed, whilst his mother had three brothers killed in Auschwitz and the fourth brother was able to escape with the help of a courageous Polish family and migrated to America. The non Jewish family that had saved him, also had to migrate to Canada because their own community turned on them for being "Jew lovers".

Andrew learnt from his mother that he lived with his parents and brother Harry in Warsaw under false Aryan papers. Neither child was aware they were Jewish as it was too dangerous for a young child to have that information which might be blurted out, leading to the death of all of them.

His mother related how the boys ran around with the other children shouting anti-Jewish slogans and as Andrew matured to adulthood, he came to understand just how readily hatred and prejudice can be taught by people who are part of a child's environment. Harry being less predictable, was more restricted in going out, causing friction at times.

Both of Andrew's parents, especially his mother, had been helped by Anton, a kindly Polish man of limited education, who worked as a labourer at the forced labour camp where Andrew and his parents were imprisoned. Andrew's parents had applied for Anton to be recognised as a righteous Gentile by the Holocaust Centre in Israel (Yad Vashem) and in the years that followed, Anton and his family were honoured by Jewish communities in various parts of the world for their courage, as they could have been killed if their actions came to the attention of the Nazis. Andrew had met some of Anton's family members many years back, and Anton died in the late 1970s.

In addition to Anton, a man who worked for Andrew's paternal grandfather assisted Andrew's father in getting false Aryan papers. However, Andrew's parents had never been able to trace this man or his family after the war and did not know what had happened to him.

It took Andrew many years to learn that he, Harry and their parents had initially been arrested and placed in a labour camp near Warsaw, when Andrew was close to two years old, and Harry had just turned ten. It was from here that they had all been helped to escape and live out the remaining war years with false identity papers. Andrew came to believe that his parents had not emerged from those experiences emotionally unscathed. Until recently he had believed that he, Andrew, had managed to overcome the trauma of those war years and had gone on to function effectively.

Andrew recalled that growing up, he often had the dilemma of not knowing whether some of his parent's behaviour that annoyed him greatly was due to their war experiences or just their personalities. In other words, did he have a right to be angry towards them, or did he have to make allowances for them? He could see how labile his parent's emotions were and saw them ranging from being fearful, to being detached and isolated, or overly irritable and prone to depression, especially when someone they knew died. Due to the war experiences and being refugees who came to a new country with no material possessions, they threw themselves into providing financial security for the family once they reached the safety of Australia.

Recently Andrew began to wonder if he had behaved in a similar fashion. Like his parents, he worked extremely long hours, available most of the time for his patients, with only residual crumbs of time free to be with his family. He consoled himself with thoughts of his children having extended family in their own lives, in contrast to the emptiness he grew up in. Vivid early memories remained with Andrew how soon after arriving in Australia he became aware of many local children having families surrounded by grandparents, uncles and aunts, making him feel very different. He found it difficult to describe how he felt at the time, except to say he felt bad. It was a strange and confused feeling, possibly akin to sadness. The family who were missing in his life felt totally lost, as if they had never existed for him. He had no memories, no photos and not even marked graves where he could pay his respects for the people missing in his family. They had been erased totally from his life.

More and more in recent times, Andrew found thoughts about the war and his family were being triggered at unexpected moments, bringing a sense of bitter losses.

Andrew remembered that after his mother talked about the family history, her mind would fester, bringing on the abscesses of nightmares. He found affection from his parents was unpredictable and at times rationed, whilst on other occasions it would come out in floods, as if it might be the last occasion that affection could be shown. Andrew found it difficult to fathom the potential of people for doing evil and when he came across the term in Hannah Arendt's "The Banality of Evil" it struck a chord within him. It became more frightening and distressing to realise that the atrocities were carried out by ordinary people, not by monsters who were different to himself. The ordinary people in the past could have been friends of their victim, lived next door, belonged to the same school or taught their victim, or may even have been doctors who treated the person they now killed.

In the past few months Andrew began to see the warning signs of being immersed in a multitude of painful experiences from the past and present. He began to realise that his negative thinking and withdrawal from most social contact was causing him to be incarcerated in a prison that he himself was constructing. He found it hard to believe how critically he was assessing himself, but realised on reflection that he was reacting to the media onslaught accusing him of killing his patient with a discredited form of therapy, and under attack not for the first time in his life. He reminded himself that it was not only he, but also Karen and the children who were suffering. The allegations that he had caused the death of his patient by using an illegal treatment continued, and each morning Andrew would anxiously scan the newspapers to see whether there were articles about him. He was aware of scrutinising people's faces and reactions to see if they had somehow judged him. Apart from his peer study group, he did not seek out social contact and in fact tended to avoid it when possible.

12.03 p.m.

Whilst taking a short break at midday, Andrew returned a call from Karen. Abruptly she reminded him that they were invited out to dinner that evening at the home of their close friends Miriam and Bert Goldfine.

'Shit, I totally forgot about it,' Andrew muttered, expressing his frustration at an unwanted outing. His frustration was matched by her anger.

'You forgot?' Karen hissed.

It didn't take a lot to annoy her lately, Andrew felt, immediately realising that it also didn't take a lot to provoke himself, and the mix was becoming increasingly explosive. He quickly adjusted and reassured Karen that it wouldn't be a problem, attempting to put out one more brush fire in their relationship. Together they decided that Andrew would keep his appointment with Dr Engel, then go home to shower and dress, before they set off for the Goldfines.

2.01 p.m.

Andrew greeted Dr Engel, who he continued to like and felt secure with. After an initial period of silence, which he knew would propel him to speak, Andrew started describing some of the thoughts about his family that he had experienced earlier that day.

Once again he expressed the anger and bitterness over the loss of his family during the Holocaust and the bitterness he felt knowing many of the perpetrators would never be brought to justice. He said that he believed he would be capable of even killing people if he was sure of their guilty identity, but acknowledged Dr Engel's point that having feelings of killing someone was quite different to actually doing it. He agreed with Dr Engel that if people were judged for their thoughts, the gaols would be overflowing. Andrew said it wouldn't be God or religion that would stop him doing it, as he did not believe in a God and wondered how people who had gone through that experience of the war could continue with their beliefs. He felt what would stop him was the knowledge that to carry out such an act would place him at the same low moral level as the people he was condemning.

Towards the end of the session Dr Engel suggested that Andrew begin thinking whether the persecution he and his family had experienced during the war years had possibly sensitised him to feeling that he and his family were victims once again in the present scenario. Did it feel to him like history was repeating itself, that once again his family was being persecuted, and could this possibly explain some of the intensity of the anger and bitterness that that was drowning him now?

Andrew's instinctive reaction was to reject the notion, but gradually, once the session was over and he was driving home, he began to feel there might be some validity to the theory. Dr Engel told him that next session he planned to follow these thoughts further, as well as getting some of the history regarding Andrew's sibs and his experiences when he commenced his schooling as a refugee in Australia.

8.14 p.m.

Andrew found himself wedged between two of the female guests of the Goldfines. He wasn't surprised that none of the six couples who had been invited to dinner that night were known to either he or Karen, as the Goldfines appeared to change their friends regularly, and Karen and he were exceptions to this pattern.He looked forward to the dinner part of the evening, as the Goldfines invariably used good caterers.

Andrew glanced down to the other end of the table and saw Karen laughing, chatting and generally animated in a way that he hadn't seen for some time. He wondered why she couldn't be like that with him and whether she really felt as happy as she appeared outwardly. She remained a striking figure and he believed that he still loved her deeply and that she probably loved him also, whatever love was. So why had she drawn away from him?

The easy banter between them appeared to have leaked away and had been missing for at least the past year or so. Physically she could still arouse him, but he wasn't sure the feeling was reciprocated. He had suspected for a while that she somehow had developed suspicions about his previous relationship with Samantha, but had never challenged him directly about it. He came close to confessing and asking for ... for what ... forgiveness? He realised that to do so would only be selfish and destructive. It would destroy any vestige of closeness in their relationship. It could just be that she was feeling the stress of all the media attention and the pending court case, and the fact that he was working excessively long hours and the kids were growing up and becoming more independent. In other words, that she felt less needed.

He suddenly realised that the young woman sitting on his right was speaking to him. She was a striking, tall lady, probably in her thirties and twenty or so years younger than himself. He had noticed her the moment he entered the room. She had high cheekbones, jet-black hair, an olive complexion and the largest dark eyes that drew the attention of every man in the room, he felt. Her dress was figure hugging with a plunging neckline that made it difficult to look elsewhere. She was not someone who didn't want to be noticed.

The young woman realised that he hadn't heard her and she repeated herself. 'I hear that you work as a psychiatrist. That must be fascinating ...'

Andrew struggled to avoid gazing at her breasts, but lost the battle whilst he was thinking of a smart reply to her query, banal as it was. 'It has its moments,' he blurted and immediately thought that his answer was inane. However, they kept on chatting and he discovered that she had trained as a lawyer, but like many in that field did not practice it. She was at home for the time being looking after two young children, but in several years' time she planned to join her husband in a small but thriving IT software business that they owned.

Again he felt himself drifting off as she spoke, wondering what it was about the female breast that fascinated so many men. Pondering that was easier than having to answer the question about himself. Was it the trauma of being pulled from the breast onto a bottle that made men so fixated by that part of the female anatomy? He doubted it being as straightforward as that.

Andrew noticed Karen glancing at him from the other end of the table and again wondered if she was thinking about the affair that he had with his patient. At the same time he realised that having this extremely attractive young woman chatting to him was something that he enjoyed a lot, but even more so, he knew that he was deriving pleasure from having people seeing her talking to him. As the evening progressed, he found himself enjoying it far more than he had anticipated. The conversation around the table was brisk and he noted that the other guests were often turning to him for his opinion about a range of issues. Like many dinner parties, the subject matter covered anything from religion to politics to sex. Occassionally he found himself actually directing where the conversation went, like a traffic cop.

He wondered if Karen would be impressed by seeing him holding the floor or whether it would have the opposite effect. Would she think she had heard it all before and accuse him of being cynical, which she had at times done in the past. The occasional disguised glance he snuck in her direction gave him no clues about her responses, nor did it slow him down. He knew that he enjoyed playing the devil's advocate and having intellectual stoushes that he felt he was adept at, but wished he could tone down some of his rhetoric and cynicism, especially the latter which seemed to have spiked in recent years.

Flippantly, he had told Karen that the thing about cynicism was that it often proved to be correct, but on the occasions he was able to be honest with himself, he knew that it could also be corrosive. Andrew found it difficult not to take on the role of devil's advocate and challenge what he saw as the asinine certainty demonstrated by advocates of a particular line of politics, religion, global warming and the like. He felt that these people at times treated the issues in an evangelical manner, very much like a religion, where they would not tolerate a difference of opinion and some fanaticism seemed to have infested their beliefs. Andrew had long felt that right or wrong, any theory should be able to tolerate genuine questioning, occasionally wondering what theories people had about him.

Just prior to sitting down to dinner, Andrew had spoken to a middle-aged lady steeped in religion and again someone he had not met before. Provocatively he had enquired whether she could help clarify for him something that had puzzled him for many years. With a choirboy look, and constructing an expression of puzzlement, he put forward the proposition that what continued to puzzle him was the issue of Adam and Eve. We get told they had two sons, Cain and Abel, so where did the rest of humanity come from if there were only the two boys? He confessed that he had read the theory that the boys might have slept with their mother, but what did this lady think? She swivelled to turn her back on him and moved away without answering. He immediately regretted behaving in this manner and felt it was a pattern that had developed in recent times, especially if he had lubricated himself with a glass or two or even more, of red.

His moment of regret was short lived as he noticed a statuesque middle-aged woman on her own and went up to speak to her. Somehow, talking to women appealed to him far more than speaking to men at parties.

'It's strange that we never met before,' he said.

'Well, we only moved to Melbourne from Christchurch in New Zealand less than a year ago.'

Feeling a little tipsy, he resisted the urge to ask her to say "six", but he didn't resist completely, drawing on the hackneyed joke that New Zealanders pronounce "six" as "sex".

'So how old are your children?' he enquired.

'Well, Sam is seven and Rita is nine,' she replied innocently.

Damn, I should have asked her a year earlier, he chuckled to himself.

With a trace of a smile on her lips, she said flirtatiously, 'You look like a very honest, stable man. Are you?'

'Well ... I –'

'I've heard most psychiatrists are crazy,' she interrupted before Andrew could respond. 'Do you agree?'

'Uh ... let me get you a drink and then answer the question,' he said, buying himself some time to think of a smart response.

Without enquiring, Andrew returned with two glasses of shiraz.

Smiling at her, he made the profound comment that he thought everyone was a touch crazy. He said that if someone was poor, they were more likely to be labelled crazy and if they were wealthy they tended to be called eccentric. He confessed that he could probably be labelled as eccentric, having just snuck in economically.

'Look, I'll give you an example', going on to describe how a few years previously he had been on his way to a birthday party where he was part of an organised roast for a friend. 'I decided to pretend to be a girlfriend of his from years back. I dressed in drag, pretending to be an old flame of the birthday boy and was about to leave the house with my wife, when the phone rang. It was a call from the hospital asking me to sign some medication orders and it needed to be done immediately rather than later. I was running late already and being part of my friend's roast I took the plunge and drove to the hospital as I was. There I was, in drag, signing the medication orders and to their credit, the nurses barely blinked. But the next day I really copped it with their teasing, which was done in good fun…not at all nasty. It went on for a few months.'

Andrew's expatriate New Zealand companion started giggling, drawing stares from other people in the room. Andrew thought to himself that Karen was probably right and that these types of interaction were a hell of a lot better and more enjoyable than heated arguments about global warming or politics or whether so and so was a misogynist or not.

However, it didn't deter him from entering into a heated discussion soon after, when he aired his views about global warming with several of the guests. Whilst he didn't deny weather change itself, he couldn't tolerate the semi-religious zeal demonstrated by some advocates of global warming, where they appeared unable to tolerate any opposing view. Andrew felt strongly that there should be room for discussion of these issues, with the ability to exchange opinions and thoughts.

Occasionally he allowed himself to be aware that he was as rigid with this view as they were with theirs. He began sharing a piece of unsolicited wisdom with the largely unreceptive audience around him. In spite of the negative vibes, he went on telling them that he had no time for the Al Gore approach of predicting impending doom, and wished he could read some balanced scientific reports to develop his own understanding of weather change and the role of carbon. His passionate argument elicited a variety of responses from the small group surrounding him. Some continued to argue about climate change, a few retreated into silence and one drunk matron chose to attack his profession of psychiatry, querying the mental stability of those who practiced it.

As if on cue, Karen came up to him and placed a large bunch of grapes on his head. 'Darling, you know we always do this before dinner, and I nearly forgot.'

Andrew couldn't recall when she had last called him darling.

Long ago, Karen had learnt how best to diffuse attacks on Andrew's choice of profession, but on this occasion Andrew felt he didn't need her assistance, as he was prepared to laugh at his own foibles, and gloss over any insults. However, Karen's response was so unexpected, that it was followed by a stunned silence, broken by raucous laughter relieving the tension.

Somewhat irritated at having been bailed out by Karen, Andrew was not to be contained. Before sitting down at the dinner table, as there was a break between each course, he fired one last arrow, summarising his points of view about global warming and simultaneously chastised himself for needing to have the last word, but the Shiraz won out. He could hear himself pontificating, telling his somewhat unreceptive audience that there should be room for discussion about climate change. His speech wasn't slurred, but there was no mistaking that he'd been helping himself to the wine, which was readily available. He elaborated further, not that he was asked, explaining that he remained unsure how much of the weather change was man-made and how much was part of the natural cycle. Like a runaway train, he ended by reciting Dorothy McKellar's poem:

I love a sunburnt country
a land of sweeping plains
of rugged mountain ranges
of droughts and flooding rains.

'So I don't suggest it rules out man made climate change,' he confided to the other guests, 'but it does suggest a regular cycle of change as well as climate change.'

His recital was met with stony silence. He regretted persisting with his argument and was relieved to be seated at the dinner table once again.

The arrangement for the dinner was to move the men to a new seat with each subsequent course, leaving the women returning to the same seats as before. Over the passage of the dinner he had chatted to two attractive women so far, and felt somewhat amazed at how many older men present were married to younger attractive partners in this group of guests.

By the end of the meal he had found himself seated next to yet another attractive young woman who explained that she was new to the area and did not know a lot of people locally. Andrew chatted mainly to her, carefully making his way through the minefield of potential topics. For a while they spoke about nothing of note. He had always been very conscious of not discussing his patients, as he felt this was privileged and confidential information. However, by this stage of the evening, the wine had loosened his tongue somewhat and he was also desperate to stay away from controversial issues, so he reassured himself that as long as he didn't mention names, it would be okay.

Once again he was asked what he did for a living, surprised that by this stage of the evening his companion didn't know, and his response elicited a nervous laugh from his dinner companion. She enquired if he could tell her about some of his more interesting cases, and normally he would have fobbed off the question and the questioner. On this occasion he reassured himself that as long as he didn't identify the patient, it would be okay.

He described treating a woman in her early thirties, who had presented with a severe bird phobia. Andrew chose not to go into the details of what brought about the phobia, in case it provided information which could identify the patient. He explained to his dinner companion how the patient was progressing quite well, so he encouraged her to bring an actual bird to the therapy session. He planned to use the bird in a process of desensitising, so that she could tolerate being close to the bird without experiencing overwhelming anxiety. This progressed well until they got to the stage where he planned to have the patient put her hand into the birdcage and touch the bird. Unfortunately the bird saw a window of opportunity and escaped through the partially open birdcage door. It flew frantically around the room, flapping its wings, causing the patient to panic and run screaming from the consulting room into the waiting room where other patients were seated. Like the plague, her panic spread, causing the waiting room to empty. Andrew and his secretary then spent one and a quarter hours crawling on the floor distributing birdseed in an attempt to recapture the bird. This was not readily done, as the room had high ceilings and the bird was as panicky as the patient had been. They finally captured the bird, but Andrew found himself running late with his appointments for the rest of the day, as the panicked patients sheepishly returned to the waiting room. The patient with the bird phobia could not be found and they finally spoke on the phone and arranged for her to return for the next appointment in three weeks' time.

'It took me several months of therapy to get her back to the point we'd reached before that bird escaped,' Andrew confided with a smile.

The young woman he was entertaining with this story, laughed out loud and he felt an inner glow, somewhat diminished by his discomfort telling him that he had probably said more than he should. Not long after, he became aware that his dinner partner had placed a small, warm hand on his thigh, and he allowed it to remain there until the desert was served a few minutes later.

At the end of the evening, as coffee was being served, Andrew engaged the table in general with his views on life. He held the floor, telling all who would listen, that he felt any group of people in any nation had the capacity for committing atrocities, if the right circumstances were in place. He shared how he felt about mob mentality and how once it took over, people were capable of committing any crime. As he heard himself speak, he realised he was setting himself up to be asked the natural question flowing from his comments.

'Well, I guess that includes you, doesn't it?'

Andrew had to acknowledge that it did. Only later did he learn that the questioner was the companion of the lady sitting next to himself.

He continued talking, telling his captive audience that it was rare for individuals to be crazy but common for groups of people, explaining how mobs allowed people to act brutally under the cover of anonymity. Again without encouragement, he shared with the table that he had stopped believing in God and was puzzled how others could believe in a God that allowed atrocities to happen around the world. He confessed that he had been amazed at his parents continuing to believe in God even after what they went through in surviving the Holocaust. Without pausing, he said that he could understand that for his parents and others like them, there was some comfort in believing that all these traumatic events were somehow part of a divine plan, rather than just random savagery.

It was just after 1 a.m. when he and Karen drove home. Although shrouded by the silence in the car, it was the best Andrew had felt for quite a while. However, any discussion he tried to bring up, Karen responded to with a grunt or minimal response. If only she would talk. He knew that there were issues corroding their relationship and driving a wedge between them, but he was still unsure exactly what those issues were. They had to be something more than the stress of the pending court case, or did they?

Because of how much alcohol Andrew had drunk, Karen drove, and in High Street Prahran, they noticed a crowd of young adolescents congregating outside a dance hall or bar. Andrew remarked to Karen that the boys look gawky, whilst the girls appeared striking in their platform high heels and negligible skirts, which had become the fashion for girls in that age group. He marvelled how in attempting to be independent and differentiating themselves as individuals, they in fact managed to look as if they were clothed in the same uniform, a homogenous mass. He had hesitated about drawing any attention to these young girls, fearing that Karen might read it the wrong way and assume that he was attracted to them – not that he didn't find them attractive. He was aware of feeling some mounting embarrassment about his behaviour during the dinner party, which was not the way he usually presented to people. But then, he didn't usually drink that much either. Some of the thoughts he had shared were his thoughts, but he realised they had come out in a manner of a performance, rather than a natural conversation.

CHAPTER FIFTEEN

Wednesday, 28 March 1990
4.48 p.m.

Andrew had finished work for the day at 4.30 p.m., dragged himself to his car, and had little memory of the drive to Dr Engel's rooms for his 5 p.m. appointment. He believed it was a reasonable hour to complete a working day, but given how he felt, he could have given the whole day a miss. In the past, he found that stopping work at 5 p.m perpetually escaped him.

'You look like a rich boy but work like a poor one. Don't we have enough money?' Karen had confronted him a few years back, but had given up telling him in more recent times. He recalled how when the boys were very young, Karen had said, 'Shhh, you'll wake the children,' and he'd replied, 'Why the hell shouldn't I, they're always waking me.' A slight exaggeration, but the kids were still asleep when he left for work, and often in bed and not to be disturbed when he returned from work. When they were very young, it was unusual not to have his night's sleep disrupted by their crying.

'I have it on good authority they're growing up,' he'd tell friends in jest. It was like the children came from a one-parent family, he sadly reflected, when he allowed himself to think about it. On the weekends Karen and the boys competed for his attention, and he became an adroit juggler of time, invariably unable to please them all.

He realised he had better remain acquainted with the person he used to be, regardless of whether he enjoyed the company of that person or not. He recalled a piece of wisdom – 'Before we can see properly, we must shed our tears to clear the way', but was unable to recall where this saying came from. Lately, he kept trying to remind himself that to alter something, one had to be in touch with it.

Arriving at Dr Engel's rooms, he knew the door would be unlocked, yet struggled to push open the heavy oak door and let himself in. He sat slouched in the waiting room chair dragged down by the recurring nightmares and thoughts from the past intruding into his sleeping mind. Five minutes later he followed Dr Engel and they sat silently in his consulting room and as usual Andrew was the first to break the silence.

'I've been thinking a lot about the past since we last met, especially how Karen and I sat on the porch of our Edwardian home in Surrey Hills. We'd been married a year or so, and it was a balmy night with a gentle breeze blowing the fragrance of the lavender over us. The passion was still there and we were filling in the gaps of what we knew about each other, which was remarkably sparse, even though we were married.' In a soft, flat voice Andrew described how he responded to Karen's request that he tell her more about his father.

'I recall saying that all I could tell her was that I never really knew my father—never did and now that he's gone, never will. I told her that he felt like a shadow I couldn't grasp.' Andrew hesitated as if unsure whether to reveal any more about his father. 'It probably sounds weird, but I always wondered if he was my real father. I know many kids go through that phase, but it never left me. I still wonder,' Andrew said, his voice now a whisper as if he didn't want anyone else to be privy to these thoughts. 'Karen reassures me that he has to be my father - we look so alike, she tells me. Maybe she's right, but during those chaotic years of the war, people connected in whatever way was needed to survive. People who knew him, including Karen, found him to be a pleasant jolly man. Probably was, but what does that prove,' Andrew queried, not expecting an answer.

Dr Engel's voice pierced the silence that followed.

'You know, Andrew, I don't think you referred to him by name at any time in this session'

'You're probably right. He never felt like a father to me. Did he love me? I don't know, as he never went out of his way to show it. I don't even know whether he liked me. I think it made me determined to be a better father to my own children. I guess that's one more broken promise, isn't it. With both my parents – yeah, I can call him a parent – it was hard to separate the "real" them from the "war-affected" them. Did I need to make allowances for the effects of the war whenever they irritated me?'

There was a brief silence, with Andrew's throat feeling as if it was seizing up, until the barriers seemed to part and a torrent of words began to escape.

'I could talk to my mother. She was intelligent and well read, but even she … how can I put it? There were times that she would hug me as if it was the last hug we would ever have – almost in desperation. At other times with her, I felt she kept me at arm's length. As I said before, with the war, survival was the main thing – probably the only thing. My parents fed me, overfed me, but there was next to no encouragement about joining social groups, or helping with activities such as schoolwork. I felt my mother loved me, but with the war, and the problems with my brother Harry – maybe there wasn't much left over for me. It was only after she died that I discovered a multitude of people who loved her – shopkeepers, neighbours, friends; they all adored her. Maybe I envied that. She was warm and interesting and certainly pretty. Yet for a capable person, she appeared to hold back from life. She and my father loved each other … I could see that and possibly was a touch jealous. So I often excused their behaviour towards me; it was the war, the problems with Harry, my brother, who I need to tell you about, and whatever else, but the fact is I felt I missed out.'

'Have you shared these thoughts with your wife?' Doctor Engel gently asked.

'The first time I told Karen about my parents, she hugged me and said, "My dad likes you a lot. My mum, well maybe, but you never know with her." I remember having trouble with Karen hugging me then as I had tears in my eyes, which I was wiping … I probably hated people seeing me crying. I asked Karen whether she was feeling sorry for me or loving me, and you know what she said? "Both."'

'I have faint memories of burying my face in my mother's chest as she hugged me to her. I still struggle to comprehend that a cultured and supposedly civilised society could aim to eradicate a whole race of humans because of their religion. Yet behaviour like this keeps repeating itself. It's such a simple word, prejudice, isn't it, and somehow it seems an inadequate word to describe such poisonous hatred over the centuries. Kids are not born that way, so obviously it's something they learn. I've tried to rid my body of the pus from those experiences, but I'm not sure that pain can ever be totally drained. I've come to realise I'm prejudiced – we all are, but I do my best to make sure it doesn't hurt others What the Germans did, I believe any other group could also do.' Andrew retreated into a long silence until he said apologetically, 'Look, I'm sorry, I have gone off at a tangent. I know I was meant to tell you about my family, but I don't think many Australians can see that there is a big difference between being called a "white bastard" in contrast to being labelled a "greedy Jew" or a "black cunt". You see, with Jews and blacks, for example, there is a history going back many, many years where their communities were victimised as a result of prejudice. So in contrast to that rhyme about sticks and stones, words can hurt you.'

Andrew became aware that Doctor Engel had said nothing for quite a while and started to feel self-conscious, wondering whether he had been rambling, but Doctor Engel encouraged him to go on and say whatever came to him.

'Let me tell you more about my parents then,' Andrew offered, 'They had three children –myself, a sister Tali, who was just under five years younger than me. That would make it 4 years younger than me, but she preferred telling people she was close to five years younger than me. Because of the anti-Jewish hatred that had taken hold in Poland during the Second World War, our parents were severely restricted in getting adequate care and assessment for Harry. They took him to doctors whenever they felt it was safe, which was not often. At quite a young age, Harry was identified as having congenital heart problems, but they took a back seat to all the other difficulties that he was demonstrating. At one point it was thought that he might be a deaf mute and on another occasion the diagnosis of chronic schizophrenia or autism was made. Because of how severe and extensive Harry's problems were, together with the pressure of staying alive in war-torn Poland as Jews in hiding, I can understand our parents having very little time spare for me and next to no time for each other. Fortunately Harry, myself and our mother Rachel all had blonde hair and blue eyes, which helped mask our identities as we lived with forged Aryan papers amongst the non Jewish community. No one told me I was Jewish, for fear I'd blurt it out, causing us to be killed. My parents said we children ran around with our playmates shouting anti-Jewish slogans with the rest of them. We survived the war and after reaching Australia, Harry was placed in a special school during the day and continued living at home at night. Harry was aged 16 when our family came as refugees to Australia in 1947, and I was eight years of age, whilst my sister Tali was four at that time.'

Andrew felt washed out with the flood of words and emotions. For many years he had believed that he had dealt with and put behind him, all the past traumas. He realised now that the flood of words and memories that poured out in today's session carried very little happiness. Dr Engel put to him and he had to agree, that far from resolving the past traumas, he had merely suppressed them and they lay covered with a scab.

Dr Engel told Andrew that the session would need to be wound up as their time had expired. He suggested however that he felt they were stopping midstream, as he believed there were many thoughts and feelings that Andrew seemed ready to describe if they hadn't run out of time. He offered to free up a time in the following day if Andrew was free to take it, rather than having to suppress so much until they next met for his regular time. Andrew appreciated the thoughtfulness of the offer and agreed to come at 3 p.m. the following day.

Once out of the office, he immediately called Rosemary and asked her to reschedule his patients to free up the time he required for Dr Engel. He had run out of fuel for the day and took to bed soon after arriving home.

CHAPTER SIXTEEN

Monday, 2 April 1990
10.30 a.m.

Strangely, Andrew felt relieved to be talking to Dr Engel. With a smile in his voice, he described how Harry had limited social skills and their parents shared stories of the many times they felt embarrassed because Harry would blurt out things that were often better left unsaid.

He recalled one occasion where friends of his parents came to the house, and Harry enquired in a loud voice why one of the female guests had taken such an ugly, drunken man for a husband. Andrew heard that other people had wondered much the same thing but refrained from saying it. His parents told Andrew that they felt like firemen putting out the flames set up by Harry and then trying to patch up friendships that his comments had damaged.

Andrew went on to describe to Dr Engel how his parents were reluctant to discuss the war years in depth, so it meant that the information he had about those years was patchy. Some of the details came reluctantly from his mother and he did not want to push her further as his mother had nightmares afterwards. Further information was obtained from family friends who were familiar with some of the history, and further gaps were filled in by studying the Holocaust Museum records in Australia and overseas. Andrew was shocked when he initially found out that he, Harry and their parents had been arrested and placed in a holding camp near Warsaw, when Andrew was about two years old and his sister Tali had not been born yet. Andrew researched the camp they had been placed in, and discovered that people held there were sent either to concentration camps and exterminated or if they were young and fit and able to work, they were sent initially to slave labour camps. He discovered that all his family were in fact sent to a slave labour camp and he was puzzled why he and Harry had been allowed to live, given their youth and inability to be productive.

He related to Dr Engel how after a year in the camp, they were helped to escape by Anton, a kind and brave non-Jewish Pole, and provided with false identity papers. He said his parents told him that they lived in Warsaw amongst non-Jews on false Aryan papers, and his parents believed that some of the locals must have suspected they were Jewish, but bravely did not betray them. Andrew said he could not personally recall the details he was describing but learnt about them from a number of sources and gradually developed images of what it must have been like.

His mother told him that he and Harry had been circumcised at birth and after their escape from the camp, they were taken to a Jewish doctor to mask the circumcision, as in Europe at that time, anyone who was circumcised was automatically deemed to be Jewish. Andrew recalled his mother weeping tears that she normally held in, as she told him about a paternal aunt who survived the concentration camp she had been sent to, but was tragically murdered after the war by a local Pole when she attempted to return to her home in a small town close to Warsaw. The man killed her as he was now living in her home, and feared that he would have to give it back to her.

Andrew said he felt that his parents both suffered with a chronic low-grade depression and anxiety, and that he had no doubt that they had both been emotionally damaged from their experiences. He related hesitantly that it was likely some of this had been passed onto their progeny, including himself. He added that he believed he had managed to cope and be productive in spite of any possible damage from those experiences, but was becoming aware that the stress of the recent media allegations and the pending court case, were slicing through the barriers he had previously constructed, making it hard for him to cope. With barely a pause, Andrew's words continued to pour out as he told Dr Engel that he had given thought to what was discussed in the previous session and tended to agree that the allegations saturating the media lately were impinging on fertile ground, giving birth to the disabling feelings he was experiencing of becoming a victim yet again.

Having commenced, the flood of words and feelings continued unrestricted as Andrew described how difficult it was for him to gaze at the images of camp inmates, seeing their shrunken faces, and looks of horror, their large staring, and vacant eyes that wished they could no longer see. He could only imagine that the glue which held together the fabric of those lives had been totally eroded, with the victims no longer able to reach out for support from their religion or their community, and certainly not from their extended family which had been eradicated. He told Dr Engel that he had often fantasised what revenge he might take on the perpetrators if they were identified for certain. He wondered if he would be capable of killing those people who had murdered his family or other families, if there was no doubt that they had done it. Other questions cropped up in his mind as to whether it would make the survivors feel any better or teach those that followed any meaningful lesson. He told Dr Engel that he had been thinking lately about the potential for evil in all people, including himself, depending on what happened in their lives.

Dr Engel kindly asked Andrew if he felt able to continue, obviously aware that Andrew's flushed face and pressured speech were flagging considerable tension within. He answered softly that he would like to go on and began to describe how it felt going to school in Melbourne at the age of eight years, having landed together with other refugees in 1947. He had missed a lot of schooling during the war years, and whilst he had been too young to recall much of those times in Poland he had vivid memories of the bullying he experienced as a migrant child in Australia. He and his family had landed in a foreign land and remained foreigners as far as his schoolmates were concerned.

As he spoke, Andrew relived the experience of being unable to speak English at first, dressing differently to the other children, having parents with an accent and food in his lunch box which was different to that of his schoolmates, and all these differences were further compounded by being Jewish. He said that he had committed the cardinal sin for a child of being different, and this is a condition no child ascribes to. On a daily basis his schoolmates reminded him of how different he was, and he felt he had not yet built up the skills or armour to help him cope. Most of the children bullying him could not have described what a Jew was, and probably had never met one before. However, it didn't prevent the insults flying regularly like missiles, calling him names such as *kike, dago,* and *bloody foreigner* as part of a new language.

> *"To market, to market to buy a fat pig,*
> *home again, home again, jiggedy jig."*

So the chorus went, playing on his differences and his Jewish identity.

> *"Go back where you came from, Jew."*

The early school years were miserable for him and he fantasised how much happier and safer he would feel if he could avoid going to school. Though the thought of not going to school was tempting, he was scared of the consequences – be they getting into trouble from the teachers for not coming or feeling guilty at letting his parents down. His parents were determined their children would get the education they themselves had missed out on. Andrew felt the teachers in those early years did little to protect him and many had an antipathy themselves to "foreigners".

Deep down, he knew that it was important to have an education, and prayed that one day things would improve – which they did. However, the scars from the frequent taunts and beltings by the other children remained to some degree. Even some of the teachers were involved in handing out physical abuse, at times, using a leather strap as punishment, occasionally for the most trivial of offences such as forgetting to bring an eraser or talking in class. Andrew believed he got more than his share of strappings.

In later years, as he matured, he often wondered why being different was a problem for others. He would fantasise that if the bullies were gathered up and transported to live in Japan, for example, then guess who would be different? He was grateful that his father had accepted altering the family name when they arrived in Australia. He said his father often told the story how they had caught a boat in Paris, filled with remnants of European Jewish suffering once the war ended, having waited for permission to come to Australia. His father had a smattering of English and when the boat landed, he allegedly was confronted by a cheerful immigration official, who slapped him on the back and said, 'You'll be right, mate.' So Sobonovski became "Wright". That was his father's story, so who would question it. However, to the kids at school, he was more "Sobonovski" than "Wright".

In Australia, as a child, Andrew said he became acutely aware of what was missing in his life. Unlike the children around him, he didn't have grandparents or uncles or aunts – there was no extended family, as if some of his limbs had been cut off. He missed the warmth of extended family that he could see when visiting other households, where they had the presence of grandparents, uncles and aunts whilst he did not even have any photographs or memories to look back on to help him recall family members. His had all perished in a killing machine fuelled by prejudice.

Even with his parents, he felt there was diminished closeness compared to what he saw in the homes of friends. He didn't doubt that his parents were caring, but they were weighed down by their own issues, having escaped without material possessions, and the pressure of Harry with his multiple problems, and Andrew felt that there was little left for himself at the end of the day. Andrew related that Harry died from congenital heart problems two years after the family had landed, in spite of the improved medical care he was receiving. He said this caused his parents to retreat even further, and they worked long hours in an obsessive drive to protect their family economically and in other ways.

'You know, Dr Engel, I haven't thought about these things for years … felt sure I'd put it all behind me. I think if any good came out of that pain, then maybe it's how it made me more independent at a younger age. I was determined that my own children would experience the time and love that I missed out on, but I've failed, haven't I? My mother – ' He quickly stopped himself, pointing out that he had kept referring to his parents without giving them a name. He couldn't recall addressing his father by his name. The name Saul felt too vibrant and real for someone who appeared as a shadow in his life

He said his mother Rachel had a miscarriage, and then saw a doctor to prevent further pregnancies. As they matured, Andrew felt that he and Tali began to relate on more equal terms.

He described Tali as being vivacious, bright and attractive to the eye. Somehow she drew people to herself and unlike many who did that, she avoided hurting them. As a result, people invariably trusted her, Andrew felt. He reflected that for someone who had so much to offer, Tali had bombed out with an arsehole of a husband, Joe.

It caused Andrew to reflect how frequently, when socialising with couples, it was difficult to like them both. You might be drawn to one, and find you have to tolerate the baggage they carried. He felt uncomfortable with how harsh his thoughts sounded and wondered aloud to Dr Engel whether he was dumping anger that belonged elsewhere onto Joe. Andrew said if he tried to describe Joe, well, he was like a shadow also, without features that stood out, but then their own father had been a shadow as well.

'Try to describe Joe to me,' Dr Engel said.

'Well, if I had to attribute colours to him I'd say they were pastel colours – nothing vibrant. The poor bugger must realise how little he has to offer. Okay, he's finished an accountancy degree and works for a large accounting firm. He earns a reasonable living for Tali and their two children, but that's all. It probably sounds cruel but all I can say he does is sleep, eat and work and be the Mr on their social invitations. He probably couldn't believe his luck in landing a prize like Tali.' Andrew shook his head and sighed. 'Surely Tali didn't marry him in desperation because she was still single and approaching 30. If it wasn't desperation that drove her, did she possibly need his dullness to feel significant herself. A bit like very attractive girls who go out socially with a friend who is … what's the word … plain, I guess, where the plainness of one highlights the attractiveness of the other. I'm sounding more and more bitchy about this, aren't I?' Andrew enquired of Dr Engel.

'We have to finish the session in a few minutes,' Dr Engel said, 'but I would like you to begin explaining to me why someone you see as being insignificant brings out such intense emotions in you.'

'Strange, isn't it – here I am working as a consultant psychiatrist and yet I don't know what these feelings about Joe are all about? Maybe the feelings have very little to do with Joe and he is a convenient canvas to paint on. If it was just his being dull, I would make allowances for that, but it's also that he treats people badly. He hates coloured people and has no generosity of spirit. He wouldn't put himself out to help someone unless he felt they were important and of use to him. Tali and her family live in Singapore where his firm moved Joe a few years ago. One thought I had was that Joe is safe and won't be gallivanting off with other women and maybe that's his appeal.'

As Dr Engel wound up the session, Andrew couldn't believe how washed out and drained, he felt yet again.

CHAPTER SEVENTEEN

DAY 1
Monday, 21 April 1990
6.58 a.m.

And so it came to pass, as in biblical terms, that the 21 April 1990 finally arrived. This was the date set for the coronial inquiry regarding the death of Mrs Coral Bentleigh, who was under the care of Dr Andrew Wright at the time of her death, so the media reported. Unknown to Andrew at the time, it marked a victory outcome for the manipulation set in place by Brett and Deborah, which had led to the barrage of media allegations suggesting that Mrs Bentleigh had died as a result of an illegal and inappropriate form of therapy called deep sleep therapy. The multitude of allegations had eventually weakened any bonds of trust that existed between the patient's family and Andrew Wright, until they joined the chorus calling for the coroner to investigate.

At first Andrew felt a sense of relief that for the first time he could fight back and present his version of events in a setting where he and his accusers were regulated by the same set of rules, but gradually the tension built up to an overwhelming level. He and his family had been left bruised by the experience of waking up each day wondering what the newspapers or television news might carry, and searching the expressions in the faces of friends and acquaintances to try and read how they were being judged. Andrew knew that even though he was the one on trial, if he was found guilty – or rather, found to have contributed to the patient's death – then people would assume that Karen had been covering for him. Likewise, if he was exonerated, then it would clear both he and Karen.

Karen told Andrew how concerned she had been about the effects of this pressure on their two sons, wondering what the stress was doing to them. Andrew felt guilty that he had been so preoccupied with himself that he did not give much thought to what the rest of the family were going through. He agreed with Karen that the boys were at a vulnerable stage of life where they were developing careers and education and forming more mature concepts about relationships with other people. Karen had also shared her concern with him that normally they would have been available to support and direct the boys as they matured, but lately it was like a train careering out of control, where the only thought for each of them was survival, and hardly any available time for anything or anyone else. Andrew knew if he was honest with himself, that he had been more removed from the lives of Karen and the boys than ever before.

As he dressed for court, Andrew reflected on the many changes in recent years where both his parents had died before this tornado had entered their lives, and in a way he was grateful that they did not have to witness these proceedings and feel embarrassed in front of their friends. However, a close friend of Andrew had died recently before the court hearing and Andrew resented that this friend never had an opportunity to see him clear his name. He wondered how Karen's father was taking it all, as he had been in poor health lately and had to retire in 1988 on the grounds of illness, which had also robbed him of a valid reason for escaping from home. He suffered with chronic arthritic pain and Andrew felt that his father in law probably had a chronic low-grade depression as well. Violet, his mother-in-law, remained much the same having long ago lost much of what was needed for a meaningful life.

As he knotted his tie, he recalled the Bar Mitzvahs of his two sons, how Jed's was a grand affair, more like a marriage, and somewhat embarrassing in its size, whilst Bobby's Bar Mitzvah fell in the midst of the media circus in 1989 and was a far more modest celebration. By 1989 they all preferred not to draw attention to themselves and found it hard to celebrate. Karen had reassured him that when she spoke to the boys about the media allegations they expressed having ongoing faith in their father. Andrew could see that both boys were doing well scholastically and had good circles of friends, but it came as no surprise to him when Karen recently told him that even though they still had faith in their father, they regretted how he appeared to have more time for his patients than for his family. Andrew knew he used to spend a lot more time with the boys when they were younger, but in recent years, they, like their mother, shared a queue with all the other issues that preoccupied him. Occasionally they joked without humour how they needed to make an appointment to see Andrew, and he wondered whether they believed their comments could possibly change things.

On occasions when he was more morose, Andrew had wondered how it would be for the boys, if he and Karen separated. He knew their marriage was certainly not going well, but was it really bad enough to bring about separation? He didn't want that, and hoped that Karen felt the same though he wasn't sure. How would the boys cope if their parents broke apart? Had the images of married life soured in the eyes pf their children causing anxiety barriers that made closeness less appealing? Both boys had girlfriends but rarely spoke about them and certainly avoided bringing them home, but he believed that was not unusual for boys anyhow.

He made himself eat what amounted to a minimal breakfast, struggling with a lack of appetite, yet knowing his body needed some fuel if it was to keep functioning for better or for worse, and thought that Karen was also unhappy and yet neither one of them seemed ready to get marriage counselling. Like Andrew, Karen had probably put it on hold. until after the court case. Or had that become an excuse for both of them to hide behind. He wondered if they were staying together because of the boys or whether there was still sufficient left in their own relationship. *Sufficient what?* he wondered. *What keeps people together?* He had not spoken to friends about his marriage and wondered whether Karen had, but then again it was not something that could be decided by a show of hands. There were only two people who could decide. *But let's sort out the court issues firstly,* he told himself.

Andrew drove Karen to the coroner's court. They had both decided that it would be better if the boys didn't attend court, knowing the circus that they might have to endure with cameras flashing and journalists pushing microphones into their faces. The boys did not agree with this decision, but had no say in it, and licked their wounds at school.

8.39 a.m.

The coroner's court appeared as a faint blur in the distance with swarms of bees buzzing around it and swarming in all directions.

'Look at those parasites!' exclaimed Karen as she realised the swarm was made up of a huge number of reporters and photographers. Andrew felt there was nothing to soften the massive brick structure of the courthouse which gave the impression it could double as a prison in appearance. Previously he had named it a monument to truth, but now ruefully wondered if the court was better called 'a prison of truth.'

He carried no resentment toward the patient's family and was puzzled how they had gone from having a warm and trusting relationship with him over the years to the state of mistrust that they now demonstrated. Andrew could accept that certain events in life he might never find the solution to — like, is there a god? How did life originate? Is there life on other planets? but the last two years were man made, had to be, they certainly weren't supernatural and there had to be an explanation within his reach. He was aware that he needed to move beyond his brain and its focus on a multitude of thoughts. There were other abilities to mobilise. He needed to look and observe, to talk and hear what people were saying, and decipher what appeared to be an orchestrated media barrage directed at himself. His eyes moistened and he felt grateful his parents, especially his mother, weren't able to witness the humiliation of the past two years.

Andrew glanced at Karen sitting alongside him, seeing the tight muscles outlining the contours of her face. Her eyes were fixed ahead like guided missiles, continuing to stare at the media swarm, partially hidden now by a mist that had appeared as if rising from steaming dog droppings. He rubbed his eyes with the back of his hand and then fiddled with his collar.

Andrew couldn't avoid thinking about his past court appearances as an expert medical witness, as this had led him to believe a lot of what occurred in court was pure theatre with a range of actors, some of whom were well rehearsed whilst others were flying by the seat of their pants. He believed that in courts truth sometimes took a back seat to a persuasive theatrical performance by lawyers or witnesses, almost a toss of the coin and hard to predict outcomes., as truth did not always win out.

The barrister representing Andrew had advised him to avoid the media scrum by driving around to the back entrance, and hopefully not having a multitude of photos taken. He knew that the average viewer still naively believed that the camera didn't lie, and the media photographers would exploit this by publishing photos where they had caught either he or Karen off guard. He'd seen photos in the media of people he was familiar with, suddenly presented as almost unrecognisable and villainous. If they photographed Karen and himself, next day the public would see photos highlighting a toxic mix of anger, anxiety and distaste in their features. Andrew agreed with his barrister that these photos would encourage the general public to prejudge him rather than weighing up the evidence, and the process of judgement by the public would commence with him looking guilty. Andrew wondered yet again if Karen believed in his innocence or whether knowing about his misdemeanour with Samantha had diminished her trust in him.

8.52 a.m.

Andrew and Karen rushed through the back door, which a kindly court attendant had opened for them. They had successfully avoided the media scrum at the front, though probably not as successful in avoiding being photographed.

Andrew had still not succeeded in clearing his mind totally of the self-recrimination of being a shadow to his children just as his father had been to him. Sure he'd been a good doctor, available at all hours for his patients, but lacking time for his own family. He felt Karen's hand grasping his gently, as if she had read his thoughts and self-doubts. Andrew and Karen made their way gingerly into court, aiming to sit in the third row behind their barrister, Michael James – close, but not too close. As Andrew looked to the side he noted Inspector Brett Maloney, the detective who had interviewed him a number of times since the coronial inquiry was announced. He had found the interviews to be unpleasant due to the abrasive manner in which they were conducted, and his lawyer who sat in felt much the same.

Andrew stared, gripped by anger and by what he considered to be an excessive number of uniformed police sitting alongside Maloney. It felt unbelievable and heavy, as if they were conducting a raid and presenting a show of force., He counted 11 or 12 uniformed police - *why did they need so many?*. It certainly wasn't a guard of honour for himself. Diverting his concern, he created a game whereby he needed to remember what the collective noun was for a group of cops. A "mess of police" came to mind. *How appropriate,* he thought, the thought weighed down by the bitterness it carried. By the time he was seated, he recalled that it was probably a "patrol" of police. But no – he remembered vaguely that it might be called a "mess" of police officers, with the word "patrol" being used for non-officer police. Whatever the correct term was, Andrew could sense hostility emanating from their unwavering stares. He forced himself not to look away, absorbing the missiles Maloney was directing at him, determined not to be cowed.

Like a dog in a rainstorm shrugging off the excess water, Andrew instinctively shook himself, casting aside all the thoughts impinging on his brain, determined to regain focus on the court proceedings, but with limited success.

Looking at people, observing their features and listening to their speech were skills he had developed as part of his work. He could not detect any softness or underlying gentle disposition in the inspector. To Andrew, Maloney showed coarse and brutal features, with cold eyes and a powerful body like a landmine set to explode. He realised that with his continuing assessment he was struggling to shift his focus away from Maloney and found himself mapping the landscape of remnant scars dotting the surface of the inspector's face - a face where any sense of kindness appeared to have evaporated. Andrew felt that Maloney's features showed a lack of cohesion and he experienced a strange urge to rearrange this facial jigsaw, creating a less threatening figure, but he couldn't say exactly what all that meant.

Fortunately coroner O'Hearn entered the courtroom dragging Andrew back to why he was there. Everyone rose in deference and Andrew's barrister, Michael James reminded him that he wouldn't be called to the stand to give evidence for at least the next two days.

DAY 2
Tuesday, 24 April 1990
7.15 a.m.

Karen brought in the morning papers. There on the second page of the Age was an account of the first day court proceedings, and the article bore very little resemblance to what they had both witnessed sitting in court. Andrew and Karen felt distressed by the blatant bias in the report, which omitted to mention anything favourable to Andrew in the day's evidence.

9.21 a.m.

Andrew's barrister drew the attention of the coroner to the article, and indicated that he intended to put the journalist involved on the stand, unless future reporting was more balanced. Out of the corner of his eye, Andrew noted the journalist squirming and the next day's reporting was far more balanced, now that the journalist had been put on notice and felt accountable.

These first two days felt very strange to Karen and Andrew. To Andrew in particular, the feeling was surreal, hearing people talk about him and describing him as if he wasn't there. He felt apprehensive about the process of the coronial court, fearing its ability to besmirch his reputation. He knew that because it was a fact finding process and he wasn't being charged with anything, it was unlikely that the court would rule that he was totally innocent and at best they might rule that he had not contributed to the patient's death. Rather, the court would aim to determine what contributing factors were involved in his patient's demise. In a coroner's court the process is inquisitorial rather than prosecution. However, if the court found he contributed to his patient's death, then he could subsequently face civil proceedings in another court. His barrister had warned him that because hearsay evidence was admissible, the danger with the poor reporting standards of some media was that mud might stick afterwards. It would be up to the court to weigh up the significance of rumours and innuendos, but the court could not prevent people being influenced by shoddy reporting of those rumours.

The majority of the first two days involved evidence from expert medical witnesses, none of whom appeared critical of his management of his patient, nor did any of them see evidence of illegal forms of treatment. Cross examinations appeared low key and straightforward, with the counsel assisting the coroner appearing professional. His approach seemed to be one of gathering accurate information about the treatment the deceased patient received, so that eventually the coroner could pass judgement on what contributed to the death of Mrs Bentleigh.

One by one the medical expert evidence stated that the treatment appeared appropriate, with no evidence of deep sleep treatment being administered. They concurred that there had been no indication for the death to be reported to the coroner. None of them was aware of deep sleep treatment being used in Victoria, though it had been used in NSW and possibly Queensland.

Andrew was impressed by his barrister's ability to get a grasp of the main issues and he believed this was reflected in the cross-examination of witnesses, where James' approach was clear and effective. A range of witnesses were called, some of them to give expert medical evidence explaining the nature of deep sleep therapy, whilst others commented on whether Andrew's treatment matched that of a competent specialist psychiatrist. They all described his treatment as being quite different to deep sleep therapy. The one exception was a female nurse, referred to as nurse G for privacy reasons., who had alleged that she worked at the hospital where the patient died and had been on duty at the time of death of the patient.

Andrew's barrister, Mr James cross-examined nurse G.

'So Ms G, am I correct in saying you're telling the court you saw Dr Wright commence Mrs Bentleigh on deep sleep therapy?'

'That's correct. I saw him start that treatment and I was shocked.'

'Well Ms G, did you convey your concerns to Dr Wright or any other staff at the hospital?'

'I attempted to, but no one wanted to hear about it.'

'Did you talk to anyone else about your concerns?'

'Yes, the day she died I went to her home and spoke to her family and told them how worried I'd been about the treatment their relative received.'

'Would it surprise you Ms G to learn that the family of Mrs Bentleigh brought her daughter to see Dr Wright as a patient four months after her mother's death? That would have been four months after you allege you went and told the family how upset you were to see Dr Wright giving Mrs Bentleigh deep sleep therapy.'

Nurse G appeared flustered but remained silent.

'Can I assume you again attempted to tell other staff at the hospital about your concerns regarding the treatment Dr Wright gave Mrs Bentleigh?'

Further silence ensued.

'Well nurse G, can you help the court understand how other staff at the hospital can't recall you working there?'

'They're not telling the truth or they've forgotten,' she stuttered.

'Can I put it to you, nurse G, that you've made up the history you've given us, and that it's a figment of your imagination.'

Nurse G looked down, avoiding the gaze of the barrister and appeared to be sobbing.

Coroner O'Hearn's voice drew everyone's attention as he informed the court there would be an hour break before they reconvened.

Andrew could not recall having ever seen nurse G before, and was staggered to hear her say that he had used deep sleep therapy illegally. He bristled at hearing her evidence, as this was a form of treatment he would never have considered using for anyone, as he felt that it had no place in modern psychiatric care. He could not imagine what motivated her to confabulate such a story. When the court resumed after the break, Counsel announced that the witness nurse G who had been in the box before, would not be able to continue as she had developed dementia. Andrew's barrister Michael James later explained that this was the only way she could extricate itself from the hole that she had dug. He then shocked Andrew further by revealing that the address she had given was that of a communal group called The Union. Though troubled by this revelation, he was still unclear as to what it meant, but felt uneasy as he was aware of the underhand methods that the sect employed at times. But why target him, he asked himself, without any clear answer.

10.40 a.m.

Inspector Maloney was finally called to give evidence. He strode to the witness box where he stood seemingly totally at ease. Giving evidence was second nature to him these days, yet in spite of all his experience he was aware of feeling uptight and his stomach was knotted and uncomfortable.

It troubled Andrew and Karen to hear him speak about a patient diary containing details that contradicted Andrew's file and recollection of events.

'So Inspector, tell the court about Mrs Bentleigh's diary and what was written there. Just before that, how did you come by the diary?'

Maloney's eye's pierced the air between himself and the barrister, without breaking the eye contact the whole time he spoke.

'I obtained the diary from the deceased's family.'

'Tell the court what information you gleaned from the diary,' Michael James enquired.

'It clearly stated that the deceased was given deep sleep treatment and that it commenced the day she died,' the inspector's firm voice answered without hesitation.

'Inspector Maloney, are you aware that it hasn't been tabled as an exhibit for this court?' Michael James quietly asked, with the trace of a smile.

'Yes, I am aware. It has somehow been mislaid but I and Sergeant Peters can both vouch for its contents, as can the family members of the deceased.'

'Inspector Maloney, you've been in the police force for many years, and yet you are treating this court with contempt,' Michael James said in voice that had become louder with a tinge of anger. Andrew was uncertain whether the barrister was really angry or adopting that role.

'The truth is that for all we know that diary never existed and you never laid eyes on it. It appears you are prepared to do or say whatever you feel is necessary to win this case. I have no more questions to ask you, nor apparently does the counsel assisting the coroner.'

Andrew looked at the inspector's face suffused with rage as he strode out of the court, without looking at anyone else. It had become apparent that the police had very possibly never viewed the patient's diary and certainly did not have it in their possession. Mrs Bentleigh's family thought they had a vague memory of her mentioning such a diary but had never seen it for themselves.

Inspector Maloney had no other evidence of note and bristled at the vigorous cross-examination by Andrew's barrister. He was livid at the implication that he had tendered evidence based on a diary without having any proof to demonstrate to the court it had ever existed.

DAY 3
Wednesday, 25 April 1990

That morning, before the court rose, Inspector Maloney requested the opportunity to enter the stand again as he felt the previous day's proceedings had reflected on his integrity, and he wanted the opportunity to clear his reputation. He had entered the courtroom with only one other policeman unlike the numbers with him on the first two days. His eyes were bloodshot and appeared to be the eyes of someone who had slept poorly the night before. In fact, he had hardly slept and had been drinking heavily most of the night. His face sphinctered with rage and to Andrew, Maloney appeared consumed with fury, which he could no longer disguise.

Andrew guessed that Maloney's anger was a consequence of being made to look dishonest and foolish, or at best, incompetent. He was aware that Maloney had created considerable damage to his career, and the second appearance proved of no advantage to himself or the court, as he just repeated allegations based on a diary that most likely he'd never seen and couldn't prove existed. It amazed Andrew that for someone so experienced in court work, Maloney would subject himself to further humiliation by asking to appear again, as there was apparently nothing more that he could add to clear himself.

Andrew realised that he was probably enjoying the inspector's discomfort to some degree, but believed there would be a price to pay subsequently and that the payback, if it occurred, would likely be directed at him and not the barrister.

DAY 4
Thursday, 26 April 1990

After several days of evidence, the court proceedings appeared to be a car wreck as far as the police were concerned, as no relevant facts emerged that could demonstrate Andrew was at fault.

Andrew felt as if he was living in a vacuum during those early days of court proceedings, as colleagues and friends appeared to be keeping their distance, with only two of his peer group ringing to wish him good luck. He wondered if many of his peer group were scared of being caught up somehow in the allegations that were being levelled at Andrew. Even Karen and he avoided saying much to each other, as if with bated breath they were waiting for the conclusion of court proceedings.

Finally it was Andrew's turn to be called to the witness box and the hostility he had sensed at the beginning of the hearing became even more palpable from the police who had gathered once more and sat together in the Coroners court. He looked in their direction and felt the cold stares pinning him down. As he rose to walk to the stand, he felt Karen squeezing his hand, communicating more than she had for a long time. He could not recall walking to the witness box, but stood there willing his mind to shut out everything except the questions being addressed to him.

Counsel assisting the coroner was a member of the police force as can be the case in coronial hearings, and as Andrew approached the witness box, there were several minutes of asphyxiating silence.

In fact, it was probably a matter of seconds, but it felt as if time had been suspended. The police sergeant leading the evidence gazed at Andrew, then looked at his papers and then back at Andrew again. Andrew knew this was a tactic to erode any defences he may have prepared, but he still couldn't avoid the discomfort it created. The scene felt surreal, and he fought to suppress the suffocating panic that threatened to emerge. From day one, he had been relieved to see that counsel assisting the coroner presented as a youthful looking man with a pleasant, intelligent face and Andrew imagined that he was studying law part-time whilst in the police force. He was probably older than he appeared, and given the hostility emanating from the police in the court, Andrew couldn't avoid being wary, though he had nothing to hide He believed the pleasant manner of counsel was no guarantee he couldn't turn but found the questioning continued to be conducted in a civil and benign manner and he answered as openly as he could over the one-hour period of questioning.

He wanted to appear calm, but his body was betraying that

impression. From time to time Andrew wiped the moisture from his brow with a tissue Karen had given him, and cursed himself for neglecting to stock his pockets with extra tissues. He wanted to appear calm, but his body was betraying that impression. The surreal feeling persisted however, and he felt as if he was on automatic pilot, floating above the sea of hostility that he continued to sense from police in the courtroom.

'So Dr Wright, have you ever used deep sleep therapy and did you use it with Ms Bentleigh?'

Taking a deep breath Andrew spoke slowly and firmly in telling the court he had never used deep sleep therapy as a form of treatment, as he viewed it to be potentially dangerous by suppressing a patient's breathing.

'Dr Wright, you heard the testimony of nurse G, what is your response to it?'

'I have difficulty making sense of it,' Andrew's voice remaining firm as he maintained eye contact with counsel and attempting to avoid looking at the police who'd formed a scrum three rows back.

'Firstly, I have no memory of ever having seen her at the hospital or elsewhere. The date she gave as having gone to visit the family of Ms Bentleigh after she died, allegedly to warn them of the "dangerous" treatment she said I was giving Ms Bentleigh, is very surprising, as the family brought Ms Bentleigh's daughter to me as a patient well after that time. I had to ask myself whether they would do that if she had spoken so badly of me. Finally I noted that the address given by Ms G suggested she was a member of a sect called The Union.' Andrew paused and added, 'I guess they are the main points I wanted to tell the court.'

'That's very orderly and concise, Dr Wright.'

Andrew looked at the counsel to see if he was being sarcastic and decided he wasn't, and had meant what he said.

'Now Dr Wright, why did you choose not to report Ms Bentleigh's death to the coroner?' counsel asked politely.

'I'd never filled in a death certificate before or since and when I asked staff and other doctors they told me the hospital where the death occurred did not qualify for mandatory reporting, as long as the doctor could see a reasonable cause for sudden death of the patient unrelated to the treatment,'

'The police speak of a diary which they've never apparently seen, but Ms Bentleigh's family believe it existed in some capacity. Have you ever been aware of its existence or seen it?' counsel enquired calmly.

'I haven't,' Andrew answered, adding a barb by saying, 'In hindsight, I am surprised, as in my interview with the police, they quoted supposed passages from that diary and used those passages to question my credibility, yet they apparently had never laid eyes on the diary – if it existed.'

At the end of the hour Andrew felt exhausted but pleased that he finally had an opportunity to face his accusers with what he believed to be the truth of the story. As he returned to his seat Karen squeezed his hand again and whispered, 'You did fine.'

DAY 5
Friday, 27 April, 1990

Further evidence was taken from the remaining medical specialists and two of the patient's family members read statements to the court expressing their distress at learning that their relative had been administered deep sleep therapy. When asked how they came by this information, it became apparent they had been approached by members of The Union. Leaving court at the end of the day, the sequence presented much the same circus as when Andrew and Karen arrived. They were ushered out the back, but as soon as they were detected, the media pack charged after them, irritated by the attempted avoidance, which they viewed as a betrayal of their reader's "right to know". Flashes exploded and microphones were thrust, accompanied by inane questions, but not for long, as Andrew drove off with Karen beside him, escaping their persecutors.

Friday, 4 May 1990

A week later it was all repeated when Andrew and Karen apprehensively returned to court to hear the coroner read out his findings, but they were weighed down by the knowledge that because a coroner is not required to find anyone guilty of an offence, they are therefore unlikely to speak of their innocence. Their role was to describe what they believed contributed to the death of the patient. If the coroner found that a doctor or treatment contributed to the untimely death of a patient, then frequently civil action could be taken afterwards by others.

As the coroner read his findings, Andrew and Karen looked at each other, their vision somewhat blurred by tears. Their reactions were ones of amazement tinged with relief. What they heard went far beyond what they had been led to believe was the best one could hope for. Unbelievably, the coroner went out of his way to state that Andrew's treatment had been exemplary at all times. The coroner emphasised that Andrew was not guilty of any negligence in his management of the patient. Andrew's barrister explained that the coroner had gone further than he needed to go and seemed determined to make it abundantly clear that Andrew had in no way contributed to the death of his patient.

Throughout the week of the court proceedings, Andrew and Karen had at times silently supported each other, sending signals of encouragement by holding hands or giving each other a brief touch of support. Now that it was all over, they felt slightly confused and uncertain what to do with themselves. It did not feel as if it was all over yet. *Was it residual stress or was it unfinished business?* Andrew wondered.

After embracing each other and thanking their barrister, they realised they needed to call the children as soon as possible. By now a neighbour would have popped in to keep an eye on them at home. They decided to go to a nearby phone booth where they could talk privately with the children, and having been cleared so extensively of any wrongdoing, they naively exited through the front door of the court believing the media would no longer see them as newsworthy, and were almost bowled over by the media pack.

They had no wish to speak to the media or give any interviews, but to the media it appeared to be an act of hostility. They were verbally abused and jostled by some journalists, though they doubted these individuals warranted the respect of being called professionals. The sour odour of hostility that Andrew had sensed at times in the court, now pervaded the air outside, polluting it. Eventually they pushed their way to the parking lot and started to drive off, only to be stunned by the bizarre spectacle of a photographer draped over the bonnet of their vehicle, much like a Jaguar emblem on a motor vehicle, as he snapped away at their faces. To Andrew it symbolised the madness of the past two years, and he angrily revved his motor dislodging their unwelcome guest.

At home there was a sense of relief that they shared with their children who continued to hang on to some resentment, still feeling they should have been permitted to attend court. They had all taken a battering and Andrew realised the heaviness that weighed them down was not going to dissipate in a hurry. Month after month they had lived with tension that stalked them in their waking moments and even in their sleep at times. There were few daily acts or thoughts that weren't hijacked by anxiety.

CHAPTER EIGHTEEN

Monday, 6 August 1990

It had now been three months since the coroner handed down his findings, stating that Dr Wright's management of Mrs Coral Bentleigh had been exemplary. Though these findings totally exonerated Andrew, the initial sense of relief that he experienced, failed to persist.

The trauma of the past two years appeared to have left its mark, as he continued to think about the events that had led up to the inquest. Giving evidence in court, and being totally cleared was meant to be the breakthrough in that nightmare, but somehow the pain and the intrusive thoughts continued unabated. Each day his troubled mind felt like a movie set, where a scene was reshot over and over again.

On some days, he would find himself thinking about the initial call from the Age journalist, shattering the peace that he and Karen were experiencing as they strolled in the streets of Brunswick and Fitzroy. At other times, like today, as he sat across the desk from his patient, he would find his concentration disrupted as he tried to make sense of what had turned the deceased patient's family against him. The patient had died from natural causes, and after her death, he continued to have a good relationship with them, and even had another family member referred to him for treatment. Then suddenly his life was turned upside down as the biased media saturation took over – but why?

He had expected calm after the court case was finalised clearing him, but instead of calm he was ravaged by headaches, painful thoughts that kept intruding, creating sleep difficulties, nightmares and lack of drive. It was a baggage he carried with him wherever he was, able to surface anywhere without warning, and like a negative roll of the dice, its unpredictability made it all the more devastating. He realised he needed to be honest with himself and face the fact that he, the psychiatrist, needed professional help.

He reflected that history was often an unfeeling creature devoid of emotion and merely documenting a series of events, and it was only when one looked back, that it was possible to attribute feelings to it. He wondered how accurate this was, as it felt to him that there had been past times when he was almost drowning in a sea of emotion. Possibly it was the manner in which history had been taught to him at school as a series of events and dates, stripping the emotion away. He realised that he couldn't afford to let his mind wander like this, otherwise he would be letting his patients down, as it was their therapeutic time and not his own that he had to focus on. However, the session was almost over and he vowed to make it up to this patient in the future, adding this to many other recent vows.

As he was about to show his patient out of the room at the conclusion of the session, his secretary buzzed him on the intercom, letting him know that the next patient had cancelled because their car had broken down. This gave free rein to Andrew's cascading thoughts, which penetrated the room where he sat alone at his desk. He thought back to the many, many months of media allegations and feelings of persecution that he and his family experienced. He recalled the loyalty of his patients who kept coming and brought with them clippings from the local media, carrying the same sensational allegations as the central newspapers.

Rapidly his thoughts shifted to his increasing suspicions that somehow the attack on him was connected with the activities of The Union, a sect that he had come to despise. He closed his eyes, reviewing the scene of a nurse that he could not recall ever having seen before, giving false evidence that she had seen him administer deep sleep therapy to his patient. Bitterly he remembered that on cross-examination, it was revealed that this nurse belonged to The Union and gradually her evidence fell apart and was clearly revealed as having been fabricated. As she sank further into the hole that she had dug for herself, the lawyer leading evidence for the coroner had requested a break in proceedings, and soon after, when the court resumed, announced that the nurse would not be able to continue giving evidence as she had developed dementia.

He recalled the image of some of Mrs Bentleigh's family members describing how they had been visited on many occasions by strangers who explained that they belonged to The Union and were out to expose abuses in psychiatric practice until gradually they were able to win the trust of family members and get them to believe that their relative had been given an illegal treatment which eventually killed her. A lie told often enough can eventually take on the appearance of truth, undermining the prior relationship of trust they had with Andrew, to the point where the family of the deceased led the chorus of voices demanding a coronial inquiry.

Andrew believed that The Union had played a major role in organising the mass of allegations against him but he could not understand why they had felt the need to do this. He also thought about his suspicions regarding Inspector Maloney, feeling that the inspector's angry attitude towards him and his false testimony in court, where he spoke of a diary he had never seen and couldn't produce, suggested that for some reason he was attempting to set Andrew up. He had no idea why this policeman would be against him, nor could he fathom whether possibly the inspector and The Union were somehow connected.

Andrew glanced at his clock and saw that there were twenty minutes before the next patient was due to be seen. Following the court hearing, Andrew had reduced the pressure of work by creating longer time breaks between patient appointments. He shook himself yet again, attempting to put negative thoughts and feelings aside. Stewing in his angry and bitter memories, he realised that the therapeutic hour intended for the absent patient was proving less than therapeutic for himself. Vaguely and briefly he fantasised that The Union and the inspector should pay for the damage they had inflicted, but it felt like tilting at windmills.

Knowing he still had fifteen minutes free, he lapsed into letting his mind ruminate further about the recent events. He gave thanks to a god he had never acknowledged, that his practice of keeping patient records indefinitely had saved him. The police had checked his records for authenticity which they then confirmed, as otherwise it would have been his word against his accusers without any written or documented evidence to support him. They even had handwriting experts confirm that the writing in the file was years old, and not merely constructed after the police got involved. He realised that the blank canvas had started taking shape, and was beginning to clarify the pain he and his family had gone through recently. He was starting to see that when something is contrived and orchestrated as he believed his case had been, then there is no way that it can make sense looking in from the outside, until further facts and knowledge are available.

Again Andrew shook himself, as if casting aside these unwanted thoughts. He needed to prepare for the next patient. He was tired of how repetitive his thoughts had become and knew that Karen no longer wanted to have him describe to her in minute details what he was thinking. About a week ago she had snapped at him to stop recounting the same things over and over again.

'I care, I really do, but I'm tired of hearing these thoughts over and over. Do something about it!' she said wearily. 'If you wrote a book and told your readers about your thoughts over and over, they'd stop reading.'

Whilst Andrew was aware that his mind was overloaded, like a computer about to crash, it seemed beyond others around him to fully understand the pressure he was under. He was aware that the powerful surge of thoughts and emotions were more than he could handle on his own. He no longer had the deep belly laugh and his humour was flat and sparse, and the best he could do was a wry smile. He realised he was quick to anger now, and even with old friends and acquaintances he was getting into verbal arguments. Everything seemed an effort and he lacked energy, drive and optimism. If a patient presented to him with these features then he'd be inclined to suspect they suffered from some degree of depression.

About a week ago he bumped into someone he'd known for a long time but never respected very much. He felt this man was pompous, opinionated and not particularly bright. They started arguing about some political issues, which he couldn't recall now, and he was glad that he had stopped himself from exploding, mindful of the old axiom that you never argue with an idiot because they drag you down to their level and win from experience. *Nothing like putting someone down silently,* he reflected.

Just prior to meeting with his next patient, he thought back to the bitterness and anger he continued to experience over a very close childhood friend dying from cancer before she could hear that Andrew had been exonerated. Their friendship went back to very early years of childhood and he knew that she had been distressed over the allegations that Andrew and the family had been subjected to. He couldn't help but feel that those responsible for his nightmare had avoided being held accountable for the pain they had inflicted on his family and himself.

He went to the door to greet his next patient.

CHAPTER NINETEEN

Monday, 13 August 1990
6.56 a.m.

More than three months after the completion of the coronial court hearing, Andrew decided to resume seeing Dr Engel on a regular basis. He was annoyed with himself for cutting the sessions prematurely, thinking he should have known better by now. Yet at the time when court was approaching he had felt there was no room in his life for anything other than a frantic need to defend himself. He could no longer deny his underlying fragility, which left him vulnerable even to the pressures of everyday living.

At times he experienced the explosive impact of a landmine within him detonating, stoked by the memories that continued unpredictably to invade and metastasise to all parts of his body and brain. He had learnt the theory years ago of how emotions could affect the body and disturb its functioning, but to have his own body disrupted so profoundly was something he felt unprepared for.

Now the court case was finalised, but the reward of calm had failed to eventuate and he knew that depression was now going hand in hand with his anxiety. If he was honest with himself, he had to acknowledge there was a degree of discomfort in seeking help from another psychiatrist, probably because he imagined people querying why he could not sort himself out. At first he had asked himself the same question, though he knew that the ability to admit there was a problem and seek outside help for it, could be viewed as a sign of strength, rather than weakness. Certainly this was what he told his patients, so why shouldn't it apply to him?

As he lay in bed, he chastised himself for allowing so many thoughts and feelings to swamp him. It wasn't only Karen who was sick of hearing about them, as he'd had a gutful also. As if attempting to soften the image of his difficulty in functioning, a positive thought somehow snuck in, as he reflected on how occasionally he would feel his energy levels and mood improving even without medication, though tinged with some sadness. It gave him a taste of how he could feel if his depression diminished.

He had woken at 6 a.m. this morning and Karen was asleep at the time. Now close to an hour later she continued to sleep uninterrupted, but Andrew realised he had better start getting himself ready for work, which required a lot more effort these days. A touch of his quirky sense of humour made him wonder if snails got depressed, and if so, how much slower could they go?

Dr Engel had slotted him in for a 9 a.m. appointment on a weekly basis commencing next week, and he suspected that this kindly psychiatrist had created an extra time outside his usual timetable, to enable Andrew to be seen promptly. As Andrew blinked, focusing on the shaving mirror, he was confronted by the image of Dorian Gray, with his sagging face and bloodshot eyes revealing the ravage inflicted by the trauma of the last two years.

8 a.m.

Andrew's first appointment at his rooms was with Mai, a Vietnamese refugee in her early twenties, who had commenced seeing him in late 1988, a few months after the devastating death of her sister, and remained loyal and trusting of him in spite of the allegations in the media.

Like many other young Vietnamese, it was difficult for the average Australian to tell her age and she could have readily passed as a teenager. Her pretty, delicate features cloaked a lot of inner pain and tears. Tight scars constricted her thoughts and emotions like so many rubber bands that could easily snap.

She had lost family members killed by the Vietcong and after South and North Vietnam merged, her family, like others who had supported the South, suffered severe discrimination. Unable to find jobs, they lived in poverty and several uncles were sent to re-education camps. Eventually in desperation, Mai together with her parents and older sister, fled by boat in late 1983, to an uncertain future. They were not aware at the time they escaped as to how many refugees were dying at sea or being raped and killed by pirates, but in desperation they would have still undertaken the risk of fleeing. They left their home country crammed in a rickety fishing boat with many other refugees, and were fortunate to avoid drowning or pirate attacks, finally reaching shore, and then spending time in refugee camps in Malaysia and Indonesia.

Andrew was aware that such a summary of the history Mai had given him was relatively sterile and stripped of much of the anxiety, fear and desperation experienced at the time. Gradually Mai had come to trust him sufficiently to slowly allow her emotions to surface in their therapeutic sessions.

Having survived the perils of escaping, Mai and her family eventually were accepted to come to Australia, arriving in late 1985, only to be devastated yet again, this time by the death of her older sister Hahn.

Hahn died in distressing circumstances in Melbourne in early 1988. Mai tearfully related to Andrew how her sister had been studying English and Commerce part-time at RMIT. Mai's body shook with grief as she described how her sister's naked body had been found in the sordid surroundings of the brothel where she worked and how the police concluded, in what her family considered to be an unseemly haste, that Hahn had committed suicide, driven to it by the shame of working as a prostitute. Whilst Mai and her family were still recoiling in horror, the investigators closed the books on the case, saying it required no further investigation. The trauma of this horrendous news shredded the family's daily life, and they rejected the finding of suicide, continuing to believe that Hahn had been murdered, and feeling distressed by what they perceived to be an obscene haste in writing her death off as suicide.

Initially Andrew considered the possibility that the family might have found it easier to accept the notion of murder rather than suicide, but eventually he came to have doubts himself, when he learned more and more details. Mai's parents had come from Buddhist backgrounds, but had left religion behind long ago, much as they had divorced themselves of many aspects of their earlier life.

Session by session Andrew encouraged Mai to allow her memories to surface and surface they did. Her distress filled the room and on many occasions he could feel moisture welling up in his own eyes. He didn't hide his reactions, as he felt she needed a real person to relate to.

Mai had been in Australia for over three years when she first came to Andrew for psychiatric care in 1988, but it was over six years since she and her family fled Vietnam. The whole region of Indo-China had been one of turmoil, suffering and persecution for millions of people exposed to over thirty years of war. The communist government of North Vietnam took control of the country in 1975 and those who had supported the South Vietnamese army suffered retribution. In nearby Cambodia the Khmer Rouge took control, killing millions of their population. There were repeated border clashes between Vietnam and Cambodia and Vietnam invaded Cambodia in 1978, ousting the Khmer Rouge. In 1979 China responded by invading Vietnam, and as a consequence, people of Chinese ethnicity were persecuted and left Vietnam in large numbers. As Mai's family were supporters of South Vietnam and in addition her mother came from a Chinese ethnic background, there was little future staying in Vietnam, and in fact they faced considerable persecution and danger.

At the time Mai commenced therapy with Andrew, it was a few months after learning of the devastating death of her sister. Both of her parents were alive and worked as cleaners at a Melbourne city hotel, leaving behind the professional careers they practised in Vietnam, where Mai's father had worked as an accountant and her mother as a dentist. There was no opportunity to resume study in Australia, for feeding their family came first for her parents, as it did for many other refugee families. Mai's parents, even more than she, were weighed down with the guilt of having survived whilst so many members of the extended family had perished in the war between North and South. The death of their elder daughter and the subsequent disclosure of her prostitution created bitterness that would never cease. Trust became a distant memory and love a luxury they could no longer afford.

Mai had tearfully confided to Andrew that while she and her parents set about rebuilding their lives after arriving in Australia in 1985, her sister Hahn had gone off the rails. With downcast eyes, she also told Andrew how Hahn had turned to drugs and dropped out of her studies. She wept as she described how the pollution of Hahn's life in the past had continued to imprison her as she gravitated downwards, moving out of home and severing contact with her family and friends. The parents were ignorant about the work she did to support herself and only later received the news of her prostitution, wishing they had remained ignorant. They drowned in the tsunami of their grief and shame, added to the trauma of not having heard from their elder daughter for nearly two years.

Mai had persisted in trying to make contact with Hahn and finally, having located her sister in 1987, about a year before her death, she kept in touch with her on a regular basis, promising not to disclose the destructive path her sister had fallen into. Mai prayed that Hahn could eventually emerge from the darkness and begin a normal life once again, though she had lost any trust in the power of prayer long ago. She knew that it was likely Hahn was trapped by her dependence on drugs, which would be difficult for her to break away from. Mai felt impotent to help her sister until eventually it became too late. The sordid death of Hahn, whose body was found in the brothel where she worked, having been sexually used yet again and then cast aside, devastated the whole family, especially Mai.

She did not accept the police version that her sister had killed herself and suspected that she may have been murdered. Mai told Andrew that she herself had no boyfriends and very few close friends, though she had been doing casual work in a coffee lounge, as well as studying nursing part-time, but remained aloof from her co-workers and students. Like her parents, Mai showed diminished trust, though for her, it was especially experienced when interacting with men.

Andrew realised that the therapeutic relationship that Mai had developed with him was vital in helping her learn to have greater trust towards men. However, outside the therapeutic relationship, the possibility of sexuality with the men she met further complicated the picture for her, making trust almost impossible as part of her interaction with them.

Andrew continued to see Mai once a fortnight for therapy and charged her only the rebate fee, as there was no other way that she could afford to come on a regular basis. In the sessions, she hinted that both she and her sister had been molested in some way whilst in the refugee camps. She said she wasn't ready to talk about this openly, but her nightmares provided a window into what she might have experienced.

Mai described many nights where she woke in terror and sweat, sometimes screaming at the shadowy figures that she felt prodding her. All Andrew could do was give her support at this stage of therapy, and allow her the freedom to share her fears with him. After five months of treatment, Mai's conscious mind started to relate what her subconscious could no longer keep under wraps. She spoke of her initial relief at having reached Malaysia and escaping the clutches of marauding pirates, as capture by them would have meant rape and death. However, in the refugee camp, malice and institutionalised cruelty took over. On a daily basis, they lived with meagre, mouldy rations, a lack of washing facilities, and minimal privacy. Soon her skin broke out in sores and she lost many pounds in weight. However, the sores and rags she wore did not safeguard her from the day that guards came into the room that she shared, telling the twelve other women to get out and pinning Mai to the ground. She disclosed that they had held her down and used every orifice that her body possessed, that she lost count of the abusers and lost consciousness. It thankfully had only happened the one time, as soon after the camp was inspected by UNESCO personnel and Australian consular officials. The wounds inflicted by the attack repaired in time to leave no visible scars, but she could no longer contemplate a physical relationship with any man after that, she confided to Andrew. It was only after the family reached Melbourne that Hahn told Mai that she had been also raped in the Malaysian camp on two occasions, but had been too ashamed to disclose it to her family.

At the brothel where Hahn had worked, a few of the other women several months ago whispered to Mai the name of the man who had been with her sister at the time of her death. They said that he came regularly to the brothel, but they didn't know his real name until they recognised him on the television news one night and heard his name mentioned. This occurred less than a year ago, but Mai said she had felt impotent to do anything with the information, or even talk about it. The news story on television that some of the brothel women had seen, reported that the man conducting an unrelated homicide investigation, was a police inspector by the name of Brett Maloney, and they recognised him to be the man who was with Hahn when she died. Almost in the same breath, the women begged Mai not to divulge the source of her information. They said that they didn't think he had killed her sister deliberately, but they felt that he had supplied her with drugs that contributed to her death, and were angered that he made no attempt at getting medical help for her before she died. They described him treating Hahn like garbage.

Mai told Andrew that she wanted revenge for what this man had done, but felt powerless to do anything about it. She knew she couldn't hit back at the men who had harmed her and her sister in the past, but this man – he was still there – and she wanted him to experience pain for what he had done to Hahn.

Though coming from a Buddhist background, Mai and her family were no longer practising Buddhists, their beliefs diluted by the traumas in their life. Doubts had eroded their core beliefs such as rebirth and reincarnation, and they were no longer sustained by their religion. As Andrew continued to see Mai in therapy, he wasn't sure at what point the thought came into his mind, but intrude it did, in the midst of an avalanche of ideas.

10.22 p.m.

Andrew sat in his study at home, long after Karen had gone to bed. He had recognised the name Mai had given him – it was the same name and the same man who he felt had damaged his own life not so long ago, who had then lied in court and appeared to be setting Andrew up. Andrew's thoughts raced in all directions, as he fantasised how he could use the information that had suddenly come his way. He worried that if he gave in to his fantasy, he could possibly be harming his patient, and his own family as well as himself. He had given into fantasy in the past with corrosive effect, such as his affair with a patient.

On occasions he had fantasised whilst watching softcore porn, and it left him feeling soiled and embarrassed, but with no residual damage that he was aware of. However, this fantasy of revenge was different, and he was aware that fantasy can seamlessly go on to reality at times. This fantasy that had come to him regarding extracting revenge, it went against every rule that had governed his life in the past – medically and personally. But what if they could get a sample of this man's sperm from one of the prostitutes he visited at the brothel? Andrew didn't know for sure, but imagined and hoped that when Hahn's ravished and lifeless body was found, police procedure would have been to take forensic samples from her body. Surely the coroner's court would have held on to those samples, but again he didn't know for sure. Was it stretching things too far to hope that a sperm sample from her sister's dead body was still available? Without that sample, it was just the word of a few prostitutes against that of a policeman, assuming that her co-workers had the nerve to give evidence, and it didn't take a rocket scientist to determine whose word would be believed.

Knowing the difficulty of involving any of the prostitutes at the brothel, he finally plunged into the decision of enlisting Mai's help. Enlisting her help – it sounded so pure and simple, but it was anything but that, and could he justify it morally? Was it crazy? Would Karen feel he was going mad? He was about to commence seeing Dr Engel again on a regular basis, but felt too embarrassed to consider divulging his scheme just yet – hell, he wasn't clear about it himself at this stage.

He had managed to stop bombarding Karen with all his thoughts and feelings, even though his stuttering mind could not hold them back from himself. Unlike Karen, he hadn't been able to turn his back on himself, or to admonish himself that he was sick of repeatedly hearing about his problems, sick of repeating himself and needed to do something about it.

Over the next week, Andrew slept restlessly and had frequent dreams, most of which he couldn't recall the next day. One distressing dream he could remember fragments of, appeared to be of his own funeral and Karen smiling and chatting during the funeral service, and at the end leaving on the arm of a man – that police officer Maloney. He had woken in a sweat and wondered if dreams could be an enactment of something foretold, but brushed that thought aside, telling himself he was being stupid.

He obsessed as to whether he should discard the crazy idea of involving his patient Mai – but it was a virus of a thought that was becoming a septicaemia, spreading throughout his being. He began to think that the moment had come where his fantasy needed to see the light of day, and as he looked in the shaving mirror, he saw a stranger to himself.

Monday, 27 August 1990
3.45 p.m.

Mai sat in Andrew's consulting room for her regular session. He gazed at her without saying anything, which was not unusual in their sessions, as he often would wait for her to speak. On this occasion he was struggling to find the will to tell her about his plan. Haltingly, he asked her,

'Would you be willing – and you don't have to answer immediately, you can think about it – but would you be willing to work where your sister worked?' Seeing the look of disbelief as Mai looked away, he rushed to attempt an explanation how she could assist in getting retribution for what this man had done to her sister. He tried to avoid Mai's gaze, which she had now fixed on him warily. He described in a soft voice that it would mean her having to accept sex with a number of customers, hoping that eventually Maloney, the policeman who had been with her sister when she died, would have sex with her also. In this way she would not arouse suspicion, he explained. The hope was that the policeman would notice her and approach her for sex.

In a whisper, he said that it would help if she was able to have unprotected sex with him. If they had sex, she would have to immediately be seen by a doctor so that a semen sample could be taken from her vagina and sent away for DNA testing. Andrew told her that he could organise a reliable doctor to do this and if she agreed, then she was not to tell anyone what they were planning. He elaborated that he hoped the DNA sample provided by Mai would match the semen sample collected from her dead sister at the time her body was found, as this would identify the man who had sex with her sister just before she died.

Andrew felt his face suffuse with heat, and his hands and face moistened, as he explained that he would arrange for someone reliable from the public prosecutor's office to collect the samples from the doctor so that it would not be lost prior to the court hearing, which he hoped would eventuate in due course. It sounded so clinical and sterile he thought to himself, knowing it was anything but that, as nothing could mask the horror residing in his request.

Having said all this, Andrew was finding it difficult to breathe as if all the oxygen had been sucked out of the room. He knew that the explanation he had given Mai had been very disjointed, and cursed himself for asking her to work as a prostitute before explaining the purpose of doing this. However, he was sure that eventually what he wanted to convey had been said and understood by Mai.

Keeping her head down, she remained silent at first and appeared particularly pale, almost translucent – though it may have been Andrew's imagination. It felt to him as if the silence went on forever, but eventually Mai looked up.

'Yes.'

At that moment, he almost wished that she had put up some argument for not doing it, as that might have assuaged his guilt.

Andrew left it to Mai to organise working at the brothel, and within a week she had managed to get approval from the manager. The way the system at the brothel worked, she was told, was that the brothel did not employ the women working there, but rather they rented rooms from the brothel. In return, they were provided with security and medical examinations as required, as well as generating the customers they serviced.   What Andrew feared even more than having to tell Mai his plan, was the need to tell Karen what he was setting in motion. More than a hurdle, it felt like a mountain that he had to scale. He avoided thinking beyond that.

7.59 p.m.

Andrew and Karen sat on the living room couch, in front of a flickering TV screen. Andrew briefly outlined his plan, aware of his racing pulse. If asked, neither of them could have given a clear description of what they were watching, as their thoughts were far removed and the sound emanating from the TV was only a muted distraction in the background. They tended not to speak to each other a lot these days. The volcanic eruption that he had predicted came on cue.

'You what!?' her voice pierced the fog that had pervaded the room. She glared at Andrew, moving away from him. 'How can you possibly be part of such a sick plan!? It's … it's immoral. It makes you no different to that cop,' she snapped, pushing even further away.

The words hit Andrew like a reverberating echo.

'That's … that's not fair,' he stuttered as he tried to fend off her attack. 'I'm only proving his guilt.'

'Yes, and prostituting a young, damaged woman,' Karen snapped, turning her head away. 'You know what? Revenge should be a four letter word … it's so *evil*,' she hissed, her face still turned away from him.

'Can't you see, that's what she wants more than anything else – to nail that guy,' Andrew defended, possibly struggling to convince himself as well as her.

'What she wants, you're telling me, is to be a prostitute. I can't believe it!' Karen yelled, as every muscle of her body tightened up. 'What she wants is not prostitution, but a chance to get back at him. Can you swear that you're not using her to get revenge yourself? I can't believe you could contemplate doing this,' she said angrily, with her voice rising.

In the face of this barrage, Andrew felt battered, his head splitting and his skin crawling, but his determination to follow through with the idea didn't diminish.

'I need to nail that bastard,' he said in a soft pressured voice.

'Where does your medical oath fit into this?' Karen hurled at Andrew, using every weapon available to her.

'I'll live with it … I'll help her live with it, but I'm not going to let that bastard get away with it scot-free,' Andrew defended, his tongue feeling thick and large.

'How do you plan to give evidence against him? You weren't there. You don't know how she died and what exactly happened!'

'I know what her family told me. This cop forced her to do things she didn't want to do. He gave her drugs and she was too scared of him to say no. I can swear in court she had told me these things herself before her death!'

Karen stared at him in silence and disbelief.

'You know that's not true. Can you really swear that you aren't using her to get your own personal revenge? You're prepared to lie and to prostitute a patient. I can't believe the man I married could contemplate doing this.'

Bruised and battered, Andrew gazed unfocused into the distance.

'No, she doesn't want to be a prostitute, but she is willing to do that if it could mean bringing justice for her sister.' He was finding it increasingly difficult to talk with his dry mouth and thick tongue. It had turned out as badly as he had feared. He felt himself staggering, though still seated on the couch, as if entangled in the labyrinth of a defence that he had desperately planned before becoming entangled in her onslaught. 'Can't you see that what she wants more than anything else is to bring him to justice? I need to nail that bastard,' he repeated again in a soft hiss. 'I'm certain the facts are accurate, except for the part about having met Mai's sister. I am certain it's what she would have told me if given the chance. That creep has gotten away with too many bad things … for far too long.'

'But Andrew, whose battle are you fighting – whose revenge – hers or yours?' Karen pleaded in a voice now softer and tinged with sadness.

'Karen, he's hurt and used people – he's got it coming to him.' Andrew's words poured out, fuelled by his mounting anger. 'You've heard the saying "don't get angry, just get even" … well, it really fits in this situation. I lost most of my family in the Holocaust, when I was just a baby. Then I came to Australia as a refugee and was bullied for years at school. Then this brute Maloney put you, me and the kids through hell with fabricated evidence and feeding material to the media.' Andrew's eyes glared, cauterising the air between Karen and himself, as if he could imprint the logic of his argument onto her mind. He confronted her with a question she had already cast aside. 'You still think I don't have "sufficient cause"?'

'I just want you to be the man I married,' Karen pleaded tearfully. 'I don't know how to live with this new person …'

'You know how I've often talked about that saying of Edmund Burke, that evil occurs when good people stand by and do nothing,' Andrew said, with eyes downcast and almost pleading for her support.

'But if what you yourself do is evil … ' Karen quickly cut in, leaving the incomplete sentence hanging. 'Can you really justify using an evil act to fight evil?' she asked in choked voice. 'It will reduce you to a shadow of the man you were, and become a shadow of the man you're fighting.'

'I need to nail that bastard,' Andrew reiterated his mantra.

'I repeat – where does your Hippocratic oath fit into this?' Karen's soft voice choked as she fought back her tears.

'I said I'll live with it and I'll help her live with it but I can't let that bastard get off scot free,' he said exhausted, wishing it could end there.

By now, the sense of sorrow filled the room like a giant brooding bird with clipped wings that would not fly off in a hurry, if ever. Both Karen and Andrew had avoided calling Brett Maloney by name, as if not naming him erased his existence.

'You know what this could do to our relationship,' warned Karen.

It was not a query as much as a statement. Andrew knew. And with time he would see. He sensed he was marching into a labyrinth of his own making, and possibly losing his way there, but not prepared to turn back. He wondered if the children were asleep - they probably were - but these days they had learnt to act out the part of sleep.

Tuesday, 28 August 1990

Andrew and Karen commenced sleeping in separate rooms. Their communication was polite but barren. Doubts started to creep into Andrew's thinking, but he was not going to let go of his plan. The accusation that Karen had made that he was no different to Maloney hurt him, as he knew he was different. The occasional doubt slipped through his guard where he questioned whether he was just being altruistic and doing this to protect society or was he getting revenge for what he and his family had gone through? He questioned whether it had to be entirely one or the other. Could it just be a mix of removing a crooked cop, protecting society and also evening the score for the harm that had been done to himself and his family?

He confirmed for himself that with suspected suicide, samples from Hahn would have been sent to the coroner. Records showed that the coroner had left Hahn's death as an open finding, as police believed it was suicide, but the coroner couldn't rule out other possible causes such as an accidental overdose, so pathology samples would have been retained in case further information became available.

As refugees, Hahn's family were limited by language and lacking knowledge of their rights. This prevented them raising the suspicion of homicide, so inevitably there was no recommendation for an official hearing, leaving the family immersed in their bitterness and grief.

Andrew found it hard to contemplate the thought that the samples taken from Hahn's body at the time of her death might no longer be available. He was reluctant to approach the police directly to check if the samples had been kept and was still available, as he didn't know who he could trust in the force. What he did know was the fortress mentality that separated police from the general community, so if one of their number was under threat, a metal screen would drop enveloping the police like a suit of armour, and protecting them from the outside world. It became a "them and us" situation. Any whistle blower attempting to create a breach in the armour would be rapidly devoured. So how could he do it? There had to be a way, knowing full well that there didn't have to be a way. He realised that he would have to take the risk of trusting someone, but who exactly?

Andrew thought back to his student days and recalled a friend from that time, who went on to do Law. This friend, Rory, was now a senior counsel and involved in a lot of coronial inquiries. Could Rory possibly check for him without arousing suspicion? The last thing that he needed was for his enquiries to become known, causing someone to feel threatened enough to destroy any existing samples.

7.44 p.m.

Andrew and a somewhat bemused Rory shared a drink at a pub close to where Rory worked in South Melbourne. After a few minutes of strained idle chatter, Rory finally popped the question.

'We haven't spoken to each other for over twenty years, so why now? Why the call? Don't get me wrong, Andrew, I'm certainly pleased to see you, but what the hell is going on?'

Andrew took a breath, grinned and plunged into the story from the deep end. There really wasn't any point in delaying it further. Rory didn't have to know everything, so Andrew truncated the story, giving out the skeleton of detail and Rory politely didn't ask him to provide the flesh. After telling Rory the basic story, Andrew enquired if there was any way that Rory could check whether the samples in question was still available and viable, without arousing suspicion.

Before Andrew had finished, Rory had already recalled the name of a man who worked in the section where samples were kept. He had represented this guy quite a few years ago, he said, on what turned out to be a trumped up charge of sexual harassment, and had successfully cleared his name. Now was the time to call in a favour.

For years Andrew had pondered and debated the theoretical question about good and evil. He had queried whether people were born intrinsically good or the opposite. When that proposition was put forward, he'd say: 'Let me answer with a question. Imagine the entire police force was on strike. The government at the time issues an edict that no one will be punished for what they do in the coming 24 hours. Now, you tell me, he challenged, how safe would you feel?'

Andrew had personally come to believe over the years, that everyone was capable of acting badly given the right circumstances or the wrong ones, he'd add. He didn't doubt that some people could act decently, even at risk to themselves, for reasons that appeared noble. He felt that some people acted decently possibly for the wrong reasons and personally, he believed that no one could say for sure how they would act under extreme pressure or threat. At the same time, he valued the importance of having a moral code, and that was something he had prided himself on abiding by. He didn't accept the argument that all good and evil was relative, and he believed that some evil things were absolute, without any redeeming features, for example, the rape and murder of a child. However, he acknowledged to himself that there were other times when killing another person was justifiable as a means of defending oneself and one's family, but not with Hahn's death, if indeed someone was responsible for the loss of her life.

Seeing how aghast Karen had been when he confided his plan to her, the distance she kept from him over the following weeks and months was not unexpected. The accusation Karen had made about him being no different to the cop Maloney really troubled him as he knew he was different. Repeatedly he ran the queries past himself, over and over again, not having anyone else to share it with.

He asked himself whether what he planned was just being altruistic, helping out society by removing this man, or was he seeking revenge for the harm Maloney had inflicted on Andrew's family and other families such as Mai's. Did it really have to be one or the other or could it just be a mix of removing a crooked cop, protecting society and at the same time evening the score for the damage this man had inflicted on a number of people, including his own family? Karen did not share his uncertainty. To her, it appeared wrong and demeaning, not only for Andrew, but would sully his family as well. She accused him of seeking revenge because of his own hurt alone, and said nothing could justify behaving in such a manner, which in her eyes could only diminish him as the man she had once respected.   Andrew treated her accusations as rhetorical questions not requiring an answer. He knew that what counted most for him was the knowledge that Maloney had hurt Andrew and his family – in fact, hurt them so badly and deliberately, that he could never forgive him.

The relationship between Andrew and Karen was now drowning in crashing waves of silence. There was no way he could give up the sting operation that he had planned, but Karen's reactions were getting him down and he felt that he was functioning at a robotic level at times.

They were now strangers to each other and the sense of humour that had always been part of Andrew's makeup was now rarely evident. Andrew had always thought of his humour as being a Jewish humour, where he portrayed himself in a self-deprecating manner, presenting as a "dill" at times. Andrew enjoyed this type of humour and felt that it had developed in the Jewish community as a defence, where one got in first before others could have a go at you. It was a humour that Karen and their friends also enjoyed, but Andrew felt himself losing the zest and humour for life, as if he was sucked dry at times. In recent times he found himself being more cutting and cynical without the gentle self-depreciatory manner of the past. The children lived in the house, but pretended not to be spectators to how their parent's marriage was unravelling before their eyes.

About a week after enlisting Rory's help, he heard back from him.

'Sorry mate, but that sample has disappeared, I've asked around a bit and got nowhere – it's weird. If I push it any further, people will get suspicious-possibly the wrong people will start wanting to know why I'm making these inquiries'.

Andrew felt a cold chill sweep through his body. Over the following days people who interacted with him tended to keep the contact brief as he was morose and irritable. Karen sensed the black storm gathering around Andrew and chose the safety of avoiding him even more than before.

Andrew decided he had to promptly let Mai know about the failure of his plans, but felt life had lost its meaning for him.

CHAPTER TWENTY

Thursday, 6 September 1990
7.45 p.m.

Andrew continued struggling to cope with the news from Rory and felt as if his life was in limbo. However he didn't feel able to build an alternate plan, if in fact there was a feasible one. In his befuddled state he put the issue on hold, doubting that such a miracle would occur.

He refused to believe that Maloney had won. There had to be another way of punishing him, but his mind was not free enough to tackle how this could be done. Gazing at his face in the mirror, something he was doing more often these days, as if measuring his progress, he perceived an image reflecting the traumas of the past as well as those still to come. More and more he saw gaunt features, with sunken cheeks, blood shot eyes and a sense of grey taking over his face. Andrew felt his face had begun showing the features of old age and life traumas etched into its surface.

The din of his thoughts surrounded him wherever he went, and he found himself obsessively dwelling on the past as if there wasn't much in the future, all the while feeling very much alone. He didn't feel he was living a real life, but hadn't reached the point of abandoning it, though the joy of life had leaked away. In the background, the bitterness and anger experienced over the previous few years, continued unabated, not able to share it with anyone, nor move beyond it. He found himself unable to erase the sense that he had been deliberately targeted by the police, especially Maloney, and probably by The Union sect as well.

Communication with Karen continued to be poor, but he put off asking her about the possibility of marriage counselling for the two of them, as he hoped things could still improve and if they didn't, then he would ask. One can rationalise most things in life, he thought to himself. At the same time he wondered why Karen herself had not asked him about counselling.

For years Andrew had questioned institutions such as religion, and whilst he always did his best to respect people's belief in God, it amazed him that intelligent people could be swept up by a concept that he saw as lacking logic. He wondered whether people needed religion to help them cope with the fear of dying and giving them some purpose in life. It had always amazed him that his parents continued to have believed in God after their war experiences, whilst his own more recent traumas had further diminished for him any possibility of believing in the concept of a loving God.

Andrew continued going to work but found himself struggling to maintain concentration and he was aware that he was spending more and more time after work dropping into a bar to have a drink or drinking on his own at home. He found himself getting very little satisfaction from any of his activities and often felt tired and needing to push himself to do things, but unsure for what purpose. He couldn't deny the mask of depression and the need to work with Dr Engel more intensively.

Andrew's instinct was to be alone licking his wounds, but he knew he'd be safer and better off with the distraction of his peer group meeting which was scheduled for that evening. He had continued attending these meetings in the recent past, but felt he was struggling to contribute as much as he used to, and often remained quiet, frequently missing a lot of what the others were saying.

Holocaust issues were beginning to intrude more and Andrew found himself visualising horrific scenes of what he imagined his family and other Jews had experienced in Europe during the war. These images came in the dark of night and the light of day and consequently due to all these intruding thoughts he was beginning to avoid going home and having dinner with Karen as he found the silence between them difficult to cope with - frequently preferring to ring and tell her he was running late and had a meeting that particular evening, and would therefore have a snack at a nearby cafe. Somehow he found the silence of the cafe easier to cope with than the silence at home. The fact that Karen made no effort to discourage this pattern of behaviour probably indicated that she felt likewise.

8.02 p.m.

The peer group always met at the home of one of the members. He felt on the periphery and though there had been some talk about his case in a previous session, the stiffness of people's interactions with him in the group showed how uncomfortable they still felt discussing it. Previously they may have been cautious, not knowing if he was innocent of the accusations, but now that the coroner had exonerated him, their reticence was harder to understand. He decided that he needed to bring back their focus on his court case to hopefully start clearing the air about it.

'Guys, I've finally run off copies of the coroner's findings – so who would like one?'

Nearly everyone there showed an interest and Andrew ran through the findings with them. It had the desired effect and appeared to free people up to discuss it with him, rather than in his absence. He only touched superficially on his suspicion of being set up and the possible role of The Union and the police. Andrew used his problem to kick off debate about prejudice in people, hoping to eventually narrow the scope of the discussion back to himself.

'Guys, I believe we are all prejudiced. We're not born that way, but all of us learn it from the things around us. I believe it's what we do with the prejudice that counts. It's puzzled me for a long time why people have difficulty accepting differences. For example, imagine we all went to live in Japan – so who would be different then? Yet we'd still be the same people. I had an Austrian patient referred to me quite a while back. I may have mentioned him to you before.

This guy had been in the Hitler Youth when young, he asked if I was Jewish and I told him I was. I treated him and we developed a positive therapeutic relationship to the extent that he sent me postcards with warm greetings from Austria. Yet at another time and another place, he may have been influenced to hate me for being Jewish. For many people, there seems to be a fine line between caring and hating. I don't know if the people setting me up and attacking me saw me as the enemy for personal reasons or whether they were attacking psychiatry and I became the target by chance.' There was quiet in the room but Andrew felt he had their attention and it was something many of them would think about for some time after they left. It helped him feel a part of the group rather than an onlooker, which he had experienced in recent meetings.

Andrew was in no hurry to go home and had drunk quite a bit at the meeting. He was sure that Karen had briefed the boys soon after he told her his plan involving Mai, and he started to sense a lot of discomfort in his sons' reactions and facial expressions whenever he tried to speak to them. It was not that he had a lot to do with his sons in recent years, but somehow this felt different, as if they were judging him harshly.

Though still sitting in the peer group meeting, his thoughts started to drift and he found his thoughts now hijacked by the query of who had set him up and why. There was no doubt in his mind that someone had organised an orchestrated media campaign attacking him. He recalled how Maloney had fabricated evidence against him in court for some reason and how the sect had manipulated his patient's family to the point where they demanded a coronial hearing. He suspected there could be some connection between the police and the sect, but as to what and why, he could not fathom at this stage. Yet what was the point of all this if he no longer had the means to identify Maloney and retaliate for what he had done?

As the meeting wound up and people were preparing to return home, Andrew didn't feel that he was sober enough to drive his car, and thought he would try to stay back chatting to a few of the group members, hoping he could sober up enough to drive himself home. Prior to the meeting he had warned Karen that he did not know what time he might return home, and he knew that she would not be waiting up for him. He asked Rick, the member he was close to in the group, whether he would join him for a few beers, effectively sabotaging the reason for staying back, which was to sober up.

Rick was of a similar age to Andrew and also not in a hurry to go home, as his marriage had broken up several years ago and he had no current partner.

10.47 p.m.

At a small pub around corner Rick and Andrew downed more than a couple of beers and Andrew realised that he was letting his tongue run loose, but it didn't worry him. Fortunately they both became philosophical rather than nasty as the alcohol entered their system.

Andrew described to Rick that he had an elderly distant cousin Joe, who was in his mid-seventies. He said that Joe had never had an opportunity to get a formal education as he was in Poland during the war years hiding from the Nazis. Having survived the war but losing most of his family, Joe fled to Australia as a refugee, and did very well financially, running a small trucking business.

'You know, Rick ... I can't help but wonder if life isn't more about surviving than achieving,' Andrew slurred. 'There are hundreds of people with Ph.Ds. in many large cities around the world who can't get jobs and end up driving cabs if they are lucky.' He could see that Rick did not appear to know what point Andrew was making nor was he interested in it.

'Okay, let's agree to disagree,' Rick said, hoping to stem the flow of conversation. With the courage of his drinks, Andrew ploughed ahead, oblivious to Rick's wish to stop this line of discussion.

'Joe has a twenty-year-old son, you know. He hasn't starred academically, but his mind and wit and creativity are very sharp. Unfortunately the kid's fallen in with a bad crowd and gotten into drugs and is not holding it together very well. So Rick, would you say he's intelligent or not?'

At this point the barman took advantage of having few customers and appeared to be listening to the conversation that Andrew and Rick were having.

'So what do you think, huh? Can intelligent people make dumb decisions?' Andrew queried the barman, having noticed he was listening in to their conversation while drying a pint glass. Andrew noted that this man's rugged, nuggety physique gave the impression he was of Irish descent and despite scars on his face suggesting he wasn't a stranger to dissent he was happy to join in and share his thoughts.

'You're dead right, you know. I've seen them come and go – judges, lawyers, doctors, all of them – no doubt they're bright, but you wouldn't believe the mess they have made of their private lives,' he philosophized, lifting the glass to the pub's dim lighting to check for any soap spots and when satisfied put it on the back bar ready for the next request for a drink with the other glassware.

Andrew took advantage of the democratic process and stated that now they had two for and one against his theory, so the theory stood, he announced. They both drank to that, further complicating the issue of driving themselves home later on. Andrew was reluctant to let the issue go and pontificated.

'All those labels we pin on people such as saying they are bright or cultured or educated – they're not worth a pinch of salt. Look at Germany during the Second World War – there wasn't a more cultured and educated bunch of people in Europe at that time, yet that didn't make people more moral. There's more to life than being intelligent,' he summed up.

An inner voice warned Andrew he had better stop drinking, and though his car was parked outside, he knew he would be stupid to drive it. He also knew he could not call Karen to come and pick him up. He decided to sit in his car for a while and try and sober up and if he still felt unable to drive, he would call a cab. He farewelled Rick and the barman, making no enquiry as to how Rick was getting home and sat himself in his car, chewing a peppermint. He was sober enough to know that there would be repercussions with Karen the next waking day, as she was also intelligent – intelligent enough to know what kind of "meeting" he had attended that evening.

Andrew felt like the structure of his life was crumbling. Revenge for what had been done to his and Mai's family seemed out of reach now. His marriage was deteriorating and like Karen, he had mounting concern about what impact recent stress was having on his two sons. They were at a vulnerable stage of life, where they would normally be building careers and concepts of relationships, *but how was that possible,* he wondered, *with the stress and chaos surrounding their family.* To Andrew, it felt that life recently was more like a runaway train careering out of control, with the main goal being survival.

He worried what it would do to the boys if he and Karen separated, and even if they remained together, what image of married life was it projecting for their sons.

CHAPTER TWENTY-ONE

Tuesday, 11 September 1990

Andrew put off telling Mai about the catastrophic news of the sample from Hahn's body having disappeared, preferring to wait until she came for her next appointment in just under a week. He knew that he could ring her and share the news over the phone, or he could bring her appointment forward, but he preferred to have time to untangle the mesh of thoughts in his own mind. As the doubts ricocheted within his head, the unanswered question that persisted was whether anything could be salvaged for his plan to still go ahead or had it been permanently aborted?

Short of a miracle, he could not see a way out of this mess. It looked grim to Andrew as he had given up on miracles from the age of six, when he woke up to discover his father putting an envelope under his pillow, and later discovered the envelope contained a note from the tooth fairy and some money. He had pretended to be asleep until his father silently slid out of the room, and he never told his father that he had witnessed the event, as he knew it would upset him and lead to his father being severely criticised by Andrew's mother.

Andrew was due to see Mai in five days' time, but today he had an appointment to see Dr Engel, which was the next hurdle to clear. Given Karen's explosive reaction when told about his plan, he was apprehensive as to how Dr Engel would react to it, but he felt there was a chance that when Dr Engel heard the plan might not go ahead, it could possibly soften his response.

Andrew continued to struggle with Karen's reaction and it was a boil that needed to be lanced. She had backed away from him when he told her of his plan and had continued to keep her distance since then. It was like living with a stranger, creating a pervasive sense of loneliness that was dragging him down. He'd read that the opposite of love is not hate, but indifference. He doubted that Karen hated him or felt indifferent to him, and it struck him that maybe like himself, she felt a sense of loneliness and fear for the future. He particularly struggled with her accusation that his plan made him no different to Maloney, as he was sure that he and Maloney had little in common. He couldn't say for certain whether he was doing it for society, by attempting to punish a crooked cop or was it, as Karen alleged, just getting revenge for himself.

Even if Karen was not caught up in a labyrinth of uncertainty, feeling she knew for sure that Andrew was driven by a thirst for revenge, he believed life was rarely that simple, and usually had multiple engines driving it. He guessed that it was always a part of Karen's personality to categorise things in a black and white fashion – that it was either one thing or the other, thus avoiding the shades of grey. It was probably a lot more comfortable than tending to be as abstract and convoluted as he was.

5.30p.m.

'You what!?' came the explosive response from Dr Engel, his voice brittle and rising, like an echo of Karen's reaction. Andrew had anticipated a negative reaction, but thought recent events might have softened the response, once Dr Engel heard the sample was missing.

Dr Engel's reaction seemed so out of character that it stunned Andrew, as the controlled, reflective tone and gentle voice that he had grown used to, was no longer there. Sure, he had predicted there might be a degree of criticism, but nothing of this severity. Following the initial explosion, a period of silence followed, building up to the point where it felt increasingly loud, until his therapist invited Andrew to tell him all about the events and feelings leading up to his decision.

'You know how the family and I have suffered for several years with false accusations and how the family of my patient were encouraged to demand a coronial inquiry,' Andrew responded tentatively. 'You also know how the evidence given in court was falsified by the inspector. We've discussed how the police – Maloney – seemed hell bent on setting me up and how The Union were somehow involved as well ...' Andrew's voice started to fragment and emitted what sounded like an angry hiss. He stopped talking and took a deep breath and then drank water from a glass standing on a small side table near him. He knew he hadn't finished and now felt able to continue. 'You know what happened to my family during the war and to me as well. Well, I thought I had put it behind me until recently when it started crashing into my thoughts. Up to now I have lived my life without planning revenge, though I certainly rejoiced if any Nazis were brought to trial for war crimes. You know how I had to put up with the bullying at school, having arrived as a refugee. Well, I'm not going to be a victim yet again without fighting back, and this time I'm not waiting for someone else to do the fighting for me. I'll certainly let the law deal with them, but I'll try and make sure that the law has as much clout and evidence, as it requires.'

'You've told other people about your plans? You've told Karen?' Dr Engel enquired in a voice that was more restrained and calmer now.

'Yes, and she hated the idea. She felt it reduced me to the same level as the people I despised for lying and attempting to set me up. Karen even accused me of prostituting my patient for my own ends!' Without waiting for any response, which he preferred not to hear, Andrew went on. 'I am not prostituting anyone. My patient also wanted revenge on behalf of her sister. Even though it was my idea to begin with, she agreed straight away. We couldn't think of any other way that we could prevent those bastards getting off scot-free. Anyhow, given that the sample seems to have disappeared, what are we disagreeing about? The chances now are that nothing will come of our plans.' Andrew waited out the silence that followed, broken eventually by Dr Engel.

'It's true that nothing might eventuate from your plan, but the problem is what the plan reflects about your thinking and feelings at the moment, Andrew. You've heard the saying "revenge is sweet but the aftertaste is bitter", and also Gandhi's quote "an eye for an eye and the whole world goes blind". So what price are you prepared to pay for doing this, Andrew?' Dr Engel enquired quietly – producing a soft landing for extremely heavy words.

'I'm really not sure … It could end up costing me my marriage. It could be that the plan fails and I end up with egg on my face and even angrier than before. So I'm really not certain what price I end up paying, but I have no other choice,' Andrew said hesitantly, as if he was wanting to convince himself as well.

'No other choice,' Dr Engel repeated. 'Can you explain that to me? If you did nothing more and didn't involve your patient, how would that be?'

In the silence that followed, and in the absence of any immediate response from Andrew, Dr Engel answered his own question:

'It would be bloody awful, that's how it would be.'

'And probably won't happen without the sample,' Andrew reminded him, 'but if it did go ahead, I guess I would have put Mai through a hell of a lot.' '

'A lot of what, Andrew? Give it a name,' Dr Engel interjected.

'Well, it's not prostitution and I'm not a pimp, if that's what you're suggesting,' Andrew hotly defended himself.

'No, I agree, but yet you are behaving like one and you plan to encourage your patient to behave like her prostitute sister. So, who ends up getting damaged the most Andrew – you or the policeman or Mai?'

'I am willing to pay a price if I can nail him for what he's done,' Andrew said with the intensity that only a quiet voice can bring.

'I wonder if you realise the actual price you will most likely pay in the end,' Dr Engel persisted. 'Look Andrew, I can be a psychiatrist with you as the patient, but given that time is so very limited with this issue, I am going to act as a friend and not as a psychiatrist. You haven't asked me, I know, but I strongly advise you to go no further with this plan.'

Andrew rubbed the side of his nose, a mannerism he'd developed over the years suggesting he was ill at ease. He respected, even admired, Dr Engel, but felt Engel had gone too far on this occasion. It reminded him of a parent scolding a child. His face felt hot and damp, and his left eye had developed a twitch, as if he had overdosed on caffeine that day. Doctor Engel rounded the session up, leaving Andrew feeling as if he had been set homework, but in essence providing him with a blueprint for avoiding disaster.

'You've got a lot to think about and decide, Andrew. Can I get you to try and do that in the next few days and call me back after that. I understand that your patient hasn't slept with the policeman yet, and I guess the next move will be delayed by trying to locate the sample. So if you accept my advice, you'll ask her to break off any connection with the brothel regardless of whether the sample is located or not. Explain to her that you have thought it through and now regret the idea, as to carry it out could damage both of you, regardless of whether it punishes the cop or not.'

'Can I call you back in a few days?' Andrew heard his distant voice saying.

'Sure. That's it for today, Andrew. Good luck with your thoughts,' Dr Engel said, as if saying a prayer for Andrew.

Wednesday, 13 September 1990
11.30a.m.

Andrew had been carrying out his daily duties in a robotic manner ever since his appointment two days ago with Dr Engel.

Today, he decided what he needed to do – he would bring Mai's appointment forward to tell her that the sample from her sister was missing. Mai agreed immediately to accept the earlier time without querying what it was about. She arrived at Andrew's office at 11.30 a.m. As she sat in front of him, Andrew haltingly, and in a monotone voice, confided what he had learnt. Mai remained silent and stayed that way for the rest of the session with no apparent emotion showing in her features, leaving Andrew uncertain how she felt about the situation.

At the end of the session as she got up to leave, neither she nor Andrew had made any comments except to confirm that she would come for her next regular appointment. There was no discussion as to whether the plan would go ahead or not. Andrew suddenly asked Mai if they could talk for a short while longer. Again without comment she sat herself down.

'I'm sorry to hit you with that news, Mai. You must feel I've let you down, after you had the courage to agree to being part of a plan that probably revolted you and yet you were brave enough to say yes to it.'

'I don't feel cheated or let down, Dr Wright, and I still hold out hope we can find a way around it. There were so many things I wanted to share and say to my sister, and I've been robbed of that. Until the time she died, I had held out hope that one day we could have fun together as sisters, and be able to share our life experiences. We had been robbed of that opportunity in the past, and now have been totally robbed of any chance it can happen in the future. I owe it to Hahn to make the man who treated her so badly pay. It's not even that I lost something I had, it's more that any chance of ever having it has been taken from me.'

Mai had expressed her pain quietly and with dignity, leaving Andrew feeling raw and desolate, with a deep sadness both for her, and for what he stood to lose in his own life. The room carried a heavy mixture of despair and hope for both of them, with the door still partially open to allow something good to pass through, before it slammed closed.

CHAPTER TWENTY-TWO

Wednesday, 14 September 1990
2.58 a.m.

Following the coronial court proceedings, Brett began drinking even more, often on his own. To an outside observer it would appear no one had emerged from these court proceedings unscathed.

At a time when most people slept, Brett sat nursing a beer, having lost count of which one he was up to. His body sank and partially hid amongst the worn down springs of his living room couch. Jenny and the boys were sound asleep in the house, and had kept their distance, knowing Brett was not a pleasant drunk especially lately. People who knew them wondered why Jenny stayed on in a marriage that was so obviously bad, but she herself realised she didn't feel secure leaving.

She believed there were physical dangers if Brett tracked her down, there was ongoing financial insecurity and most of all, she reflected, there was a lack of self-belief. She felt she didn't know what was needed to make a good marriage and doubted she had what was required.

Though the TV was playing, the screen only showed drifting snow, the product of a TV devoid of programs as it was now close to 3 a.m. Since the coroner read out his findings, Brett had continued struggling to contain his anger, which had long been an issue for him, but now readily flared up even more. The pin of the emotional grenade was close at hand, ready to be pulled. One day he'd even the score with that bloody psychiatrist. Previously targeting Wright had not been personal, but that had now altered.

Brett hated looking in the mirror and seeing the decrepit signs of aging; the bags under the eyes, the skin blemishes and the veins on the surface of his nose from his drinking and lifestyle. He'd thought about leaving Jenny but knew he wouldn't, as he doubted another woman would stick it out or be as accepting of him if he only threw a few crumbs in her direction.

The sober part of his brain knew his career was shot, and he sensed that Deborah felt he was of little use to her now. She seemed to still view her plan as a victory, for even though Dr Wright had been cleared, Deborah believed he had not come out of it unscathed. She'd heard his marriage was on the rocks and emotionally he wasn't coping that well, so that he was no longer focused on doing something about The Union. Brett himself did not feel as confident that it was time to celebrate, as his years in the police force left him feeling uneasy that something could still go wrong.

There had been other issues Brett had to deal with lately. Two weeks ago Ralph died, still not having found an organ donor. Brett hadn't anticipated it would touch him, but it left him feeling uncomfortable. Guilt was not an emotion he could readily identify, but something had snuck in that that was causing him discomfort. Soon after Ralph died, probably two days after, he drove to Deborah's commune and she appeared far from pleased, telling him never to come again unless she requested it. There was no sex between them and no invitation to stay the night. She appeared annoyed at his performance in court, and he gauged her feelings to be an indicator that he was not someone she considered useful in the future.

Brett had got Jesse to join and live with The Union people over a year ago and bumped into him that night he came unannounced. Jesse had taken to Deborah's sect, and she to him. For someone as deprived as Jesse, it had clearly felt like a true home and Deborah felt like a mother who wanted him, so much so he'd expressed that he was trusted to do maintenance work on the property and also mentioned he'd he'd been given something of an ill defined role as an enforcer, where he ensured Deborah's orders were being carried out.

Monday, 17 September 1990
8.30 a.m.

Andrew had just completed a session with his first patient for the day when his secretary interrupted to say that there had been an urgent call from Mai. She had asked to speak to him when he was free to do so. His normal approach was to wait until the end of the day to return calls, unless they were very urgent, but his curiosity and uncertainty as to how urgent it was got him to ring her immediately before seeing the next patient.

Mai's tense voice told Andrew that even though it was urgent, it could wait until after his last appointment, and she wanted to tell him face to face what the issue was, but wouldn't discuss it over the phone. Andrew didn't push her, hearing the tightness in her voice and arranged to meet with her at the end of that day's work. She asked if they could meet at a cafe some distance from Andrew's medical rooms, and he agreed without asking her to explain.

5.46 p.m.

Upon arrival, Mai suggested they go to a nearby park so that they could speak privately, unrestricted by fear of being overheard or noticed. Andrew drove them to the empty park where they stayed in the car. Without being prompted, Mai started to speak rapidly with her words tumbling out and tripping each other up at times.

Andrew didn't interrupt, understanding her need to speak, without his questions disrupting her train of thought. Her pressured, buffeting speech described a current relationship that she had been in for about 10 months. As she divulged this, her profuse apologies followed almost seamlessly. She lowered her eyes as she confessed to Andrew that she felt terrible about having kept a secret from him and that it was not the way she normally behaved. Her speech became even more pressured, bordering on a stutter at times, as she attempted to explain that she had always been very open in their sessions together except for one fact.

Andrew felt an urge to question Mai, but held back in response to the signals and pleas that her pressured speech emitted, asking for her words to be granted the freedom to tumble out before questions were asked.

Mai pleaded that everything else she had told him so far had been true, as the shame of her omission brought a flush to her cheeks. She reiterated that the history she had previously given of being traumatised by men and mistrusting men in general was true. With downcast eyes, she described that she had been seeing a man who was kind and gentle, and gradually, together with the help of her therapy with Andrew and the support of her boyfriend, she had learned to trust this man. With embarrassment, she explained that the reason for not telling Andrew about Richard, came out of concern that if he knew she had a boyfriend, he would disbelieve everything she had told him about the past traumas with men, and tend to think she had exaggerated these experiences. She had also feared that Andrew might judge her as being promiscuous, and added that there were still difficulties sexually between her boyfriend and herself, as if she hoped this fact would be more believable, given the history she had given Andrew in the past. Shyly she added that her relationship with Richard was improving sexually and emotionally. At this point, her story became even more halting, almost to the point of stuttering, as she confessed yet another bombshell to Andrew, that her boyfriend was a policeman. Richard moved in with her about five months ago, she added.

Though startled by the revelations that had poured out, Andrew had refrained from interrupting, and allowed her words and emotions to spill out, which they did. He was transfixed by what she was telling him, feeling her account was taking on the appearance of a storyline in a novel, with Kafka-like qualities. If he was having difficulty getting his head around the story so far, what followed next almost decapitated him.

Mai revealed that her partner Richard – or Dick, as his colleagues called him at work – was a detective in the Victorian Police Force, and had been one of two police called out when her sister was found dead. Andrew gently encouraged Mai to describe Richard's involvement when her sister's death was reported. Mai related how Richard had told her that he had his doubts about her sister having committed suicide, which was the official line at the time, but because he was a junior then, and certainly lower rank to the policeman that took over the case, he felt there was little he could do about it.

Mai described how Richard told her he felt ashamed about accepting the official line, rather than firmly expressing his doubts. At first he had voiced some tentative queries, but his words were promptly squashed. He then retreated and did as much as he felt was safe. He was concerned that Hahn's forensic samples taken after her death might disappear, so he took steps to secure the material and keep it viable, as best he could.

He explained to Mai that the forensic material from the autopsy had been put in three bags; one bag for skin scrapings under the nails, a bag for hair and the third bag containing a swab with sperm analysis from the dead girl's vagina.

Andrew reflected to himself how difficult it must be for Mai to be describing the sampling of her sister's body parts, and he admired her strength.

Mai went on to describe that Richard had gently explained to her that her sister was known to the police for prostitution and drug addiction and minor petty crimes, so they readily assumed that her death was suicide, with little interest in pursuing it further. The coroner faced with this history of drugs and prostitution, together with the police stating strongly that they suspected suicide, was disinclined to have a full hearing and left it as an open finding in case new evidence cropped up. The coroner had stated that he could not be sure that it was suicide, as he could not rule out an accidental drug overdose given that blood tests taken from Hahn revealed a toxic level of amphetamines and significant levels of sedatives and heroin, as well as some alcohol. None of these findings motivated the police to investigate Hahn's death further and they did not indicate to the coroner that there was any suggestion of foul play. As Hahn's family were migrants, they were unaware of their rights to ask for a full coronial hearing.

Richard was nominated by his superior to be the informant (whose duty it was to collate information for the court). Richard's superior told him to "deal with it". Richard was unsure whether his superior wanted to get rid of the samples to cover up for someone or whether he just wanted the samples to be disposed of, to avoid the possibility of his assessment being open to future scrutiny and possibly showing that he had erred in his finding. Richard realised that he was meant to remove the samples and not keep them – but keep them he did, in a manner that he believed preserved the integrity of the forensic material.

Mai said that Richard had told her that he didn't know what he would do with the samples when he secured them, and even now was unsure, but for him it felt like a psychological shower that helped cleanse some of his guilt at not having pressed his doubts regarding the official police assessment. She said that Richard explained to her that he believed that if the samples were kept dry, it would preserve their integrity.

Tearfully Mai described to Andrew how painful it had been to tell Richard about the plan that her treating psychiatrist had come up with, confiding to her partner that she had agreed to do it, and how the plan had now been shattered by finding out the samples had disappeared. Sobbing, she recounted explaining to Richard that without the material from her sister's body they could not hope to prove who was with her at the time she died, and who may well have contributed to her death. Mai said that at first Richard attempted to comfort her and as her distress continued, he had told her the startling news that the samples could now be retrieved, and were in his possession.

Taking a tissue offered to her by Andrew as a gesture acknowledging her distress, Mai went on to share how she hugged Richard, begging him to try and understand that it was the only way she could possibly prove what happened to her sister, and most of all, enable investigators to possibly identify the man involved.

Mai recounted to Andrew that Richard continued to feel extremely uncomfortable with the idea of the plan, but reluctantly accepted her need to do it as he struggled to understand the emotion driving her. Intellectually, he could make some sense out of her feeling that she owed it to her sister, and that it really had nothing to do with sex except as a vehicle for eliciting the truth. But here the brain and emotions parted ways, and whilst he did not attempt to stop her, he struggled painfully with the idea. He hinted to her that it created images in his mind that he had difficulty erasing. He told her that he feared what it might do to her emotionally, as well as being fearful of what it could do to their relationship. He queried whether one of the prostitutes in the brothel couldn't achieve the same goal.

Mai explained to Dr Wright that she attempted to get Richard to understand how risky involving any of the women working in the brothel would be. She knew that the prostitutes feared crossing the policeman who had slept with her sister, and there was no guarantee they could carry out the plan adequately.

Andrew looked at Mai, and saw a childlike figure with downcast eyes, and here he was, encouraging her to undergo the degradation of allowing unknown men to use and abuse her body in ways that could soil her emotionally forever. His thoughts and emotions were like dodgem cars colliding in all directions, but Andrew remained determined to carry on with the plan.

As if reassuring Andrew, Mai described how Richard reluctantly came around to the idea, and told her that he understood her feeling that she couldn't take the chance of the plan being sabotaged by someone else, but there remained a significant gap between what he understood intellectually and the revulsion that he felt emotionally.

After hearing all this from Mai, the silence between Andrew and her hung in the air, casting a dead weight in both their chests, as if the oxygen in the room was being soaked up. During the silence, Mai waited for Andrew's response, trying to guess what he was thinking and feeling. Andrew decided to keep his doubts to himself, but silently worried whether Richard could really be trusted and whether the sample in Richard's possession had in fact maintained its integrity and would still be accepted in a court of law.

Mai and Andrew continued to be silent, at least externally, for inside both, the turmoil created a heavy din of its own. The uncertainty was endless if Andrew gave it free reign, such as wondering if it would prove to be Hahn's sample and not from anyone else, until he lectured himself that in the absence of proof to the contrary, he needed to trust Mai's assessment of Richard. Having scaled that mountain, he quickly made the decision that the sample would best stay with Richard for the time being.

He couldn't resist re-enacting the scene he imagined would occur in court, when attempts would need to be made to tender the samples as evidence. Mai could only guess at what was occurring behind the wall of silence in the car, but realised she was part of that silence and eventually cut herself loose from questions that had no immediate answer.

CHAPTER TWENTY-THREE

Friday, 21 September 1990
10.30 a.m.

Mai decided that she would take herself to the brothel where her late sister had worked. Now that she and Dr Wright, who she referred to as "Andrew" these days, had made the decision to go ahead with his plan, she saw no reason for delaying commencing work there.

She was aware that the longer she put off going to the brothel, the more difficult it would become. She felt immersed with a sense of dread, fearing what working as a prostitute might eventually do to herself and to her relationship with Richard, and apprehensive about her parents' ability to handle the discovery that their remaining daughter had also turned to prostitution. She had already decided not to tell them at this point, believing there was nothing to gain and concerned they would pressure her to give up the plan.

Over the years, Mai had been hurt by many people, especially men, but those who had harmed her in the past were not people she could retaliate against, as they were too far removed geographically and in time. But this policeman Maloney, he was someone she could fight back against, and she was determined to do so at any cost, and she knew the cost could be considerable.

As Mai tentatively pushed open the heavy door, entering the brothel where her sister had died, she felt the beginning of a wave of nausea rising in her throat. Not for the first time she questioned her sanity in agreeing to work as a prostitute. Sure, she could mount an intellectual argument for doing it as a way of seeking revenge, yet here she was receiving psychiatric care in an attempt to overcome her mistrust of men and heal the scars from past abuse, but now about to open up these wounds again from further humiliation. Was she about to sabotage any progress that she might have made in therapy so far? She realised the contradiction whereby the therapist treating her, was the same person encouraging her to working in a brothel.

As she entered the brothel, she saw several young women scantily dressed and glancing with curiosity in her direction. They appeared friendly and most smiled at her. She saw an older woman approaching her and assumed that she must be the madam in charge of the brothel. She was wearing tortoiseshell glasses perched on a largish bulbous nose, with a creased face and bright red lipstick extending beyond the boundaries of her lips.

'You must be Mimi then. Let's go into my office...'

They walked through a larger room blighted with mirrors and chandeliers past their use by date. Somehow Mai found the room unsettling. Just off this space was the office, a minute room without windows and only containing only a small desk, two rickety chairs and a dinted filing cabinet. The room had no cross ventilation and the air was stuffy as they both sat facing each other. The madam introduced herself as Mona, a name Mai had already heard from some of the other women working there. The conversation informed her that the name of the brothel had altered a number of times over the years, but was currently called Sweet Orchid. The arrangement was that all the women working there or "girls" as they were referred to, paid rent to the establishment and essentially worked for themselves. In return, the brothel provided security, assistance in generating customers and organising regular medical checks for the workers. Whatever the women earned, in theory they kept; the only expense was the rental, which essentially took about 40 per cent of their earnings.

Mai didn't tell the management that she was related to Candy, though a few of the women working there knew of the relationship, some because she had visited her sister in the past and others she had confided in lately. She wondered later whether it was wise to have confided but she had hoped they might be able to give her more information about what happened to her sister.

Mai found the initial interview with the madam and her female offsider harrowing and humiliating. It felt as if they were groping her body verbally, as they went through a checklist, asking whether she did anal sex, oral sex, whether she demanded the man wear a condom, what positions she found acceptable during intercourse, would she do blow jobs, did she accept being tied up, was she prepared to have a client all night, had she ever had venereal disease, did she do drugs, had she ever been in jail and so the questions continued, initially embarrassing and even angering her, until numbness set in.

Gritting her teeth, she told them that she was willing to have unprotected sex, not revealing the reason being her knowledge that the policeman she had in her sights always demanded this from the women he had sex with. She also agreed to being tied up during sex as the other women told her this was something that he enjoyed. It was explained to Mai that she could choose the hours she worked, provided she gave the office prior notice. She experienced a poverty of dignity during the interview with the madam, and realised there was more of the same to follow, which could well cauterise her soul. Having told Andrew about Richard possessing the material taken from Hahn's body after her death, Mai saw no reason for delaying what she had become driven to do. The longer she put it off, the more time it would give Richard to stew over it. She was determined to try and avoid having Richard involved at all, and driving herself to the brothel was part of that decision. She did not believe that would stop Richard fantasising about her work, but that was something she couldn't completely control.

5.30 p.m. 22 September 1990

Returning to Sweet Orchard the next evening, Mai parked her car in the space that the madam had provided her with. Her heels clicked on the pavement as she approached the entrance at about 5.30 p.m on

Saturday night. She already strongly disliked the building located in Richmond, and appearing as a massive lump of bricks totally devoid of charm – it could readily have doubled as a warehouse or cheap office space, she felt.

Mai expected there would be about fifteen or so women working that evening, and she had met a few of them already, the day before. Only two or three of the group were Australian-born as far as she could recall. Probably over half of the women were of Asian background and the remainder were largely from Eastern Europe. There was one younger girl, possibly under twenty years of age, who was a student and was using the money to pay for her education, or that was the reason she gave. However, the brothel – being somewhat seedy – tended not to be a place where students went to work

Mai walked through the front door and towards the back room where the women did their makeup and showered. The cracked, coloured walls cast a red glow on their faces and bodies. Dim lighting hid a multitude of faults – both in the building and in the people that worked there. Scattered around the back room were eight women in various states of undress, some because they were getting themselves ready and others because they had no intention of covering any more of their body. Mai saw another young girl, going by the name "Hibiscus" who said she was eighteen, but no one bothered confirming whether this was accurate or not. The owners appeared immune to any action being taken against them by the authorities that monitored brothels in Melbourne.

Another woman, going by the name of "Petals", smiled in greeting and said hello to Mai. As far as Mai would find out from a short conversation, this woman was from Thailand, pushed into prostitution by her family because of the severe poverty they all struggled to exist in. Mai felt that Petals would have been pretty once, with features that had contained laughter lines from years long gone, but now partly erased. Her oval shaped face had lost its weight far too quickly for the skin to shrink, leaving her with flaps on her face and most probably on her body. There was nothing subtle about the approach the women used with potential customers, the majority performing the same choreographed dances and seductive movements – which appeared to work due to the usual combination of customers drinking to excess and dim lighting.

Mai reflected on how these women once had parents and possibly siblings, but now the only family they possessed were the other prostitutes. Some of the women still cared about the way they looked and made varying degrees of effort, some even competing amongst each other, but many of them appeared to be beyond caring. For the majority of them, there was a past forgotten, a future avoided and the present numbed with drugs. In fact drugs were often the cause of them becoming sex slaves desperate to maintain their drug habits. A few of the women sensed that Mai was somehow different to them, but most attempted to be supportive and wished her good luck.

Mai had some food brought in before commencing work that night. She had told Richard that she wouldn't be home until the morning and he remained silent, eventually kissing her on her cheek. She strolled around the brothel, briefly introducing herself to many of the women who appeared supportive of her and wished her good luck, even the few who had initially seemed envious of her. A few of the older workers reassured her that in the brothel she would not feel a victim, but rather would find that she was the one in charge. She was not sure that she could really believe this. Some of the other women as well as the madam, told her that if a client became threatening, each room had a buzzer that she could press to get help, which came in the form of a massive man mountain by the name of Mike.

For the first two weeks, Mai attempted to detach herself from what her body was being subjected to, but this was not fully successful and there were times when waves of nausea would hit her. But gradually she developed the knack of being "Mimi" rather than Mai, whilst she was being groped and penetrated, at times submerged under layers of fat piled up in men who rarely washed and some who did not see her as a human being. She had given up on religion years ago, but couldn't resist thinking ironically how she had been taught at a young age that humans were created in God's image, which encouraged her to ask some invisible teacher as to which image that was.

Mai continued to accept unprotected sex in case the prey she was attempting to snare turned up unexpectedly, demanding someone who would have sex without a condom. She worked for five nights a week, including the weekends and took Monday and Tuesday night off, feeling that this improved her chance of enticing the policeman to have sex with her. It troubled her that she had not seen her target for the two weeks she had worked there.

Not for the first time she queried in her own mind why the women there were called "girls", whilst their customers were referred to as "men". To Mai, it seemed just another way of diminishing the value of women. How language dealt with women had often puzzled and troubled her, and she noted that in the brothel and in the outside world, many swear words originated from the terms used to describe female genitalia and lovemaking.

When customers entered the brothel, the women were expected to line up so that customers could choose, which Mai felt was demeaning, as if they were in a cattle yard. Another option for the customers was to indicate to the madam what they were looking for, and she then directed them to the girl she felt would be suitable.

The first night Mai worked, she was picked out by a fat unkempt man who looked to be in his forties. He paid for an hour with Mai for which she charged him $200 that had to be paid up front. She instructed him to have a shower, which was encouraged in the brothel but not always adhered to, and she showered separately, which he was not happy about. Some of the women working in the brothel had advised her that she could delay things by stretching out the showering time for herself. When she re-entered the room, she found her client standing naked, hairy and potbellied and suddenly rushing towards her. She told him to wait until they were both in bed where she found his hands excitedly groping her body. She tried to engage him in some conversation about what he did for work, to which he responded irritably, telling her that he didn't pay good money to chat. She knocked back his demand of a blow job, so without delay he entered her and came almost immediately.

From the beginning of working in the brothel, Mai attempted to numb her body and mind, but found memories of being molested in the refugee camp piercing her defences and forcing their way in. Over the coming days there were occasions where she was more successful in detaching herself, but there were other times when painful images from the refugee camp, images of what she imagined her sister had experienced also, and thoughts of how her parents would react to finding out that both their daughters had turned to prostitution, attacked her mercilessly.

Friday, 12 October 1990
3.10 p.m.

'He's an important officer … name's Brett. He wants to see you tonight,' said the madam.

Somehow, all Mai's pain had suddenly became worthwhile.

At first Mai was puzzled how he could possibly know about her, but finally concluded that the madam must have offered her as someone new who was willing to have unprotected sex. It had taken "Mimi" three weeks to land her trophy.

Mai told the madam that she would be available but felt she should go home in the meantime and rest that afternoon as she had a migraine. She had decided on this strategy previously so it would reduce the risk of contaminating the vaginal sample by having sex with a number of men as well as the policeman.

When Mai arrived home, she rang Dr Wright to alert him that she would be sleeping with "the man", the policeman Maloney that night, and said she would tell him soon after it happened. It all sounded so calm, organised and clinical, but she was aware that her body was betraying the calm she was attempting to project, as the tautness of her body, the slight tremor of her hands and the dew of sweat on her skin revealed a mixture of fear and anxiety coursing through her body. She didn't know how to fill in the hours before returning to work and knew that sleep would escape her. In fact she was scared to go to sleep because of the nightmares that could occur.

Finally she settled on taking a mild sedative, which she had used sparingly to help her cope with working in the brothel. She then turned on the TV as a background noise. Here she was about to get the prize she had really wanted, but at the same time revolted her. This was the toxic mix she experienced that evening.

1.01 a.m.

Mai had taken another sedative one hour before going to the brothel for her appointment with Maloney, but it failed to restrain the heavy sound of panic as she waited for her client. Soon after, the madam pointed her out to a heavily built man that she could barely look at, and she heard him ordering her to follow him, rather than the other way around.

He had roughly taken control, chosen the room that she followed him into and told her to strip. Impatient with the speed of her undressing, he yanked her bra which she had just undone and threw it onto the floor, and then ripped her underpants from her body.

Various phases of her life from the past and the present competed with each other for space in her emotions and thoughts.

Roughly, he shoved her onto the bed and stood above her, forcing her mouth to give entry to his penis, and then aggressively moved her head up and down whilst he stayed inside her. He pulled out before coming, and let his full weight fall onto her, forcing yet another entrance into her body. Mai made herself respond as best she could, as this was the moment she had planned, determined that his orgasm would provide the sample she had traded her humiliation for.

He seemed able to delay coming until twenty minutes later when she felt his body arch, and his breath exhale, as he punctuated his orgasm with a loud grunt, whilst she hugged him to her body in case he had wanted to withdraw too soon. Without any exchange of words, he rolled off her, dressed rapidly and left.

Mai dressed, wiped the moistness from her eyes and waited several minutes in case Maloney had loitered, and then dashed to the phone to call Dr Andrew Wright as they had arranged. The word "now" was all that needed to be said before hanging up.

She waited for Dr Wright outside, trying not to think of either the past or the future, but only what she needed to do now.

CHAPTER TWENTY-FOUR

Saturday 13 October 1990
2.15 a.m

The jarring scream of Andrew's phone pierced the fog of his sleep. Groggily he fumbled for the clock on his bedside table. Struggling to emerge from the vapours of his deep sleep, he stumbled out of bed into the privacy of the bathroom, clutching the phone to his face.

'Yes?' he whispered.

He heard a soft, just audible voice carrying a message that was anything but soft. 'Now.'

'Now,' Andrew repeated the word to himself.

'Now,' he repeated once more as if fearful to let it go.

His body urged him to lie down again, but his mind registered the phone signal and he was now wide-awake.

'Now.'

He felt the surge of adrenaline stretching his body's soft tissues and nerves and was grateful that in spite of the hurt created by having to sleep in separate bedrooms, it had enabled him to receive the call without waking Karen. Now – only a single word, but loaded with meaning, as this was the signal that he and Mai had agreed on to warn him that she had just finished having sex with "the man". Neither Mai nor Andrew could bear to give him a name, not wanting to humanise someone they viewed as less than human.

Mai and Andrew had agreed that following her signal he would call the doctor that he had previously briefed and organised for this moment.

Dr John Edwards was someone Andrew had known for many years, in fact, since the time John commenced training to be a doctor, working as a junior resident at Fairly Hospital under the partial supervision of Andrew. Andrew had respected John even back then, viewing him as a socially minded, intelligent young man, and their mutual respect and friendship continued over the following years. John had gone on to specialise in Obstetrics and Gynaecology, and when approached recently by Andrew, he had agreed to cooperate with the plan that Andrew described in detail.

John reassured Andrew that he would be available to examine Mai no matter what time he was contacted. He promised that if the call came during patient consultation hours, he would ask one of his colleagues to take over for him in examining the patient he was seeing, whilst he would make himself available to examine Mai. After the gynaecological examination was completed, Andrew planned to take the vaginal samples and personally courier them over to the Government Forensic Pathology office, where he would be met by the pathologist after Andrew alerted him to their imminent arrival.

Andrew had previously briefed the public prosecutor and planned to leave a message for him the following morning. It had taken all of Andrew's persuasive skills to obtain the cooperation of the prosecutor and pathologist as the prosecutor was concerned about becoming involved with a case that he might not win, and the pathologist could visualise a scenario where his work and private life might be disrupted by hordes of journalists, publicity and being called to give evidence. He was also worried that he might be accused of being part of a set up.

As Andrew quickly dressed, preparing himself to drive rapidly to the brothel where he had arranged to pick up Mai, his mind kept reviewing the sequence of events and whether there was something vital to his plan that he might have forgotten to do. He had almost finished dressing in the small empty bedroom down the corridor when suddenly, like a stunned rabbit caught in the headlights, he faced Karen, silent and grim, with her intense stare cauterising the air between them. The bright lights of the room and corridor were now exposing him fully, as if naked. He addressed the question that she had not yet vocalised – 'It's just a patient. A very anxious lady, she needs support,' he explained in staccato fashion. There were still no sounds emerging from Karen.

The silence made Andrew feel even more pressured, forcing him to speak.

'That's why I gave her my private number, on the understanding that if she was at the end of her tether and felt suicidal, she could call me at any time. I'm sorry. I should have warned you it could happen.'

'Do you have to go out then?'

A caring question delivered in an uncaring tone. But then, this was the tone that he had been encountering more and more since confiding in Karen about the sting operation he was setting up. The shards of broken glass had seemingly severed a lot of the warmth in their relationship.

'I'm afraid so, but it shouldn't be too long. I'll just make sure that she will be okay until tomorrow morning when I see her for a longer session. If it turns out to be worse than I think, I'll have to arrange for her to be hospitalised tonight. If that happens, I'll let you know.'

The last few words were probably not heard by Karen who had already turned on her heel and was heading for bed. Andrew finished dressing in the spare bedroom and then went to the kitchen and quickly poured himself an orange juice before heading to the garage.

3.02 a.m.

It was still dark and there were few cars on the road, so the drive to the brothel took only about eighteen minutes, driving rapidly but not to the extent that he risked being pulled up by the police for speeding. As he drove, rather than experiencing a sense of victory which would have been premature, he began to think and imagine what Mai must have endured in the few weeks since he formulated the plan and obtained her acceptance of it. Before, when he reviewed the plan and sequence of events, it had all felt so clinical and detached, but he realised he could not avoid acknowledging her pain any longer. How many men had she been obliged to service during that time? All types of men groping, searching, humiliating and invading her body

Arriving at the brothel, or rather, around the corner from it, Andrew saw the slight figure of Mai largely hidden by darkness. He stopped and without a word being spoken, she got into his car. He sensed that she was reluctant to talk at this stage and he hoped that his eyes and face would communicate the support he wanted to offer her. After Dr Edwards examined Mai and took the samples, Andrew drove her home, arranging to see her first thing that morning at his rooms. He then couriered the samples to the pathology office, before heading home for two hours of troubled sleep prior to consulting at his medical rooms. Andrew was aware that there would be no immediate answer and all he and Mai could do was to sit it out as best they could.

Sunday, 14 October 1990
9.29 a.m.

They sat facing each other in Andrew's office, neither saying a word – he couldn't say for how long. He had a strong urge to go over to Mai, pull her slight frame to him and hug her, comfort her as best he could, but he knew he shouldn't, and he didn't.

Being a Sunday, the building was unoccupied except for Andrew and Mai. They had planned for this day, whenever it fell, and for what hopefully would follow in court. Somehow, all the planning couldn't remove the sense of isolation and emptiness that he felt, and he suspected Mai did as well. Whatever the outcome, and obviously there was no guarantee that Maloney would be charged and found guilty, Andrew felt they had at least succeeded in creating a scenario that would draw media attention – lots of it.

Even if he escaped conviction, Maloney could not escape severe damage to his reputation as the public focused on his evil acts, repeatedly publicised in the media. That was Andrew's fervent hope.

So, conviction or not, he envisaged Maloney would pay a price, with damage to his career and to himself personally. But what would happen to their own lives – his, Karen's, their children, and Mai and her family?

Andrew was aware that he had developed strong feelings of caring for Mai. If he was honest with himself, he also felt physically attracted to her. But was this love, or more likely, was it two wounded people clinging to each other, licking each other's wounds? But he didn't live in a vacuum and Karen was the mother of his children. He had loved her intensely when they married, no doubt about that. Even though the flame of this love might be flickering, it had not blown out completely. Things never remained the same. Could his relationship with Karen be rekindled to what it was before? Possibly not, but there was probably enough still there that was worth fighting for. Like a DVD that he replayed and then put on fast forward, covering so much in so little time, Andrew told himself that the future was not his decision alone. What guarantee did he have that Karen would want him back? And Mai, what gave him the right to imagine that she would be compliant with any decision he arrived at? For God's sake, wasn't she living with a partner at the moment?!

So they sat in silence, gazing at each other – two wounded people who had forgotten how to celebrate.

CHAPTER TWENTY-FIVE

Monday, 15 October 1990

In a robotic fashion that had become increasingly familiar to him, Andrew again forced himself to go to work. It was two days since Mai had sex with Maloney and Andrew felt like he was treading water, knowing there would not be any immediate answers. He and Mai, especially Mai, had done everything possible to make his plan work and now they would have to wait. He had always prided himself on his ability to cope, and felt weak in floundering at this stage.

Karen was aware that Andrew had come home in the early hours of the morning, but did not allow herself to think about where he might have been nor let herself ask him directly. These days she did not trust his answers and knew they should see a therapist together, but still did not feel ready to do this. They were two strangers continuing to share the same house.

By late afternoon, Karen sat herself down and tried to read a magazine but found it difficult to concentrate. Andrew had mumbled that he would not be coming home to dinner as he had a meeting and would probably come home quite late. There was quite a deal of noise in the house as her two boys had invited friends over and it felt as if they were occupying the whole house, apart from the couch that she was on. She had not discussed the difficulties that she and Andrew were experiencing nor had the boys questioned her about it, although she was certain they were aware that things were not right. In the past she would have enjoyed the happy noise and laughter that the boys and their friends were making, but today it grated on her nerves like a fingernail dragged across a blackboard.

Karen decided to take herself out of the house and walked to the nearby park where she sat alone on a bench overlooking a small lake. Though rugged up with an overcoat and a scarf, she still shivered, and knew that she needed to make important decisions about her life and where she wanted it to go, but continued to feel that she wasn't ready to do so. That's the thing about decisions, she thought bitterly to herself, you then have to carry them out. She felt it was bizarre the areas that her mind was revisiting these days. There were thoughts coming from all directions into her mind and she allowed them to take her hand and carry her back in time. She knew that she didn't believe in God and hadn't for many years, and reflected that religion had not been a big feature of her parents' lives either – well, certainly not for her father. She felt her mother had always threatened to believe in God and had commenced going to church after Karen left home. Her father had come from a non-observant Jewish background, whilst the mother came from a Presbyterian family who were largely non-observant as well. Karen had been sent to an Anglican school where she recalled attending religious instruction classes just because everyone else did.

Her memories drifted back to the time she met Andrew and she had no doubt that she experienced love and passion back then – but now, now she was unsure about what kept her in this marriage. She thought there were still love somewhere in the background, whatever love was, but wondered if it was mainly loyalty that held her there. *Did he deserve loyalty?* she silently asked herself. She recalled that when they were about to marry, Andrew had made it clear that even though he was non-observant it was still important to him that she convert to Judaism before the marriage. At the time she had some difficulty in understanding why, matched by his inability to explain, but she had no doubt at the time that his wish for it to happen was very strong. In time, she realised that part of it seemed to be for his parents and for maintaining tradition, and that a major factor was his determination that in spite of Hitler's genocidal intent, the Jewish race would continue to exist.

Karen recalled how back then she didn't mind converting for Andrew sake, and gradually tried to educate herself and understand how traditions that went back centuries were important to him. He had explained to her at the time that if her mother had been Jewish, then Karen would have automatically been classed as Jewish, because with a mother, there was no doubt whose child it was, whilst with a father, it was not as clear whether it was his progeny or not. So she became a Jewish wife and the boys had Bar Mitzvahs, not that long ago. At first her own family were surprised and some of them scoffed at her decision, but it didn't trouble her. She thought back to the many discussions that she and Andrew had, pondering what it meant to be a Jew. Was it a religion or was it a race or could it be both?

They sent their children to a Jewish school and gradually Karen felt accepted by the wider Jewish community, though she did sense that some of them doubted her Jewishness. That didn't trouble her, but what did upset her was the fact that she finished a degree in law and then put her career on hold to have a family, and never returned to the career.

As the children grew up, she had toyed with the idea of returning to Law or another career, but felt too much time had elapsed, so she ended up persisting with being a home person and supporting Andrew's career. From time to time, doubts would spring up as to the wisdom of putting her career aside and she recalled how she bristled when people asked her what she did, and after her reply, she noticed the questioner losing interest in her, having heard that she only worked at home. Even now, thinking back, she felt herself being irritated by those reactions, as it made her feel as if she was a non-person, even though Andrew told her repeatedly that her career at home was the glue that kept the fabric of their family life together. In recent years it became harder for Karen to see herself as a binding force or glue holding the family together. As the years went by, her capacity to glue and be a cohesive force in the family had gradually evaporated—or maybe it was a myth to start with. Maybe, just maybe, it took many family members working together to create that glue.

She recalled that whilst she regretted the loss of her career and almost grieved for it, at the same time Andrew had confessed to her years ago, that he envied her time with the children, feeling that it was time he was missing out on. Karen tended to believe that people often hanker for what they don't have, but rarely take the opportunity of acquiring it by giving up what they possess. She wondered with a tinge of sadness whether she had accommodated Andrew's needs to an excessive degree and given away some of her identity and aspirations in the process. Yet she had been comfortable doing this until recently, when she became aware of Andrew's affair with a patient. She had begun wondering if she was still married to the same man. Sure, everyone changes with time, but his differences appeared corrosive, where he had evolved into a person consumed by anger and a thirst for revenge. The tenderness and trust in their relationship appeared to be lost, and she knew she didn't want this life but could not be clear what alternative life to aim for. *Maybe it was time to attempt shaping events rather than being the passive recipient of what came her way.* Her thoughts created a chill in the air around her and caused her to shiver.

On the spur of the moment, Karen decided to check if some of her girlfriends were free, and if so, to go out with them. She felt a glow of anticipation, like a schoolgirl buoyed by the knowledge that friends seek her company, and happily arranged with two girlfriends to go to the movies that evening.

6.30 p.m.

Andrew walked through the front door and loosened his necktie. As he placed his car keys on the kitchen bench, he noticed a white piece of paper:

> *Gone to the movies with friends.*
> *-K.*

Andrew paused for moment, before throwing the note in the bin. He made himself a sandwich and sat in the lounge nursing a beer.

The TV was on in the background but he could not have told you what he was watching because he wasn't. It just served the purpose of background.

Like Karen, his thoughts wandered all over the place mainly remembering times gone by. He recalled that for many years of the marriage they had both enjoyed the intimacy of sex with each other – at least it felt that way to him. He recalled many of his friends grumbling about their sex lives becoming insignificant in their marriages, and occasionally these complaints raised doubts in his own mind as to whether Karen might be faking having an orgasm to protect him from feeling that he had failed. However, he had always reassured himself that she would not behave in that way as she was honest to a fault.

Lately Andrew had taken to thinking about the many areas that had altered in his life over the years. There was a time when he had many friends and socialised regularly, both individually and as a couple. There was a time when he went out regularly with Karen and spent considerable time with his two sons. There was a time when he followed his sporting interests and played golf and tennis and swam, as well as pursuing his interest in photography, music and literature. Somehow, all those times had been swallowed up over the years as he became more and more immersed in his work, and he felt a marked sense of sadness over losing a large part of his past life.

Andrew recalled a particular episode about seven years ago where a close friend of his at the time, Peter, also a psychiatrist, was describing the boredom of his sex life with his wife Romy. At the time Andrew had counted his blessings, feeling that his own marriage and relationship was so much more successful than many of his friends. Peter described to Andrew how Romy no longer made any pretence of being interested or involved in having sex with him. He lamented that during sex he would lie on top gazing at the featureless white sheets, whilst beneath him Romy would be looking over his shoulder watching a TV program that was playing in their bedroom. Andrew remembered that he squirmed on hearing this, wishing that Peter was not divulging so many details. Peter had gone on to say that not surprisingly his own interest in sex had waned and he had become increasingly impotent, creating a problem for Peter and relief for Romy. At first Peter attempted to console himself with the thought that there was more to their relationship than sex, but gradually it stopped consoling him and he started facing the fact that the poor sex was eroding the remainder of their relationship. Romy had rejected the idea of any counselling and Peter confided that he had begun wondering whether he should obtain sex outside of the marriage to supplement it, but feared that would be the beginning of a downward spiral.

Andrew wondered why he had gone back to that specific interaction when there were so many other issues in his life at present. Possibly his friend's relationship, that had appeared so different to his own at the time, was now creating a sense of familiarity. He recalled that he and Peter had discussed that both of Romy's parents had died within a couple of months of each other and that possibly Romy was showing evidence of some mild depression. Romy's relationship with her parents had been poor for many years and now that they had died, she had to face the fact that it could never improve. He remembered Peter telling him that he was concerned how Romy was starting to question the point of life and whether we are just born and eventually die, leaving no meaningful legacy behind.

Andrew felt uncomfortable with the realisation that a scenario that had appeared so very foreign to his own at the time, was now taking on aspects that he could begin recognising in his own marriage. He downed his fifth glass of beer, aware that he was continuing to drink excessively, and decided that he would put himself to bed rather than wait for Karen to come home.

CHAPTER TWENTY-SIX

Friday, 19 October 1990
7.30 p.m.

Brett rang the brothel where he had slept with Mimi several nights ago. He was puzzled to hear that she no longer worked there and that no one seemed to know where she had gone or why she had stopped working. This uncertainty festered as he became more and more troubled by the situation, which didn't ring true to him. When he thought about it, Mimi had appeared from nowhere and had now returned there. Something felt very wrong, and the major part of Brett's life had been lived responding to and dealing with suspicion. It tainted the air he breathed and the water he drank. He rarely attributed unusual events to chance.

Brett rang his partner Vladimir and asked him if he knew anything more about Mimi, and was told he had not heard from her, but after a pause, corrected this, saying she had in fact left a note stating that she wouldn't return, without giving a reason. This had become a suspicion that Brett couldn't turn his back on, and he began asking around, mainly talking to many of the girls who worked in the brothel. Having learnt nothing more, he made some discreet enquiries from people he knew in the Victorian Vice Squad. There appeared to be a vacuum of information, Brett decided, becoming increasingly irritable, and a sense of threat started to pervade his thoughts. He was not going to let this go and decided some of the girls in the brothel must know more, but weren't sharing the information.

Feeling like a wound up spring, he weighed up the best approach and chose to target Tess, having been told she was someone Mimi had befriended during her brief stint working. He decided to combine pleasure with work and booked a time with Tess. He'd had sex with her in the past and thought she was a bit like a cow, appearing totally passive and submissive, not very bright, but with a good body.

It was about 11 p.m. when he entered her room, pleased to note her wide-eyed fear and slight trembling of her hands. This aroused him, and he demanded unprotected sex from her, as he had done in the past. Though Tess was familiar with his demands, with a stuttering voice she still attempted to stand her ground, stating that she preferred he wear a condom, as if this slight rebellion might alter the balance of power. Brett's angry glare, and his demand that she "get on with it'", caused her meagre protest to fade as she rapidly complied with his demand.

He was deliberately rough with her, slapping her face and flipping her over, before painfully entering her unprotected body. She whimpered as he pounded away, verbally abusing her at times and warning that he needed to know everything about Mimi, and unless she levelled with him, she would pay for it big time. As her fear escalated, distorting her features and speech, Brett became more and more aroused and entered her one more time. As he sat astride her, he again demanded that she tell him everything.

Tess recalled hearing of girls who had disappeared in the past, and remembered rumours that they had been killed or tortured. Her voice stumbling with fear, she told him that Mimi was in fact the sister of Candy, and he didn't need reminding who Candy was or had been, but she denied knowing why Mimi had come to work at the same brothel that had once housed her sister.

Several punches to her abdomen doubled Tess over, clearing her memory, and between sobs she confessed that she didn't know why Mimi had chosen to work at the brothel, but she had heard that Mimi wanted to have sex with the detective and was angry at how he had treated her sister Candy. She pleaded that he let her go as there was nothing more that she could tell him. A further slap to the face and

Brett let her go with the warning that if he found out she had known more without telling him, then she would pay for it. She mumbled that she had forgotten to mention that Mimi was a patient of Dr Wright. Brett's antennae went up, as he had been in the game long enough to realise that he was possibly being set up; there were too many coincidences, far more than could be explained by chance alone.

Monday, 21 October 1990
9.05 a.m.

Brett decided to make some enquiries and obtained the names of the two policemen who had been involved in taking forensic samples of Candy to the storage area at the coroner's court. He spoke to the senior of the two and was told that the samples were duds, and that as the senior in charge, he had arranged for his junior Dick Redford to dispose of them. After Brett stormed off, the senior rang Dick telling him that Brett wanted to meet with him. Dick in turn told Mai what had eventuated and together they formulated what he would tell Brett when they met later that day. They decided it would be best to lie and have Brett believe the samples no longer existed.

6.52 p.m.

Dick met with Brett in the back room of the local pub, and found him to be belligerent and sullen. The meeting lasted close to 15 minutes, with uncomfortably long periods of silence until Brett abruptly terminated the meeting and exited the room without any greeting or comment. Richard left very soon after, unconvinced that Brett had accepted his story and increasingly suspecting that he hadn't.

Following the coronial hearing, Brett had been livid at being made to look so inept in court. Meeting later with Deborah calmed him somewhat, as she told him this had been the first round, and they needed to keep their ammunition dry for the rounds to follow. He sensed however that her attitude towards him had dampened, and suspected it might be partly related to criticism of his performance in court. In time he became increasingly aware that she no longer saw him as important for her future plans. What particularly troubled Brett was Dr Wright's barrister suggesting Brett may have doctored the evidence. *Doctored was just the word,* he had thought sarcastically at the time, but Deborah was right, there would be other opportunities to make Wright's opinions and words suspect and not to be taken seriously. For the moment he felt he had to live with the knowledge that the court case might have damaged his career prospects.

At the time he and Deborah had attempted to set Dr Wright up, it had not been personal but merely a way of protecting their interests. The humiliation he experienced on cross-examination by Wright's barrister changed all that and he looked forward to a future time when he would make that prick Wright pay. As he mulled over what Tess had revealed, he knew the time of reckoning might not be far away.

CHAPTER TWENTY-SEVEN

Thursday, 25 October 1990

Andrew raised the Bible in his right hand and swore to tell the truth and nothing but the truth. His body was tingling and he felt tense but determined. He had arranged for media contacts in the meantime splashing Detective Brett Maloney's name across many headlines. Whilst the journalists were cautious, given that legal proceedings had still not been finalised, they were able to mention that the detective was standing trial on charges of corruption, including illegal drugs, profiteering from prostitution and failure to render medical aid to Candy as she was dying.

Now Andrew stood in the witness box as the defence counsel, Kevin McCarthy approached. He felt nervous, but this trial was what he had wanted for a long time.

'So Mr Wright – no, it's Dr Wright, isn't it?' the defence enquired. 'But as a medical doctor, how is it that you had one of your female patients prostitute herself to gather evidence against my client? Would you consider that ethical? Is it legal?'

'I believe it to be so,' Andrew answered in clipped tones.

'You believe it to be so – I wonder how the College of Psychiatrists would feel about that?' McCarthy enquired. 'You would do anything to hurt my client, wouldn't you? Why didn't you get the police to investigate this matter – it's their job, isn't it?'

'No, that's not so,' Andrew responded. 'This man is a policeman himself and that will complicate any investigation by police. I was told what happened by a patient of mine who was the sister of the deceased.

I don't believe the police are always thorough in investigating other police members.'

'So psychiatrists are more thorough in investigating these matters, is that what you're saying,' McCarthy confronted, with a statement rather than a query. 'And what you know is second hand, isn't it?' McCarthy stated, sounding a trifle more belligerent than he had been before. 'Has anyone who was directly involved at the time your patient's sister died spoken directly to you?'

'The sister of the deceased is a patient of mine, as you know. Her work name at the brothel was Mimi and her real name is Mai. I have always found her to be totally reliable.'

'I must remind you that's all second hand information, isn't it, Dr Wright? You saw nothing and heard nothing directly from the deceased prior to her death, did you?' In the absence of a response, the defence council responded testily. 'Please answer the question, Doctor Wright.'

'I can prove Detective Maloney had sex with Candy the night she died, and some of the other workers at the brothel have told my patient Mai about his giving drugs to Candy and not getting any help for her when she was dying,' Andrew responded, keeping a cap on his smouldering anger.

'Inspector Maloney doesn't deny having sex with Candy, but he does deny giving her drugs or being there when she was dying. We believe your accusations are vindictive. We may find that the Victorian Medical Board will have issues in the future with how you encouraged your patient to work in a brothel. It's not my area, but how do you believe it will impact on her ability to relate with partners, with friends and with immediate family?'

Andrew woke in a sweat, the nightmare having been so real.

He was experiencing nightmares most nights now, especially since things had deteriorated in his marriage and for a little while Karen had been pressing him to consider living apart. He had even made some half-hearted enquiries about properties he could rent, but hated the idea of making such a break from his family. He felt like he was already living alone, but did not want to translate this into reality. As long as Andrew stuck to his plan of using Mai to get back at Maloney, Karen believed he should move out, giving her space to evaluate things, including their marriage. She was not prepared to be a witness on a daily basis to Andrew acting in a manner that she considered evil.

Having been woken initially by the nightmare and then kept awake by the alarm that he had set, Andrew forced himself to get up. He had already cancelled his patients for the day, as he had an appointment at 11 a.m. with the public prosecutor's office to discuss the evidence he had accumulated and what action might be taken. After he showered, he put on his bathrobe and went into the kitchenette to make breakfast. As the hot water for his coffee boiled he went to the front door to collect the day's newspaper. There was no paper to be seen, but in its place sat the horror of a dog's head with teeth bared obscenely, greeting him. He felt himself shaking and couldn't believe the B grade movie that was playing out in his life. He picked up a note that had been taped to the doorstep and saw that it had been typed and had no signature attached. It felt surreal as he read to himself:

> We know where you are, we know where your wife and kids are. Stop causing trouble if you know what's best for you.

Suddenly there was no demarcation between the nightmares and what was happening in his daily life. Was there anyone he could talk to or trust enough to discuss the horror he was living in? He felt very alone and vulnerable. He thanked the god he no longer believed in that Karen and the boys were still asleep, and he rushed to bury the obscenity that had greeted him. Eventually he would have to tell his family about it, but that was not as bad as the visual image that confronted him.

Almost on automatic pilot, he dressed and had a cursory breakfast. He was about to leave the apartment and head to the garage where his car was parked, when the phone rang. It was Mai, wanting an urgent meeting with him as far as he could gather, because her sobbing drowned a lot of her words. He decided to try and move his appointment with the prosecutor's office to next morning if possible, as the quagmire of recent events made it even harder to plan a course of action, and he was able to secure an 11 a.m. time for the next day. He needed to be clear about what was happening with Mai as well as sorting out how best to cope with the threats he had received.

2 p.m.

Andrew sat in his car in the nearby train station car park where he had arranged to meet Mai who arrived half an hour later, somewhat dishevelled and flushed. She tearfully described to Andrew a threatening letter that she had found on her doorstep that morning.

The typed note warned her to forget everything or she would meet up with her sister, and also threatened her parents. She told Andrew her parents had suffered enough, and she was no longer prepared to be part of any legal action against Detective Maloney. She described that since she had worked at the brothel, Dick had been polite to her, but somewhat distant and they no longer had any sexual relationship. All the passion in their relationship had evaporated. When the threatening letter arrived, Dick pressed her strongly to give up on the plan to prosecute Maloney. He was now convinced that Brett hadn't believed the story he told him about the forensic samples taken from her sister, and he warned Mai that even with his help, it would be impossible to totally protect her parents from the threat that had been made. Mai found herself increasingly fearful that she risked losing her parents and her relationship with Dick, and was not prepared to take that risk.

Like dark storm clouds breaking open, her words tumbled out interspersed with sobs, as she described receiving a call from Tammy, a brothel girl she had come to know whilst working there. Tammy warned her that Tess, who also worked at the brothel, had blown the whistle out of fear, showing signs that she'd spoken under duress, and had told Detective Maloney that the Mimi he had slept with, was in fact Candy's sister, Mai. On hearing this, she felt shattered and vulnerable, and Richard insisted the plan had become too dangerous for her to continue being involved. He convinced her that if she continued with Dr Wright's plan, it would jeopardise every important thing in her life, including their relationship. Mai had always been aware that if she proceeded with Dr Wright's plan, it would feel devastating to her parents to know both their daughters had been involved with prostitution, but she was prepared to deal with this, believing that if the plan succeeded, her parents would eventually forgive her. But now, the whole thing had been blown out of the water and everything dear to her felt exposed and at risk.

CHAPTER TWENTY-EIGHT

Sunday, 28 October 1990

Andrew felt devastated on hearing the developments Mai described. He doubted that Mai would consider leaving Richard – nor should she, he thought in a moment of clarity. Given the intensity of her feelings, there was no way he would attempt trying to alter her mind in a bid to encourage her sticking with the plan he had devised. Realistically, he couldn't guarantee her safety nor that of her parents, and he now felt he had to respect her wish to avoid damaging her relationship with Richard any further.

It was as if Andrew and Mai had both stepped back and taken stock, realising the damage that could eventuate if they continued as before. She had previously been willing to risk her parent's reaction if working as a prostitute enabled her to avenge what happened to her sister. However, the risk had dramatically increased now, and threatened not only her parent's feelings but also their lives. Whilst Andrew understood and respected Mai's decision, he couldn't avoid feeling crushed by the thought that once again that rogue cop Maloney had won out.

Andrew had just moved out the day before into a short term, one bedroom rental apartment, and had not yet told Karen or the boys about the threats that were being made. Living away from his wife and children would protect them far more than if he was at home. The visit with the prosecutor had been set up for 11 a.m. next day with the intention of presenting the evidence that had been collected about Maloney and Hahn. It all seemed pointless now, and he wasn't sure what he could say to the prosecutor when they met.

There he was, stranded and totally on his own without Karen or the children, crushed by his failure and the price it had extracted, and no longer having the support of Mai. Though devastated by his sense of failure and feeling very alone, pride still took hold and he was relieved there was no one to witness his flood of tears overwhelming his controls. Mai had left after telling Andrew she could no longer be part of his plan, and he began to crave having his family around him to help fill the void that had started to engulf him. like a bottomless pit.

He started his car and drove rapidly from memory, and was fortunate to have survived the trip without incident. Just prior to starting the car, he jotted down in his small notebook, the events that had occurred and the options open to him. It was not that he was likely to forget these points, but it had been a pattern developed since a young age. Most times he never checked again what he had written, but the obsessive ritual of doing it reduced his anxiety about the possibility of forgetting. For those who didn't have this compulsive pattern of behaviour, it was difficult to understand, but for Andrew it felt that in some magical way the act of writing imprinted the facts in his memory bank, and he felt calmer for doing it. As he drove, his vision was blurred by the tears that kept flowing and his concentration was minimal. Looking back later he realised he shouldn't have driven at that time.

6.03 p.m.

Andrew arrived at Karen's home, which used to be his home, or rather, a home that they both shared, and rang the doorbell. As if she had been waiting on the other side of the door, it promptly opened and the minimal restraint he had was lost as he sobbed uncontrollably with his body heaving. Without saying a word, Karen held him tightly to her chest. He couldn't say how long she held him, but it felt like it was for hours, as if comforting a newborn child. Finally he was able to get the words out, describing how he had failed.

Gently she consoled him, telling him that to cease doing evil is a success not a failure. Karen gave him a blanket, draping it over his shoulders, and it felt to Andrew like the first caring gesture she'd demonstrated towards him for a long time. As he lay back on the couch Karen had led him to, her support gave him hope there could be more to come in the future. He was aware his sons were in the house when he arrived, but they kept out of sight, and Andrew imagined they were mature enough to give their parents some space to interact, and hopefully start sorting things out..

Karen explained that Andrew could visit her and the boys regularly, and eat with them, but she felt it would be wise for him not to move back in just yet. She explained that she wanted to work with him on repairing the damage to their relationship and that they should consider joint counselling, where they would see a counsellor together. Whether they could repair their relationship sufficiently to make a go of it, remained to be seen, she felt. She acknowledged that they had both been injured, and gently suggested that it was a time not for blame but rather to face realities and work on them. She believed that somehow this crisis had opened doors that had remained closed for far too long.

About an hour later, Andrew woke and again was hugged by Karen. As he showered and dressed he somehow felt buoyant, as if his world was starting to make sense.

Monday, 29 October 1990
11 a.m.

Andrew sat facing Assistant Prosecutor Wilson.

'I can't go on with the accusations and evidence against Maloney,' he explained in a fractured voice. He was startled by how readily his decision appeared to be accepted without question. Reflecting on it later, it felt to Andrew that possibly the prosecutor's office had hoped for this outcome all along.

'That's fine, but don't believe that Maloney gets off scot-free,'

Wilson said in his professional soothing voice. 'He's now on our radar and we'll go over him with a fine toothcomb. We don't need people like him in the force.'

Andrew had not been to work for close to a week now and intended resuming at the beginning of next week. It was time he got back to helping others and in the process, himself.

Over the days that followed Andrew threw himself into his work, commencing at 7:30 a.m. and going home at 8 p.m. After a couple of weeks he forced himself to stand back and examine how he was behaving. He drew the blinds of his mind attempting to be brutally honest with himself. He confronted the question of whether he was using work to hide behind. He wasn't certain but suspected that he might be, and in fact that he had done this for many years in the past. He realised that if he was totally honest with himself whilst helping people in his work he was also nourished by their gratitude and praise. So what else was there in his life, he queried, taking on the role of consultant psychiatrist and patient in an alternating manner.

Sadly, he realised that outside of work his life had progressively shrunk over the years. By the time he'd get home the children were either in bed or getting ready for sleep, and as they got older his arrival barely caused a flicker as they continued with their own activities and their own friends. He generally felt too drained to offer anything to Karen and at times felt irritable if she attempted to tell him about her day. All he sought was the opportunity to vegetate in front of the television set without having to talk. He wondered why Karen had put up with it for so long. Had she given up on him or was she being supportive by drawing back? It pained him to face the fact that he had become a stranger in his own house and that it was his own doing that brought it about. Still Karen had remained loyal and made allowances as if he was a child.

At the same time he had minimal contact with friends unless they initiated it or Karen organised something. He still attended clinical meetings with his peer group and probably enjoyed those because he felt he had something to contribute and was good at his work.

Andrew had been aware for a long time that isolation was one of his major fears.   In addition he was apprehensive about the ageing process and the onset of early dementia. He felt his main attribute over the years had been his intelligence, and if he lost that, he feared he'd become an empty shell, increasingly dependent on others. He realised that if one of his patients presented with a history like this, he would probably conclude they were chronically depressed and hiding from life and in need of therapy. In contrast, as he observed Karen's life over the years, he felt her personality was vibrant and warm. She appeared intelligent , involved with people and enjoying a range of interests and a desire to face life rather than hiding from it.

Whilst shaving in the morning, he continued to see a disturbing image reflected in the mirror. It was his face and yet it wasn't. The rugged features with stubble revealed early signs of ageing starting to creep in and take hold. Fine red spider vessels had begun occupying his cheeks, whilst the loose skin under his eyes was sagging, witness to the ravages of time.   Within, he was aware of memories that he needed to live and grapple with, as well as memories stolen from him and forever lost.

He began to ask himself not only whether Karen would have him back but was he certain he wanted to return. He believed he did though he could not answer for Karen whether she hoped he would return in time. One thing he did know was that a relationship could not be mended from a distance, in the same way nothing worthwhile could be grown without tilling the soil and making it fertile. It was close to a month now since he moved out of home and he had forced himself to keep in regular contact with Karen and the boys. He was still unsure whether they wanted him or mainly felt sorry for him.

Whichever it was, he realised that for his marriage to have a chance to be repaired he and Karen would need to see a counsellor together for a while. As someone in that profession himself, it didn't feel easy to seek help from another therapist, but he had no doubt that was the only chance they had of making it work again. For it had worked once, that he didn't doubt. Even after the initial passion had cooled to some degree there was a mutual caring or whatever love is. He admitted to himself the remnants could be nutured.

It amazed Andrew that with all his training and years of living he still could not really explain what love was. How could a four letter word be that difficult to comprehend? He had read multiple explanations and essays on the question of love, and there was no doubt that it was a word grossly overused. If he believed half of what he read then what he felt in loving Karen ranged from a chemical reaction to a primal need and bonding. It had always fascinated him how these explanations ended up substituting many words for that one four-letter word leaving the reader none the wiser.

Andrew decided that he would put the idea of joint counselling to Karen when they next met face-to-face. At present he was going to the family home two or three times a week for dinner and had accepted and going to a friend's place for dinner tomorrow. They had avoided going to parties lately as neither one of them had discussed openly with friends the fact that they had separated. From time to time he had bumped into friends on his own and had the impression that they knew from whatever source, but felt very uncomfortable bringing it up. He had commenced entertaining the idea that he and Karen needed to speak openly about their separation and felt it would be good for them and also far more comfortable for friends.

As the barriers began to weaken, the kernel of an idea had the freedom to germinate about the possibility of confessing to Karen something that she probably already knew – namely his affair with his patient. He was still uncertain whether this would be wise or would it just be him shifting the pressure on to Karen and appeasing his own feelings of guilt. Rehearsing what he would say if he went on to confess, he decided that he would not attempt to excuse it or shift any blame on to anyone else.   If he did confess, he planned to state that he chose to be seduced, regretted it and had no valid excuse, but could only promise that it would never happen again to the best of his ability. He adjusted his thinking feeling it would be better just to say that it would never happen again.

Friday, 2 November 1990
8 p.m.

Andrew and Karen pulled up outside the Freeds' house, where they had been invited for dinner. This was the first dinner party they had gone to together since the embarrassment at the Goldfines' – a place where he had dominated the evening and made a pork chop of himself. He was determined to make this evening work and was reassured to some degree by the fact that the Freeds were a pleasant, quiet couple and not part of a trendy crowd. Unlike the Goldfines, they had long-term friends rather than intense relationships that lasted for limited periods of time.

Andrew had offered to pick Karen up and drive to the Freeds' home, and was startled to hear her accept, as she had avoided any sign of depending on him for a while now. How long, he couldn't say, but it felt like it went back over a year now, and probably even longer. He warned her that when they were at the Freeds' home, he meant to bring into the open the elephant in the room, namely that they had separated. He explained how he believed their friends already knew and were uncomfortable around them whilst the secret remained, but he reassured Karen that he would only do it if she didn't object. Karen agreed silently, nodding her head.

The Freeds ran a small toy importing business, which was obviously successful, as their Malvern house appeared substantial but tasteful. Karen and Andrew had known Peter and Jenny Freed for many years and enjoyed their company, though only socialising occasionally. As the Wrights entered, it appeared to them that all the other guests had already arrived. As if a fuse had blown, there was sudden silence and discomfort pervading the lounge room where everyone sat. Looking around, it appeared that they knew three of the couples and the fourth couple were introduced to them.

'Don't let us break up the party,' Andrew quipped in an attempt to pierce the silence.

The sound gradually filtered back as Andrew and Karen sat themselves down. The chatter continued until Andrew threw a time bomb into the room.

'I think you guys know that Karen and I have separated for the moment. I can confess here and now and that I see myself being the primary cause of the breakup. I imagine you know I've been accused of doing terrible things to a patient. Anyone who gets the newspaper or listens to the radio would have seen how Karen, myself and the kids have been subjected to years of harassment through the media, and I guess it wouldn't surprise you to know that its taken a toll on all of us, culminating in a court case where the truth finally came out and I was totally exonerated.' Andrew paused and looked around, noting that everyone appeared to be concentrating on what he was saying. 'I'll explain very briefly that from the court proceedings we realised that an attempt had been made to set me up. Now, I guess everyone at times in their lives has thoughts or fantasies about getting even for some perceived act of unfairness.

'With me, I need to admit, it went a bit further – no it actually went a long way further. It became an obsession that I somehow had to avenge what had been unfairly done to myself and my family. There are a lot of sayings about revenge I can relate to now are more along the lines of Gandhi's statement: "An eye for an eye and the whole world goes blind". I've come to realise how destructive revenge can be not only on the target but also on the perpetrator. For me it became an obsession and I acted in ways that were totally wrong and out of character I hope. I did things that I am ashamed of now and I won't describe, but it changed the person I was, and altered Karen's perception of me to a degree that separation was inevitable, hopefully not for ever,' Andrew said smiling gently at Karen. 'Well, there you have it and I guess this must be what a confessional is like,' he added as he reached for his glass of wine, not yet having the courage to examine people's faces, apart from noting the look on Karen's face which appeared more gentle and relaxed than he had seen it for quite a while.

A wave of sound and movement suddenly entered the room as the other partygoers came over to Karen and Andrew, expressing warm support and hugging them. Somehow Andrew's words, though formal and awkward at times, had managed to remove the shackles from the other guests who now seemed to relate far more comfortably to he and Karen. After a while the conversation returned to the normal chatter of dinner parties, but the obstacles were likely to stay removed allowing people to feel more comfortable with each other.

Seated at the dinner table Andrew found himself placed next to a very attractive young woman in a blue figure hugging dress with a plunging neckline, sitting on his left. He chuckled to himself, wondering if she'd been sent out to test him. Not only was she attractive but also appeared intelligent, working in the research section of the science faculty at La Trobe University. He made sure that he listened as well as looked, and not for the first time pondered the question of whether women dressed like that for men, for themselves or for other women. Most of his female friends assured him that they dressed only for themselves, but the sensual presentation at times made him wonder if that was accurate.

On his right side sat an equally pleasant lady who appeared far more matronly and he made sure that he divided his time equally with both. He was pleased to hear the attractive young woman, who had introduced herself as Phoebe, begin speaking about issues related to the confession he had recently shared with the room.

'So, do you see that obsessive drive for revenge as being an illness?' she enquired.

Andrew restrained himself from cracking the gag that came to him, that being blind, he wouldn't be in a position to see it as anything. He knew that her comment warranted a proper response.

'I do actually see it as an illness,' he responded, 'and I believe it often requires treatment with a skilled therapist. It is more than just a question of perceiving things incorrectly, though it can distort the way a person views the world. I'll give you an example,' he went on. 'This turned out to be rather funny, though in its own small way the distortion of perception I'll tell you about caused me to be really angry, and unwilling to question whether the way I was looking at things was accurate. It occurred probably one and a half or slightly more, years ago. I was sitting at home with a beer in my hand, feeling sorry for myself and watching or rather just gazing at the television. I can't recall the program, but suddenly an advertisement appeared which stated that the Sapphire clothing store was having a 60% off sale. This was a Camberwell men's clothing store that I liked and shopped at from time to time. I immediately hopped into my car and drove down to Camberwell. I entered the shop and enquired from the salesman whether all the items were for sale at 60% off. He looked at me strangely and said, "We don't have anything for sale at present." I angrily queried this, saying I knew for certain that they had a sale, and we exchanged further pleasantries until ultimately I stormed out of the store in anger. It was only when I was driving home, that it suddenly hit me, realizing that the program I was looking at was something I had recorded quite a while back and therefore the advertisement with it also related to some time ago. I might have realised my error sooner if I hadn't fallen into the trap of thinking that here again the world was treating me badly and I was being screwed.'

Phoebe started chuckling. 'That would be so hilarious if it wasn't so sad at the same time.' Others in the room looked around when they heard her chuckles but Andrew didn't feel like sharing it with the whole room at that time. By the end of the evening Andrew reflected how different the night had been compared to the time they were at the Goldfines'. He hadn't hogged the conversation nor had he been deliberately provocative, and the evening turned out to be a very pleasant one, far more pleasant than he had anticipated. Even gazing at his dinner partner's breasts was reasonable, he reassured himself, as he believed it was normal to have fantasies and what you did with the fantasies was the important thing. As these thoughts jiggled around in his head, he couldn't avoid some twitching of his left cheek reminding him that fantasies were not always safe-that some fantasies can on occasion translate into reality.

'I think we should see a counsellor ...' Karen said gently, her eyes fixed on the dashboard. 'Working on our relationship from a distance isn't the way to go about fixing us.'

'I really want that,' said Andrew. Unexpected tears pricked the inner corners of his eyes.

Karen turned her head and smiled at him.

'But ...' choked Andrew, 'I need to tell you something first.'

The smile quickly evaporated from Karen's lips. 'What is it?'

'Andrew felt his teeth clench 'If we're going to make this work, we need to be completely honest with each other ... Late yesterday she called me.'

'Who?' Karen whispered.

Andrew close to tears felt his throat tightening.

'Samantha ...'.

'Samantha,' Karen echoed, her eyes darting back to the dashboard.

'The patient I had an affair with – that you know about – I'm pretty sure I never mentioned her name to you before, probably because it made it more real.' Andrew was almost stuttering, feeling his skin was moist and pierced by prickles. He pulled the car to the kerb and stopped. He began talking immediately, describing the call from Samantha 'She ... Samantha... rang me yesterday out of the blue and sounded really angry, spitting her words out - "I want you to know my relationship broke up a week ago, she told me. Tim, my partner...*was* my partner, to be more accurate. Turned out he was no different to all other men and I caught him cheating on me with my best girlfriend.'

Andrew cautiously glanced at Karen, and saw her staring through the side window He was almost stuttering as he forced his words out,

'She told me that for the first couple of days after her partner left, she started thinking about me and what had happened when she was seeing me. "I had this idea I should report you to the medical board," she told me. "What would they do to you if they found you guilty?", she'd enquired in this calm voice.'

Karen made no sound, so Andrew continued, hoping he was doing more good than not by being so forthright.

'Her question caught me by surprise. Until now it had been a monologue and suddenly she wanted me to speak. I told her I would admit I was guilty, as I shouldn't have allowed it to happen. That she was my patient and I had let her down. What would they do to me? I guess they'd suspend me from practice for several years. She said nothing, so I told her how sorry I was that I had permitted it to develop.'

'Why do you think she rang to tell you that?' Karen asked, now looking at him through moist eyes.

'I'm not sure,' Andrew said hesitantly. 'If I had to guess, I'd say her initial impulse was to retaliate for what Tim had done. She couldn't get at him, so hitting out at another man-me-would have to do. I was truthful when I told her I've regretted it ever since and vowed I wouldn't let it happen again. I apologised and told her I was sorry. She said "thanks", nothing more.'

'What happens if she does report you and you get struck off?' Karen asked anxiously.

'I have a gut feeling she won't make a formal report, and blames herself as well as me, though I told her the blame lay totally with me.' Andrew replied gently, as he tentatively put his hand out to touch Karen's hand. 'If I do get struck off I'll find other work until I can practice again. I want my life to have dignity and honesty in the future.'

Karen didn't take her hand back, even gently rubbed her thumb over one of his knuckes.

'I'm sorry to have brought this up,' Andrew said apologetically, 'but I felt I needed to warn you' if anything were to happen. I want there to be no secrets, not anymore.'

Karen had continued to let Andrew's hand rest on hers. As she gently spoke, the hint of a smile started returning to her lips.

'I still want you to move back and have us work together on the relationship,' she said reassuringly. 'From now on we work in tandem on things as much as possible.'

As if let out of gaol, Andrew nodded, happily and silently agreeing, as they opened the door to her home and to the opportunity of it becoming his as well, once more.

ARTHUR KLEPFISZ

Arthur Klepfisz came to Australia with his parents as refugees from the persecution and killing taking place in Europe during WWII.

Born in Poland, he had no English skills on arrival, and though it was his second language, he acquired the skills rapidly to the point where English became his top subject at school. At Melbourne Boys High School, after scoring 100% in English literature, his teacher suggested he consider writing as a career. He deferred doing this and studied medicine at Melbourne University, going on to specialise in adolescent and adult psychiatry. He wrote mainly medical reports, short stories and occasional material for talks and newspapers.

In spite of a very busy psychiatric practice, he enrolled in a creative writing course at Deakin University with author Andrea Goldsmith, and found the course to be stimulating and inspiring. He obtained a distinction and was reminded that whilst medical reports involved 'telling', creative writing involved a more complex process of using words to describe a character and experiences.

Apart from his family, he became increasingly involved in photography and helping young people understand issues related to prejudice, bigotry and bullying and the importance of taking a stand to assist those under attack.

Gradually he freed up more time to write about issues close to his experiences and work as a psychiatrist, examining many of the factors that contributed to the behaviour of people and how they related to the world around them. Interspersed with darker aspects of life, he used an ongoing sense of humour, at times biting and on other occasions gentle, as a means of dealing with the vicissitudes of life.

I want to thank my family, Andrea Goldsmith who reactivated my love of literature and writing, Ian Grinblatt who commenced the process of editing and the staff at Brolga Publishing who helped bring it to life. I also want to thank forensic pathologist Professor David Ranson for helping ensure the integrity of forensic issues in the book.

AN EYE FOR AN EYE

Arthur Klepfisz

			Qty
ISBN: 9781925367713			
	RRP	AU$24.99	.....
Postage within Australia		AU$5.00	.....
		TOTAL★ $_____	
		★ All prices include GST	

Name:..

Address: ....

....

Phone:...

Email: ....

Payment: ❏ Money Order ❏ Cheque ❏ MasterCard ❏ Visa

Cardholder's Name:..

Credit Card Number: ....

Signature:..

Expiry Date: ....

Allow 7 days for delivery.

Payment to: Marzocco Consultancy (ABN 14 067 257 390)
PO Box 12544
A'Beckett Street, Melbourne, 8006
Victoria, Australia
admin@brolgapublishing.com.au

Be Published

Publish through a successful publisher.
Brolga Publishing is represented through:
• **National** book trade distribution, including sales,
marketing & distribution through **Macmillan Australia.**
• **International** book trade distribution to
    • The United Kingdom
    • North America
    • Sales representation in South East Asia
• **Worldwide e-Book distribution**

For details and inquiries, contact:
Brolga Publishing Pty Ltd
PO Box 12544
A'Beckett St VIC 8006

Phone: 0414 608 494
markzocchi@brolgapublishing.com.au
ABN: 46 063 962 443
(Email for a catalogue request)